Main

Apocalypse Then

Apocalypse Then
STORIES

Rick DeMarinis

SEVEN STORIES PRESS
New York • London • Toronto • Melbourne

Portions of this book previously appeared in the following publications: "Dead Men"
and "Bête Noire" in the *Antioch Review*, "Desperado" in *Blackbird*, "Svengali" in
Epoch, "The Bear Itself" in *Iron Horse Review*, "The Horse Dealer's Lovers" in
Measures of Poison, "The Missile Gypsies" in *Mamaliga*, "The Life and Times
of a Forty-nine Pound Man" in *Open City*, "Why the Tears, Miss Earhart?" in
Paris Review, "Apocalypse Then" in *Photographers, Writers, and the American Scene*.

Seven Stories Press
140 Watts Street
New York, NY 10013
www.sevenstories.com

IN CANADA
Publishers Group Canada, 250A Carlton Street, Toronto, ON M5A 2L1

IN THE UK
Turnaround Publisher Services Ltd., Unit 3,
Olympia Trading Estate, Coburg Road, Wood Green, London N22 6TZ

IN AUSTRALIA
Palgrave Macmillan, 627 Chapel Street, South Yarra VIC 3141

LIBRARY OF CONGRESS CATALOGING-IN-PUBLICATION DATA
DeMarinis, Rick, 1934–
Apocalypse then : new stories / Rick DeMarinis.— Seven Stories Press 1st ed.
p. cm.
ISBN 1-58322-637-0 (alk. paper)
1. United States—Social life and customs—Fiction. I. Title.
PS3554.E4554A86 2004
813'.54—dc22
2004012305

College professors may order examination copies of
Seven Stories Press titles for a free six-month trial period.
To order, visit www.sevenstories.com/textbook/
or fax on school letterhead to 212.226.1411.

Book design by India Amos

Printed in Canada
9 8 7 6 5 4 3 2 1

For Jim Welch
1940–2003

↡

CONTENTS

MOSS

ↆ

the last god we trust
the radioactive sun
hangs in generated haze
bright as a new dime

no one now remembers
your first words or last
or how your simple light
kept us clean and just

now we have stolen your fire
little prometheans chained
to the fuse of blind desire
under your helpless gaze

—Kyle DeSmet

Apocalypse Then

The man ahead of me smelled of cleaning fluid. Fumes rising from his body stung my eyes. My nose itched. I gagged. My sneeze exploded into the back of his neck. He turned and gave me the look of a man who wants to let you know he has suffered.

"Sorry," I said.

He was wrapped in crusty rags that might have been actual clothes at one time. His long yellow hair twisted out of his head in stiff ringlets. Shirley Temple hair, dipped in yellow bile and stiffened with glue. There were dried cuts on his neck, as if he spent his nights sleeping on coils of razor wire. It was late afternoon and the line for government commodities was still half a block long.

We were on the sidewalk outside the distribution center, taking advantage of the generosity of our welfare system. I was eligible for a handout because of my low income.

"No problem," the man said. Philosophical amusement crinkled the parchment skin around his eyes. He apparently expected gratuitous abuse, something he lived with. I sneezed again but managed to turn my head. "God bless you," he said.

"What's that smell?" I asked.

"Toilet cleaner," he said.

I sneezed once more—this time into my hand.

"They poured it on me as a joke," he said.

"Poured?"

"From a bottle. I could be poisoned. I feel a little unstable. I might get dizzy or pass out before this line moves again. If I do, would you hold my place?"

I was wearing a blue knit sweater and clean beige slacks. My hair was washed and combed. My aftershave smelled like nutmeg and rum. I was the neatest, best-groomed pauper in the line.

"Kids," the man said. "They poured it on me while I was sleeping, down by the river, in the park. I might have swallowed some. They thought of my face as a toilet."

He took a deep breath and looked at the sky. It was late October and there was a touch of winter in the air. The sky was hard blue, clear as day one. Blades of evening light slashed red pathways between the peaks of the mountains. "It's learned behavior," he said. "Look to the parents."

"Uh huh," I said.

"The kids get roughed up by life, and so they're mean in return. It's becoming more and more common, I'm sorry to say."

Sociopathic Disorders 101. What I didn't need just then was another lecture. I was one semester short of graduating with a BA in math and physics. I'd applied for a defense job in Seattle. If I got it I'd soon be making a decent wage. It looked like things were going to work out for me after all.

Corliss, my wife, had begun to surface occasionally from her wretched depressions. The new pills seemed to be working. After I got out of the air force and started school as a twenty-two-year-old freshman, things were pretty grim between us. I sold our car, sold her grandma's silver service, sold my blood. But now my prospects were good. We even had sex now and then. Depressed sex, maybe—sex followed by tears, remorse, and long silences, as if in relenting she had acted out an ugly childhood memory—but at least it was sex. Bad things had happened to her, but she never talked about them in specifics.

The bum put his fissured hand on my shoulder and smiled. His smile was surprising. The few teeth he had were clean and rooted in healthy gums. Under his stained beard there was a strong jawline. His pale blue eyes were still capable of sharp focus, suggesting dependable mental activity. His forehead was straight and tall, as if housing a large, noble brain. One of Mother Nature's more elaborate jokes. I couldn't hold back a small laugh.

"I appreciate your concern," he said, ignoring my amusement. "You seem to be a decent young fellow."

"Thanks," I said. We had an audience. Several people behind and ahead of us were leaning out of line to take in our little dialogue.

"Never sell yourself short," he scolded. "Have you read Bishop Peale? You have untapped potential. You need to think positively. That's the secret to a successful life.

Fill your mind with truth and you will cast out error."

Like a fragment of bark from a rotting tree, a piece of his clothing fell off. It might have been a scarf, a sleeve, or a jacket panel. He didn't notice, and it didn't seem to decrease the mass of rags encasing him.

"I've read Bridey Murphy," I said. In fact, I was halfway through the book. Corliss insisted I read it. Reincarnation was her thing this year. She believed she was the reincarnation of Cortez's doomed Aztec mistress, Malinche, the Great Whore of Mexico. She'd dyed her hair black and wore Mexican jewelry. She adopted a pose that in profile made her seem like a pale *mestiza*. She had even started signing her name "Corliss Malinche Westhaymer-Moss." I'm the Moss.

Corliss spent her first ten years in the tropical Tampico-Tuxpán area of Mexico. Her father, Bill Westhaymer, was a Pemex petroleum engineer. I met her in San Antonio when I was stationed at Lackland Air Force Base. We both had limited experience with sex. It teased us with the promise of endless erotic adventure. So it made sense to get married, though we had nothing in common. She wasn't so depressed then. But she was only eighteen and the black flower of mental disease had not yet bloomed. It was 1956 and the country was prosperous and orderly and the people gave no outward sign of being troubled. But by 1962 we had inched toward the edge of an abyss. Cuba had medium-range missiles aimed at the soft underbelly of our nation. That's why I was applying for defense work in Seattle. The Pentagon couldn't throw enough money into planes, submarines, and missiles. The defense contracts were pouring in.

"Don't read that reincarnation hokum," the bum said. "Read Doctor Peale. If you take his lessons to heart, you can make something of yourself, son."

"It worked magic for you," I said.

He gave me his long-suffering look again. "That wasn't necessary," he said.

I shrugged.

The line lurched ahead. We shuffled, one step at a time, up the stairs that led into the distribution center. Inside we were given slips of paper and pencil stubs. "Write down the things you need most," an old volunteer said. He was a skinny, lipless man with a thin, judgmental nose. Like many veterans of volunteer community service, he was officious and intolerant. He enjoyed, in his joyless way, the moral superiority implied by his position. I wrote down Butter, Eggs, Bread, Powdered Milk, Cheese, Macaroni, Beans, Rice, Canned Vegetables, Canned Soup, Canned Ham, Canned Turkey.

He took the bum's slip, then mine. "Butter, eh?" he said. "I suppose margarine won't do?" He assessed our worthiness with quick, impatient glances. He didn't like our looks. The bum only triggered his contempt; I made him suspicious. "You're not working?" he said to me.

"No. I'm a student," I said. "At the U."

He studied my list of requested food. "This is quite an order," he said. "You have no income?"

"I'm on the GI Bill, but that barely pays our rent and utilities. My wife can't work."

He studied my grocery list as if deciphering a cryptogram. He tweezered his small pointy chin between his thumb and forefinger. Meanwhile, another volunteer, a plump, red-faced woman, filled a cardboard box with the bum's request. All he wanted was bread and butter, powdered milk, canned fruit, and strawberry jam. The woman gave him two pounds of butter.

"I'm okaying everything except butter," the old volunteer said to me.

"Why not butter?" I said. "My wife has to have butter. She likes butter on her string beans, and on her toast. She can't eat margarine. Margarine is hydrogenated fat. She says the free radicals in it will give her ovarian cancer."

He gave me a long squinty look. "We're running short," he said.

"You gave *him* two pounds!" I said, indicating the bum who was now walking out of the building, carrying his box of food.

The old man shrugged. He read the request slip of the next man in line.

"What does he need with butter?" I said. "He lives down by the river, probably in a cardboard box. What the goddamned hell is a bum going to do with two pounds of butter?"

The old man gave me a stern look. "That will be enough of *that*," he said.

"The hell it will! That bum doesn't even have a place to keep it cold. It'll turn rancid in a couple of days. You've just thrown away two pounds of good butter, you goddamn incompetent!"

"He isn't very grateful, is he?" said the plump woman filling boxes. She gave me one of those dark sneering smiles that if it came from a man would mean things were going to get ugly.

"I'll call the police if you don't leave these premises immediately," said the old volunteer.

I left with my box of food. The bum was high-stepping down the side street that led to the river. I followed him. The street ended in a vacant lot. A well-worn path through the lot descended toward Riverfront Park. The bum disappeared into some tall shrubs. Then I caught sight of him moving along the river bank toward the grassy area where swing sets, slides, and monkey bars oxidized in the damp air. At the far edge of the grass a stand of cottonwoods leaned toward the river. He went into the trees and once again disappeared from view.

I crossed the grassy play area and went into the stand of cottonwoods. The bum had a cozy set up: a lean-to made of scavenged plywood with canvas draped over the open ends to keep out the cold autumn wind and the eyes of the curious. I heard him in there organizing his loot.

"Knock, knock," I said.

He quit messing with his jars and boxes. He was quiet as a mouse discovered in the pantry.

"I want to make you a deal," I said. "Hello?"

He poked his head out of his canvas door. "It's the Bridey Murphy man," he said.

"I need a pound of butter. I'll trade you a can of yams for it."

He shook his head vigorously. "No, I need my butter. I need the vitamin A for this arthritis." He opened and closed his scabrous hand.

"I'll give you a can of turkey along with the yams," I said.

I stepped into his hovel. He was a pack rat: stacked magazines and newspapers sat against a makeshift wall. Coils of half-rotten rope, pieces of scrap metal, stacks of plastic throw-away flowerpots, a box of rusty bottle openers, expired calendars, a shelf with a dozen books: *The Power of Positive Thinking* along with other books with titles such as *Think Your Way to Wealth! Plan for Retirement Now! Earn a Steady Income This Easy Way!* There was barely room for his sleeping bag, a Sterno cooker, and a small kerosene heater.

"Take it easy, young fella," he said, taking a defensive stance.

"One of those pounds of butter is mine," I said. "Hand it over."

"I told you, son. I need it."

I didn't like him calling me "son." In the air force a certain type of southern boy would call you "son" in a certain way when he wanted to put you down. I tackled Learner Paris who was from Baton Rouge because he wouldn't let up on the "son" crap. He won the scuffle but we both got Article 15 court martials. I went from airman first to airman second. Learner didn't lose a stripe but got twelve weeks of KP, along with me. He stopped calling me "son"; I stopped calling him "peckerwood." We became drinking buddies.

I felt a rush of blood heat my face. I reached for the butter. The bum put his hand on my wrist, the feeble arthritic grip more plea than restraint.

"I'm taking the butter," I said.

"Go ahead, take it then," he said, thrusting the butter toward me. "Take my butter."

I did. I had to think of Corliss. If I came home with margarine, she'd go into a black funk and not surface for days, pills or no pills.

"I'll give you a can of ham for it," I said. I dug into my sack pulled out the four-pound can of water-packed ham.

"Keep your ham," he said. "I can't eat it. I'm Jewish on my mother's side. A man has to be accountable to the memory of his mother, doesn't he?"

"Then take these dried prunes. They'll keep you regular."

"I'm regular as Big Ben," the bum said, but he accepted the bag of prunes.

Our business was finished but I had more to say. I couldn't just walk out of his lean-to, leaving him to think the worst of me. Why did I care what this old Positive Thinker thought? Maybe because he had mentioned his mother, which led to the improbable thought that this rag-swathed wreckage was once a loved and pampered child—a child with no inkling of what was in store for it. I fished in my pocket for loose change. I gave him a handful of nickels and dimes. Maybe half a dollar's worth.

"You're full of negative thoughts," he said. "You have destructive attitudes toward your fellow man."

"That's not true," I said.

"You think about it," he said.

I walked the rest of the way to University Housing carrying my load of groceries. Corliss was sitting in our tiny kitchen drinking coffee. She was sloppily dressed—raggy jeans, sweatshirt, and flip-flops. Her long, unwashed hair was limp and sheenless. Her eyes were black with the complex and ruinous history of another person. La Malinche. She wouldn't look at me.

She poked a finger at a large white envelope on the table. "They're going to make you an offer," she said.

I picked up the envelope, ripped out the letter. It was from the Seattle defense contractor. If I accepted the forthcoming offer, I'd report to work a week after my final semester. Quality Control Specialist, Grade Three.

"Hot damn!" I said.

"I'm not going," Corliss said.

She was in one of her bleaker moods. I ignored it. "Look, honey," I said. "I got a pound of butter for you."

I handed her the wax-papered package.

"What's this?" she said, studying it.

"What's what?"

"There's a thumb-print on it. It's disgusting."

I looked at the butter. The bum had pressed his thumb into it. His black thumbnail had pierced the wax paper wrapper. The thumbprint was brown. Brown with God only knew what.

"I won't eat this," she said.

I peeled the wax paper with the brown thumbprint off the butter and rewrapped it in a clean sheet of foil. "It'll be fine," I said. "Did you take your pill today?"

"Seattle is where they'll strike first," she said. "Because of the defense plants. We can't go to Seattle."

"Get used to the idea, Corliss," I said. "We're going to Seattle."

"We won't have to. I'll get a job, right here in town. I can still type sixty words a minute. We'll be safe here."

This was pure fantasy. No way could Corliss work with other people. She could barely talk to the mailman.

"I don't want to be safe here," I said. "Safe but poor—no thanks. I'm not going to stand in line for commodities the rest of my life."

"You only *only* think of yourself! This is what you always only do. It's always me me *me*. Why don't you ever consider my feelings? Do my feelings mean nothing at all to you?" Abundant tears streaked down her cheeks and pooled on the Formica top of the dinette table.

I'd stood in line for an hour to bring her food. I'd taken shit from the pious volunteers. I'd forced a bum to hand over his butter so that she wouldn't have to worry about getting ovarian cancer from margarine. But it wouldn't do any good to point this out.

Corliss saw things one way and one way only. Her world had one center: her bundle of neuroses.

"Take another pill, honey," I said.

I opened a can of turkey and made turkey hash for supper. She wouldn't eat. I watched the news. The Russians had a naval convoy steaming toward Cuba but Kennedy was going to cut them off with a blockade. The fleet was sailing back from the Mediterranean at flank speed. B-52s were aloft, ready to fly over the North Pole and bomb Russia into radioactive ash. Everyone was on edge, from Washington, DC, to Seattle. World War Three was on the horizon, a horizon banked with poisonous mushroom clouds.

After the news, I put on my coat and headed for the door. "Where are you going?" she said. "I don't want you to go."

"I'm meeting my study group. Can't let them down."

"Let them down this once, please."

"I can't. We've got to get ready for midterms."

"Bastard," she said.

I went to the Stockman's Bar uptown. They were waiting for me, Richie Yang and Don Barstow. Richie was from Taipei on a scholarship. Don Barstow was a cowboy with a talent for math and science; beyond that he was a complete ignoramus. They raised their mugs of beer in mock salute. "The ball and chain cut you loose?" Barstow said, puffing on a hand-rolled cigarette.

"Not exactly," I said.

We drank and played pool for a couple of hours, then Richie said we ought to go up to school and break into the physics lab and finish our projects so that we could all go out again tomorrow night and get drunk without having to worry about an unfinished project.

We entered the physics building through a window in a men's room. The window was at ground level and easy to jimmy. We walked up the unlit stairwells to the third-floor physics lab. It was dark and empty. We turned on the lights. Our projects— oscilloscope kits—were sitting on a bench like gutted TV sets. There wasn't much left to do. We had to solder in some resistors and capacitors. It took about an hour. During that hour a loud bell clanged every two or three seconds. It was annoying but it didn't interfere with our work.

A graduate student came in carrying a radiation monitor. "You wingnuts have had it," he said. "You've caught yourselves a major dose." He was a tall skinny genius, the pet of the department, headed for big things in theoretical physics. His tall narrow face was white with alarm. There was a motto silk-screened on his sweatshirt:

We Create So That
Others Might Destroy

It was either protest or brag, I didn't know which.

"What you mean?" Richie Yang asked him.

"We had the linear accelerator running downstairs," the grad student said. "Dr. Habib was bombarding beryllium. High-velocity neutrons have been ripping into this room for the last couple of hours. What did you mental cases think that bell was for? The shields only cover the outer walls of the energy ring. No one is supposed to be *above* the target area. That's why we lock up the building at night."

"How were we supposed to know what the damn bell was for?" Don Barstow said. "Why didn't you two-bit Einsteins post a sign?"

The basement-dwelling linear accelerator was the toy of the professors and their select graduate students. The undergrads knew it existed but not much more.

We got out of there and dragged ourselves to the Student Union for coffee. "We're dead men," I said.

We drank our coffee at a small table in the nearly empty Union, imagining our bodies riddled by atomic bullets. The heavy neutrons would pinhole our organs, our blood cells, our marrow, make Swiss cheese of our brains. If we lived, our disorganized DNA would make us father monsters.

"Shit fire," Don Barstow said. "I was about to get out of here and go to work for 3M before going on to grad school." He pulled his bag of Bull Durham out of his shirt pocket and rolled a cigarette with one hand. We studied his skilled fingers with the morbid fascination of condemned men watching butterflies mate outside the death-house window.

"And Richie here just got accepted by the Cal Tech PhD program," I said.

Richie moaned. He started to speak with manic intensity. The sheer velocity of his words moved us but we could not understand him. He had reverted to Chinese. Terror had made him lose his grasp of English.

"Killed by a damn neutron," Barstow said. He took a long drag on his cigarette.

We knew about the neutron bomb. It had been in the news. It was the bomb that kills people but leaves real estate unharmed. The perfect weapon for our grim new world. The underlying value system of a world that could dream up neutron bombs held that real estate was more valuable than people. No national leader could come right out and say it. None of them could say, This type of weapon means that people are less important now than the things people have made. We still wanted to believe in the individual: his freedom, dignity, and self-reliance, qualities we admired and hoped to preserve. But the opposite was becoming true. People were trouble. People had crazy ideas that didn't fit in with the larger goals of governments. People who lined up for welfare commodities were only the most obvious parasites. The fact was, most people were parasites in one way or another. These parasite populations needed to be controlled and sometimes selectively reduced. They were expendable. What better device to carry out that program than the neutron bomb?

I went home. Corliss was watching *The Untouchables*. "I may have been fatally exposed to radiation," I said.

She didn't turn from the TV set. "You've been drinking with your so-called study group," she said. "I can smell it."

"All of us were radiated by high-velocity neutrons."

"You're just trying to upset me."

I sat down next to her and took her in my arms. I was shaking a bit. I kissed her and she didn't resist. She felt my tremble: it made her tremble. She kissed back, hard. I undressed her, slowly, the way that makes her wild. Someone undressed her that way a long time ago, when she was twelve. She told me that, but not who or why. I suspected the worst.

We went to bed. We made love like only damaged people can. Predictably, she went into a blue funk afterward.

"Don't make us go to Seattle," she said. Then she redirected this plea to God. "Please, Jesus, don't make us go to Seattle."

But He did.

The job was good and it paid well. I worked on the quality control of vendor supplied parts for intercontinental ballistic missiles, then moved up to reliability engineering. I tried to think positively: the more missiles we make the less likely they'll be used. It was Pentagon logic. It made sense to me.

Now and then I recalled something the old bum had yelled at my back as I hauled his butter away: "What are you a captive of? Can you even name it?" I couldn't and still can't, but I think about it often.

We bought a house in a Seattle suburb, sold it, moved to other places, other jobs. Eventually we had a child. Corliss's mental health improved. She gave up on exotic spiritual notions. She put on weight; she became a functional homemaker, a dedicated consumer.

Sometimes the worst doesn't happen. I didn't get sick and die from exposure to high-velocity neutrons kicked free from beryllium by a partially shielded linear accelerator. Don Barstow and Richie Yang didn't get sick and die either. They went on to big things in applied and theoretical physics.

Best of all, the doomed world did not end.

The Bear Itself

A few of us went to Flathead Lake seventy miles north of town. We had fishing gear and swim suits and a case of Highlander longnecks. We also had a fifth of Lemon Hart rum. Richie Yang, the genius from Taiwan, was behind the wheel. It was Astrid Custer's '57 Chevy Biscayne, a gift from her parents, but Richie needed to hone his driving skills and Astrid was willing to let him.

Richie passed the bottle of Lemon Hart back to me. I passed it to Astrid, who was sitting next to Richie. Astrid passed it back to Richie. Richie took a long hit then passed it over his shoulder to Roddy Custer, who was sulking in the back seat next to me. We all gagged and wheezed—the sort of noises that must have been heard in the trenches of Verdun after canisters of phosgene had exploded in them. Lemon Hart is 150 proof, undrinkable without being watered down with mix, but it was the end of the semester and we were reckless and ready for adventure.

"What good are grizzly bears anyway?" Roddy Custer said. "All they do is kill cattle and sometimes people." We hadn't been talking about grizzly bears, but Roddy was in one of his combative moods. Roddy was from Phoenix. Astrid was from L.A. I think he was resurrecting an earlier argument he'd been having with her.

"You've got a point, Roddy," I said.

My job, as I saw it, was to ease the tension between Astrid and Roddy. I didn't want them to wreck the afternoon. I was in a good mood and wanted to keep it.

"They're cute," Astrid said.

"That's rich," Roddy said. "Grizzlies are cute, alligators are cute, dinosaurs are cute. Astrid thinks all animals are cute."

"I do not," Astrid said. "I do not think that camels are cute, okay? Rhinos are definitely not cute. Hyenas? Good God, I've never seen a cute hyena."

"She has all these stuffed animals on our bed," Roddy said. "Tigers, wolves, bears."

"I bet they're cute," I said.

Roddy laughed. "Spoken like a true mountain man." Since I was the only one from Montana, he liked to call me "Mountain Man."

I leaned forward and said, "Turn left into that pull-out, Richie. The little cove's down below those bushes."

Richie hit the brakes too hard and I slid off the back seat. Richie had finally passed his driver's license test after three tries. He was a genius in physics, tops in our class, but the rules of the road mystified him.

Astrid said, "God, you're so *drunk*, Richie."

"Not drunk," Richie said. "Reflexes far too quick for shitty backwoods Montana road. I am fast-track man."

"That doesn't make sense," Astrid said.

"That's because you don't understand the incongruency between shitty backwoods roads and a fast-track man," Roddy said. "I think Irish is dead," he added.

Arashmidos Dowlatabadi, the Iranian, was asleep next to Roddy Custer. We called him "Irish." We started out calling him "Arash," but it soon became "Irish." No one could pronounce his real names, first or last. He too, and against his religious principles, was drunk.

We'd been drinking since before noon, nonstop, and it was now three. We started at Stockman's Bar. After we got bored with pinball and shitkicker music, we decided to drive up to Flathead Lake. Spring semester was over. All we had left were finals. The cold war had shifted into high gear and I had enough science and math to land a good job in the defense industry.

Arashmidos was also a physics student, but his main course of study was partying. He loved to party and he loved America. The USA was his playground. He was a little guy from a wealthy

Tehran family and he had an eye for statuesque Nordic blondes. Astrid, a statuesque Nordic blonde, had called him cute. "Oh, Irish, you're cute as a damn bug," she'd said. She said it in Stockman's. She'd had two boilermakers and was feeling global and happier than I'd ever seen her. She was the life of our little party. She gathered Arashmidos in her arms and gave him a big hug and then a kiss. "I adore Persia," she said. She was careful to say "Persia." Arashmidos didn't like to be called an Iranian. "We are the Persians," he'd insisted.

The kiss bothered Roddy. Things hadn't been going very well between him and Astrid, and the kiss—booze-fueled and sloppy—didn't help the situation. Roddy was a racist—the intellectual kind, the kind that clothes his rabid opinions in selective science. He had nothing to say against Persians—("The ancient Medes were a great people")— but had frequently offered unsolicited critiques of Negroes, Jews, and American Indians. After today, I figured he'd probably include the modern Middle Eastern populations in his catalogue of inferior races. He liked Richie and so had nothing negative to say about the Chinese. He was, in fact, a Sinophile. From Chinese food to Chinese philosophy, Roddy had nothing but high praise. He didn't think much of the Communists but believed they were a passing phase. Communism was something the greatness of the Chinese people would assimilate and eventually transform.

Roddy wasn't a good student. He'd taken Differential Equations twice and still only managed to make a C. He did all right in Mechanics, Hydraulics, and Electricity, but Vector Analysis was a complete mystery to him. Which was unfortunate since the Vector Analysis professor shared Roddy's views on race. They became friends and often had coffee together in the Student Union, shaking their heads in agreement about the Communist underpinnings of the civil rights movement. But Roddy couldn't get past Stokes's Theorem and the professor, much as he liked Roddy, wasn't going to pass him.

I'd signed up for a couple of grad courses in math, but I soon realized I was over my head. Undergraduate math was easy enough, but once you got into graduate work the rules changed. I got through the seminar on Fourier Series, but Topology was my Waterloo. I didn't get it, and knew I never would. My brain wasn't capable of pure abstract reasoning. I had job applications out, from Seattle to Los Angeles, and had received three offers.

Richie managed to stop the car short of putting it into the lake. We piled out and skidded down the steep embankment to the narrow, driftwood-covered beach. I'd discovered this beach the previous summer and felt possessive about it. You couldn't see it from the road. From the road the lake seemed remote, protected by steep cliffs. And this was true until you realized that there was a gap in the cliffs created by a stream that fed into the lake. For about fifty yards on either side of this stream there was a stretch of gritty sand and driftwood, a hidden paradise. All you had to do to access it was climb down through a tangled screen of bushes.

"Moss's Cove," Roddy said, giving me title to the place.

I accepted the honor. "Welcome," I said.

We changed into our swimming suits, deciding we'd fish later in the afternoon when the landlocked kokanee salmon started feeding on the crepuscular bugs. We were drunk enough to lose our modesty and stripped behind bushes that gave only partial cover. Astrid, though, was drunk beyond shame. She pulled off her shirt and Levis, unhooked her bra, stepped out of her panties, and stood at the edge of the brilliant water like a Scandinavian goddess who'd materialized out of the pages of some ancient Viking saga. We all acted as if this were a normal everyday sight, but I felt as though the air had been sucked out of my lungs by a nuclear blast. I was sure Arashmidos and Richie were struck in the same way, but they were acting cool about it, too. Cultures apart, we were all stunned by Astrid's radiant unashamed beauty and cautious enough to pretend we weren't.

But not Roddy. He carried her one-piece Esther Williams–style bathing suit to her and waved it in her face. "Jesus Christ," he said. "Put this on, will you?"

Astrid answered him by diving into the shallow green water and swimming out to where the water was dark blue. Roddy threw the bathing suit down and opened a beer. He was still in his clothes.

"Come on and skinny dip, you cowards!" Astrid yelled from fifty yards out.

"She's been drinking," Roddy said.

We looked at him. "You think?" I said.

"Lately, I mean. She's been drinking a lot lately. I go to school, she goes out to Eddy's Club or The Flame for drinks. I come home, she's on the couch with a beer or a glass of Chianti reading some goddamned poetry book or watching soaps. Supper? Forget supper. Don't come wandering by my apartment looking for supper."

"She's just bored," I said.

"No she isn't," Roddy said. "She's taking a poetry writing class Monday nights from that big Jew in the English department."

"What big Jew would that be?" I said. Truth was, I didn't know anyone in the English department and was surprised Roddy did.

"Joel Barger, the poet they imported from New York."

"Poetry," Arashmidos said, "is very important to us Persians."

"China invented poetry," Richie Yang said. "Poetry is inward vision of sage. Listen—poet sees truth in single grain of sand!" Richie picked up a handful of the gritty beach and let the coarse sand sift through his fingers. His eyes were glassy. I figured he was close to passing out. He waved the bottle of Lemon Hart in front of him as if he were hearing the cadence of some ancient Chinese poem. Then he put the bottle to his lips. The white-hot liquid spilled down both sides of his chin. His knees buckled. He straightened himself, and after a moment he put the bottle down carefully, adjusting it so that it would stay upright on the sloping beach. Then he stripped off his trunks and fell into the water.

"Hooray for Richie!" Astrid yelled.

Arashmidos stepped carefully into the cold lake and waded out to waist-deep water. His baggy trunks ballooned with air as the water rose around them. He held his arms crossed against his chest. His skinny brown body shuddered.

Roddy sat down on a sun-bleached log with the bottle of Lemon Hart. "I think she's messing with the big New York Jew," he said.

"I doubt that very much," I said. "Astrid wouldn't do that. She's your *wife*, man."

Roddy looked at me like I was the village idiot. "She told me she'd decided to become a poet. She said poetry was her life. I said the *hell* it is. I said you're my wife, period, my helpmate. End of story. I reminded her of her wedding vows, which I happen to take very seriously. Love, honor, and obey. She said—now get this, Moss—she said, Go screw yourself, Roddy. That's what she said. Can you believe it? That's not what a decent wife says to her husband, is it? If we ever have kids is she going to talk that way in front of them? Where did she learn to talk like that? I'll tell you where. From that big Jew poet from New York City, that's where."

Arashmidos came out of the lake shaking. "Too cold," he said. He put on his shirt and sat down beside Roddy and me on the bleached log. Astrid's golden head bobbed on the water two hundred yards out.

"Look at her," Roddy said bitterly.

Arashmidos and I looked at her. Neither one of us felt bitter.

"Look at *this*, if you want proof," Roddy said. He pulled a scrap of paper from his back pocket. "She wrote this for the big Jew's class."

I took the paper from him. I read:

Camp smoke in the air
yet the salty perfume
of your bear-like hair
lifts me into dreams
of the promised garden—
your fierce touch
draws out my honey.

"That is very very beautiful," Arashmidos said, slapping his thigh.

"It's pure pornographic filth," Roddy said. "It's degrading. 'Ode to the Dream Grizzly,' she calls it. Dream grizzly my ass! I guess I *know* who it's an ode to!"

"She could be writing about you, Roddy, you fierce bear-like bastard," I said, trying to inject some humor into the waning afternoon. I understood now what Roddy's anti-bear sentiments were all about.

Roddy snorted. "Baloney! If she wrote that about me, don't you think I'd know it? And if she was writing about a dream grizzly, why'd she say bear-like instead of bear? You don't say bear-like when you mean the bear itself."

"It is extremely beautiful," Arashmidos said. "In Persia, we eat and breathe poetry. Omar Khayyaam, if you recall, was a poet. And not only a poet, but a famous mathematician and astronomer. Omar wrote a very important treatise on algebra—an invention, by the way, of my culture."

"Your culture probably invented the ballistic missile and the transistor radio, too," Roddy scoffed.

Arashmidos gulped some Lemon Hart. His big Persian nose was aglow. He said, "Listen to this:

In the silence of the temple of desire,
I am lying beside your passionate body,
my kisses have left their marks on your
shoulders, like the fiery bites of a snake.

"These are the extremely beautiful words of Forugh Farrokhzad, one of our finest women poets. So you see, Roddy, such feelings are universal. You have no need to take Astrid's poem as anything but the metaphorical expression of very beautiful and sensitive thoughts."

Roddy looked at Arashmidos but didn't say anything. I believed he was visualizing Astrid's and Arashmidos's sloppy kiss in

Stockman's. His eyes narrowed with distrust. He said, "Maybe she was writing about you, Irish."

"If only it were so," Arashmidos said. His dreamy smile had too much hope in it.

Roddy got up and made a move toward Arashmidos. I caught his shirt and spun him around. Roddy growled at me. I growled back. I pulled his shirt until the buttons flew off. He grabbed my trunks and yanked me down the sloped beach. I lost my footing and fell. I tried to kick his ankle but he danced away. We were both winded.

"Where's Richie?" Arashmidos said.

The alarm in his voice froze our combat. I waded out to the place where the lake bottom dropped away to blue-black depth.

"Hey Astrid!" I yelled. "Where's Richie?"

Her head turned on the smooth surface of the water as if it were on a lazy Susan. "I don't know!" she yelled back. "Isn't he there with you?"

We knew he wasn't, but we looked around the beach anyway. We searched carefully behind the shrubs, as if we were looking for a wallet.

He hadn't come in. I scanned the lake again. I saw him—he was at least two hundred yards beyond Astrid. He disappeared and appeared—going under, coming back up. When he came up, he waved his arm. His mouth was open, but if he was yelling I couldn't hear him.

"Behind you, Astrid!" I yelled. "I think he's in trouble!"

Astrid's floating head turned again on its lazy Susan. When she saw Richie she said, "I'll get him." She swam easily and powerfully toward our drowning friend.

"She swam the last leg of the four-hundred-meter medley for Long Beach Junior College," Roddy said. "They get great swimmers at Long Beach JC. Summers, she worked one of the lifeguard stations at Venice Beach."

I resented his casual tone. It was as if he were telling us what she had for breakfast. I dove into the water. I wanted to help Astrid get Richie back safely, but I wanted to get away from Roddy more.

I'm not a great swimmer. It took me too long to get to them, and by the time I did they were halfway back to the beach. Astrid was on her back swimming with one hand while holding Richie's head out of the water by his hair. Her strong scissoring legs were enough to propel them shoreward at a good rate.

"What should I do?" I asked.

"Just stay clear," Astrid said. "I've got him."

When we got to shore I helped Astrid drag Richie up on dry sand. Richie had turned a pale shade of blue but he hadn't taken any water into his lungs. He was shaking hard from cold and exhaustion. Astrid knelt down beside him. "Just relax, Richie," she said. "I'll get some blankets out of the car." Her tight nipples brushed Richie's cold chest as she bent to kiss his forehead. "You're going to be just fine, Richie." She got up, a bit shaky herself.

"Jesus Christ!" Roddy said. "Will you please put on some clothes, you goddamned whore!"

If a handful of words can end a marriage, Roddy had found them. He tried to defuse them in the ensuing silence by changing the subject. "I'll get the blankets for Richie," he said. "I'll get the fishing gear, too. The silver salmon should be rising any minute. Let's build a campfire! Irish, collect some wood!"

But no one felt like fishing. Our day in the country was over. We drove back to town, subdued. Astrid sat up front with Richie, only this time she was driving. Arashmidos sat in the back between Roddy and me.

Roddy shifted around in his seat uneasily. He wasn't so stupid to not realize what had happened that day. His mood was repentant, but that wasn't going to be enough. He called me "Mountain Man" once or twice, wanting to restore the festive atmosphere we'd started out with.

"Grizzly bears," he said, growing desperate. "I guess if they keep to their habitat I could put up with them. They're no worse than wolves or mountain lions. It's all a matter of degree." I let him talk to himself. He'd be doing a lot of that from now on.

Richie, wrapped in a blanket, nodded in and out of consciousness. Arashmidos was dozing, his head on my shoulder. Astrid held the wheel with both hands and leaned forward in her seat, her teeth clenched. She was determined to get us back to town and nothing more. She turned on the radio, found Ray Charles singing "Drown in My Own Tears." She turned the volume up full blast. Arashmidos sat up, suddenly wide awake. He leaned into the front seat and pointed excitedly at the radio as Ray cried and shouted of lost love and unbearable loneliness.

   "*This!*" Arashmidos said, as if playing the trump card in an argument he'd been having with one of us. "*This* is the true American poetry! *This* is who you are! There is nothing more to say about it!" He looked at us, one by one, daring anyone to fault his reasoning. No one did. Then he went back to sleep.

The Missile Gypsies

Moss loved his truck. It was a nearly new
'63 Ford pickup, shiny blue, with four-wheel drive capability. He'd
washed and waxed it before he'd headed for Charlie-9, the silo
that had a problem. The truck gleamed like a blue sapphire in the
tan landscape of North Dakota, but the muddy road he'd been
on for the last ten miles had coated it gravy brown from wheel
hubs to door handles. And now, to complete the insult, he was
stuck in a herd of cattle. He'd turned through a sharp curve and
there they were, on the other side of the hairpin, jammed into
a bottleneck between the high bank on the left and a wire fence
on the right.

Several hundred head squeezed past the truck. They bent the
side mirrors, made the truck rock on its groaning springs, laid
a sloppy pavement of green manure he'd have to drive through.
Moss, not much of a country boy, liked a good steak but didn't
think much of cows. It appalled him, sometimes, to think that
a mouth-watering medium rare T-bone had its origins in one of
these drooling sloe-eyed manure machines.

The cowhands touched the brims of their straw hats in polite
salutation as they passed by on horseback—nice guys—and Moss
nodded back at them, affable, understanding, but behind his smile
was the complaint: Who's going to clean my truck? Who's going
to fix the bent mirror mounts? A passing Black Angus looked
into the cab with the devoted eyes of a sleepy lover. Moss told it
to go fuck itself.

It wasn't Moss's truck. It was the Company's truck. But it was
assigned to him and he'd use it as long as he was stuck out here
in the boonies, driving from one Minuteman silo to the next,

climbing down access holes to collect U E R s—Unplanned Event Records—from clipboards left by other Ford-driving engineers and technicians, all of whom were overseeing the installation of missiles that could incinerate half the world.

Moss had been the sole driver of this particular truck for four months now, long enough for him to feel possessive. He'd broken it in gently, as if he were the one making payments on it. The Ford had his stamp on it. "As the twig is bent, the tree's inclined," was one of his favorite quotes. If the truck was anyone's, it was his.

That evening, after washing his truck and attempting to straighten the mirror mounts, he told the story of the cows and the cowboys to his wife, Corliss.

"I'm glad your life is interesting," she said.

"I thought you'd be amused."

"Oh, I am. I'm very amused. I'm thrilled. I'm surrounded by amusing and thrilling things. I can hardly wait to get up in the morning to be amused and thrilled all over again."

Moss did not pursue this conversation.

Corliss hated North Dakota. She felt violated by being spirited away from Seattle by the whims of the aerospace company her husband worked for. Back in Seattle she'd been learning how to play the cello and she'd taken a course in creative writing from a novelist who was down on his luck and needed to supplement his flagging royalties with a monthly paycheck from Green River Community College. Corliss had been seven months pregnant when they came to North Dakota, and the baby, Teller—named after the father of the H–Bomb, Edward Teller—was born in Minot. The constant distractions of motherhood, combined with exile to the hinterlands, sabotaged whatever hopes she had of doing something meaningful with her life.

Moss had to go where the job took him. He had two choices: Go to the wheat fields and cattle ranches of North Dakota where the company was installing Minuteman I C B M s in government-appropriated land or get laid off. He went. He was now classi-fied as a Reliability Field Engineer, Grade One. The pay was larcenous—almost double what he had made in Seattle, thanks to a generous per diem allowance, dislocation pay, and as much overtime as he wanted—but the living conditions were not ideal and there were few amenities. And after the work here dwindled, he'd be transferred to some other bleak landscape where more Minuteman missiles would be installed. And after that, who knew? Most likely he'd be sent back to Seattle. If not, he'd follow the missiles wherever they took him. Maybe he could get in on the Polaris contract, the submarine-launched ICBM being developed by Lockheed. Lockheed Missiles and Space was located in Sunnyvale, California, just south of San Francisco. Corliss would thrive in Sunnyvale.

For the last six months, Corliss and Teller had been stuck in the single-wide "Kit" mobile home on the grounds of Minot Air Force base. She wouldn't go out other than taking the baby for short excursions around the trailer park in his stroller despite the constant prairie wind.

The wives of the other field engineers had formed a club, but Corliss wouldn't join. "I don't know how to play canasta," she said. "I don't like gossip. The only things those women read are romance novels and diet books." The other women reacted predictably to her aloofness: They stopped inviting her to their gatherings and snubbed her whenever an opportunity presented itself.

"Aren't you being a little snobbish?" Moss had said. "It can't be all that grim. There has to be a few intelligent women in the club. You know—women who listen to classical music and read serious books, women who know a Picasso from a Pissarro. Women like yourself."

"You mean neurotics. No thank you. Besides, I can't haul Teller to bingo games or garden parties, can I?"

"It's not as if you're the only mother here. I've seen some kids running around."

"Kids, not babies. You know how Teller is. If he's not within reach of a lactating nipple he gets hysterical."

Moss had gone to the Sears outlet in Minot and bought a big TV set for Corliss and Teller, but it could only pick up one channel even with the antenna he'd attached to the roof of their trailer. Corliss had planted Teller in front of the big TV in his high chair. The snowy images of Captain Kangaroo and Cecil the Seasick Sea Serpent could not hold his attention. As soon as he was deposited and belted into his high chair he arched his back, turned red, then began to scream. The boy was practically grafted to Corliss, but Corliss—a nervous chain-smoker—had limited patience and no talent for mothering.

The pregnancy had been a surprise, the result of a carelessly inserted diaphragm after they'd both had four or five mai tais, and Corliss could not rid herself of the notion that she'd been singled out by a perverse fate for the unlikely role of motherhood.

Corliss didn't like to breast-feed. She'd tried to wean Teller to the bottle but he cried in dismay whenever she offered him the rubber nipple. He'd turn his head away and compress his lips, offended by the artificial device. Nothing but the genuine article was acceptable to Teller. "He's going to be a great success in life," Moss had quipped. "He's never going to settle for second best."

Corliss had a hard time delivering Teller. She was narrow in the hips and Teller's bowling ball cranium found no easy passage. His head would crown, then withdraw—crown and withdraw—a kind of see-saw torture that didn't end until the slow-to-act obstetrician opened the way for Teller's oversized head with surgical scissors, widening the birth canal. The episiotomy took weeks to heal, but it was only the flesh that healed. The wound went deeper than flesh.

Corliss and Moss had a reasonably satisfying sex life before Teller came along. Now all that was history. Moss understood that he had to be patient, that Corliss's sex drive would return as the memory of Teller's hellish delivery faded, but in the meantime he'd grown a bit desperate.

Teller, at four months, was a big baby with big features. His nose was broad and dotted with large white pores. His eyebrows were dark and promised to become thick, like his namesake's. His ears were pretty as satin roses. He had stiff yellow hair that swirled up from his head like spun sugar. His mouth was wide, the red lips generous.

Neither Moss nor Corliss had generous lips. They had small mouths and tight dry lips that had been evolved in sub-arctic environments. They had both come from thin-lipped northern tribes among whom full-lipped sensuality was rare and signified, when observed in others, a lapsed morality. Moss felt that Corliss had succumbed to this frigid genetic mandate—a temporary condition, he hoped.

Teller's searching blue eyes were always moving, as if on the lookout. Sometimes Moss believed he could read his son's ratcheting eyes: The baby didn't trust them, perhaps even thought Moss and Corliss were not his parents at all and that the genuine article would show up soon to rescue him from these impostors who didn't even like each other very much.

Whenever Moss and Corliss argued, Teller would turn splotchy red and sob himself into an inconsolable hiccupping fit. Teller seemed to have concluded, even though he was an infant, that love between human beings was as uncommon as hate between the angels. Moss had read about a Southeast Asian civilization that believed babies were emissaries from heaven and remained so until they were a year old. If that were true then Teller's disapproval of his circumstances was nothing less than *heaven's* disapproval. Moss thought this was an amusing notion but he hesitated to share it with Corliss. In her present condition, Corliss would hold on to the symbolic possibility inherent in such an idea and would dwell, in an unhealthy and obsessive way, on its implications. And this would compromise the effects of her Valium tablets—which, on the other hand, didn't have much impact on the darker reaches of her mood swings. Corliss had an active imagination. Moss believed this was a talent but also a liability.

Moss had bought Corliss an IBM Selectric and a ream of bond. Corliss loved the machine and typed every day when Teller was down for his afternoon nap. She felt she had learned enough from the Green River novelist to begin a novel of her own. She

wrote a thousand words a day, faithfully. There was no narrative
continuity between each day's work but this didn't bother her:
Each day's writing was a fresh start. Start on what? It didn't matter.
What mattered was the sound of steel striking the pure surface
of the twenty-weight bond. What mattered were the words, the
strings of words, the blocks of words. As the paper blackened
with words, Corliss felt she'd accomplished something real. In
those moments she felt justified.

Moss read her efforts dutifully every evening, and in spite of
the fact that he knew it would be a mistake to offer criticism, he
was actually impressed with the quality of her writing. He hid
his surprise, but his enthusiasm was genuine. To test his honesty
Corliss asked him to be specific, and Moss was able to pinpoint
compelling phrases, images, and witty snippets of dialogue
between characters roughly based on people they knew back in
Seattle.

He'd say something to the effect, "You've got the goods, babe,"
and then they'd have a drink and smoke cigarettes on the steel
mesh deck of their trailer while Teller, grunting with pleasure,
pulled his sustenance from Corliss's reluctant breast, his big
red lips squeaking as they produced powerful vacuums over the
chapped nipple.

"Lover man," Corliss would say, taking a deep drag on her
cigarette.

Moss drove his truck through the already opened gate and into
the parking lot of the Delta-flight operations building which was
still under construction. The building was the size of a California
bungalow. Moss entered and took the elevator down to the launch
control capsule eighty feet below the surface where the clipboard
with its sheaf of UERs would be.

The launch control capsule was the tiny room where two air
force officers would eventually control ten ICBMs, each missile
packing a one-megaton warhead, enough power to flatten any
city on the planet. There were five launch control capsules per
squadron and four squadrons in the Wing. Two hundred missiles

would eventually sit in their silos under the prairie when the project was completed. It could be a daunting thought, but Moss didn't let it bother him. He believed the missiles would never be launched. Human beings were out of control, but not *that* far out of control.

Moss was not religious in any orthodox sense, but he felt the world operated under the direction of a Universal Manager who would always prevent humanity from annihilating itself. This belief in what amounted to a spiritual "trigger-lock" made his job ordinary everyday work, not a prologue to Armageddon. The Universal Manager allowed all sorts of horrors to walk the planet, but only up to a point. The reins were slack, but they were reliable.

Melba Fish was in the capsule, filling out a U E R. Melba worked for Autonetics, a Los Angeles–based company that was a contractor for the Minuteman inertial guidance system. She was an electrical engineer, a little older than Moss. She was a tall brunette with a long stride. She had high cheekbones and a sharp slender nose. Her nostrils were so narrow Moss wondered how she was able to breathe without keeping her mouth open. She wore heavy glasses that slid down her nose, pinching the already pinched nostrils. She spoke with a nasal twang.

"Buy me a drink at the officers' club, Moss?" she said.

"Sure," Moss said.

He knew better than to think she was interested in him. Melba was married to an air force pilot stationed at Vandenburg Air Force Base, in California. Even so, Moss wondered what she looked like under her denims as he followed her truck back to Minot.

In the bar she said, "Tony asked me for a divorce."

"I'm sorry," Moss said. He'd met Tony Fish once, when Fish flew to Minot in an F-104. He was a short, broad-shouldered light colonel with a chest full of medals. Moss remembered him as the kind of asshole who looks you in the eye as if he were staring through the ring-sight of a .50 caliber machine gun, waiting for you to look away first.

"He wants to marry a nineteen-year-old recruit. A baby slut in air force blue."

"The man's not worthy of you, Mel," Moss said. Moss thought of his own situation. Was he worthy of Corliss? Was Corliss worthy of him? Was anyone ever worthy of anyone? What a pompous notion! He was sorry he'd said this to Melba. It was a dumb thing to say.

He had three drinks to Melba's four. Then Melba said, "Help me get even, Moss."

Moss was offended. "You want to use me," he said.

"I've seen you looking at me. You're not bold enough to go beyond looking, so I'm being bold for you. Besides, that desperate scowl you carry around makes me think you'd like to use me, too. Here's your chance, Buster."

They had another drink then went to a downtown hotel, registering as Dr. and Mrs. Edward Teller. Melba looked as good under her denims as he had imagined.

Moss drove home in the dark, inventing excuses.

Corliss was in bed, smoking. "So, what's her name?" she said. Teller was sleeping at her side making strong sucking noises against his chubby wrist.

Moss presented his elaborate lie. It was a good lie, replete with technical jargon. But his tone was wrong. His tone was too defensive, too stylized. His tone told the truth.

"You bastard son of a *bitch*!" Corliss said.

"Don't get crazy on me, honey."

"I can fucking *smell* her!"

"It was an unplanned event," he finally admitted.

Moss spent the rest of the night in his truck telling himself he was a good man with poor judgment. He had no personal trigger-lock. The Universal Manager had no interest in providing personal trigger-locks. Let the impulsive little people put their lives in the toilet. It didn't concern him. He was concerned only with the big picture. For the Universal Manager, the self-destructive antics of the little people provided jolly entertainment, nothing more. Maybe some of the more tragic undoings of the little people made him weep, but the Universal Manager enjoyed a good cry now and then, too. Sadness completed the rainbow of emotions he wanted to experience. After all, what was Creation for? Bird-song, sunsets, and starry nights? This was the basis of Moss's belief system. In moments of doubt he called it an *interim* belief system—something better might come along some day. But for now this one worked for him.

When the sun came up Moss hosed yesterday's dust off his truck. He started the engine and listened to the soft rumble of the big V-8. The throbbing revolutions of the idling engine obliterated thought. Moss let himself sink into the sound, until there was only the sound.

Payback

Corliss finished her novel but couldn't come up with a title that covered the book's themes. She asked Moss for help.

Moss hated it. He'd read it twice. He hated it more the second time through. He hated it because it was about a marriage that looked very much like theirs. It portrayed intimacies that would be seen as autobiographical. The novel was well-written, clever, even witty. And this depressed him because he saw that these qualities alone made it publishable.

"Call it 'The Son of a Bitch in My Bed,'" he suggested.

"I want you to be serious. Surely you've seen it's not just about us. I'm using marriage as metaphor. American marriage, I mean."

"Metaphor for *what*?"

"For wish-fulfillment—our national obsession and failure. The way we think we're getting one thing and find out too late it's something very different. It's always an ugly surprise. Yet we keep falling for the illusion. Most politicians depend on this weakness."

"So what you're saying here is that *I'm* your ugly surprise?"

"'Ugly' is too strong a word, but we did surprise each other, don't you think? I thought I was getting my hero, a man who was good-looking and brainy, who hadn't buried his feminine side totally and so could be intuitive and gentle at the right times, and so on."

"And you got . . . ?"

"A man who was gentle because he was weak, who was smart enough to get by, but without any analytical ability. I got a man who saw his feminine side as a threat, an unexploded grenade."

"That's why you made Ted Endicott a pervert?"

"Ted Endicott isn't *you*, honey. He's a prototype with a lot of you in him. I used you as a model. I took some liberties with the image, as all artists must do."

She'd been referring to herself lately as an "artist." Moss found this amusing at first, then annoying. ("As an artist, I tend to think motivation alone never explains the deed it inspires." "As an artist, I understand how the shadow-self weaves the tale of our lives while we children of light bury ourselves in side-issues.")

Moss knew that he'd fallen for an illusion, too. The girl he married was concealing a future obsessive-compulsive neurotic who equated love with safe haven, sex with obligation, self-respect with self-righteousness.

But Ted Endicott was a plainly a creep, and Moss resented being the model Corliss based him on. One particular perversion of Endicott's was watching his wife, Adela, have sex with men she picked up in bars. Endicott would sit in a chair next to the bed taking Polaroid photographs while Adela and the stranger went at it. Moss thought this was unbelievable and wanted Corliss to cut it out of the manuscript.

"Too close to home?" she'd teased.

"Not close at all. If I walked in on something like that I'd load my .38."

"But you're not a violent man," she said.

"All men are violent, when push comes to shove."

"No they're not. Men in prison camps during wartime often go humbly to the firing squad. They've got nothing to lose in fighting, but they go docile to their deaths anyway."

"I wouldn't be as docile as this Endicott moron if you were like this bitch Adela."

But it wasn't about *him*, she insisted. All men have beyond-the-pale sexual fantasies at some time or other in their lives. It comes with the territory. The homoerotic impulse is common among heteros, ask any psychiatrist. Bestiality—not the rarity you'd think. She reminded him that just the other day they read about a man who was arrested for having sex with another man's horse.

The police found an incriminating jar of Vaseline in the mare's stall—evidently the pervert had a high opinion of his apparatus! And sex with children? It happens all too often. Incest? Good God we've had enough confirmation of *that* in the last few decades. There are isolated areas where the groom's father believes that being the first to deflower his daughter-in-law on the wedding night is his somber familial *duty*. I'm not talking about Borneo either, she said, I mean right here in Backwater Flats, USA. What I'm saying here is there's no such thing as normal when it comes to sexual impulse or the constellations of tribal customs that define its expression. Her approach to these subjects, she said, was anthropological—the deeds were well documented.

She argued with passion, even though she knew there was nothing original about her ideas. Freud, Krafft-Ebing, Kinsey, Masters and Johnson, they turned over all the rocks a long time ago, but the subject excited her and her excitement made the argument seem fresh.

"This is payback, isn't it?" Moss said, opening another beer.

"I don't know what you mean."

He pointed at her typewriter as if it were a lethal instrument. "Payback," he said. "This is payback."

Corliss scoffed. "You think I'd waste my talent on something as stupid as *that*?"

"Yes."

"You flatter yourself."

"Maybe."

"That's not what artists do."

"I bet that's exactly what artists do."

Corliss stopped the argument before it got nasty by going back to reading her manuscript.

"Call it 'Payback,'" Moss said, but Corliss was not listening.

Structure

Moss eventually agreed to attend the healing service at the Church of Galvanic Grace with Martina Benyo, his wife's best friend. Martina claimed her neurosis had been "pruned" (not *cured*) by Doctor Italo Tutta's "Logic Battery." After only seven weekly sessions her skin had cleared up, her stool had firmed, her hair had stopped falling out, and she'd gained three pounds. She believed her overall health had improved. She felt she could embrace life again, without the usual sinking feeling that the embrace would not be returned.

The Logic Battery generated "square-wave" pulses of varying electrical potential. The "supplicant" sat in a wooden chair and electrodes were taped to the "serial deltas" on his or her body. When a switch was thrown, a rheostat adjusted, a high-frequency circuit tuned, and the resulting series of shock waves "severed the flowering branches if not the roots" of the "channel-blocking mindweed"—the cause of the "bifurcated energy drain" which eventually led to the "spiritual indolence," popularly—and mistakenly—known as "depression."

Even though the claims were modest ("no ill is ever completely cured, and supplicants must always be on guard against the windblown spore of recurrence"), Moss scoffed. Charlatanry, modest or outrageous, annoyed him. He was, after all, trained in the sciences. The Scientific Method was his bible, orthodoxy, and church. Dr. Italo Tutta's mix of pseudoscientific, religious, and horticultural terminology was not even *good* charlatanry—the mumbo jumbo too earnest, too eclectic, too goofy. But he agreed to let Martina take him there because he was lonely and frightened and willing to try anything once. He didn't believe his condition could be "pruned" even a little but Martina kept after him until he saw that the only way to stop her nagging was to let her have her way.

He was lonely because his wife, Corliss, had left him, and he was frightened because he believed he had symptoms of prostate cancer. He didn't especially like Martina—she was loud, dramatic, bossy—but she was close to Corliss and was therefore a conduit of information to which he would not otherwise have access. ("Is she sleeping with anyone?" he'd asked. "Not yet," Martina replied, her arch, sidelong glance suggesting, even welcoming, the possibility. In fact, she knew that Corliss had gone salmon fishing, *twice*, with Draco Valilis, a radiologist from Tacoma.)

Moss blamed himself. Who else? He was the instigator. He'd been feeling trapped for no reason he could justify. His life was good by any standard. I'm a self-pampering ingrate, he told himself. There are people in the world who pick through garbage dumps to live! Most people on the planet have never seen a paycheck! There are fanatic police states where people have their hands cut off for stealing bread! He should have been thankful for what he had. His health was good, his job was interesting, he was making decent money, and, if he played his cards right, his future would be secure. Yet he felt locked inside invisible but impenetrable walls, and the walls were closing in. He felt put-upon. He felt resentful.

He also felt stupid. But he wasn't stupid. He *understood* his complaint was an all too familiar one. But knowing he was traveling a well-worn path didn't lessen his anguish. It made it worse. The anguish was as real as it had been when it first surfaced, however many American decades ago. It had become a polyp on the national spirit. Moss had patriotically pursued the founding fathers' ideal, Happiness. But Happiness eluded him. *Is this all there is?* he asked. But this was the pampered ingrate's classic question. It had no merit. He despised himself, and the many before him, for asking it.

And then, out of nowhere, he was blindsided by sudden emotional outbursts. A piece of sentimental music, popular or classical, could trigger it. Once while driving home from the aerospace company where he worked, he almost veered off the freeway when

the DJ he'd been listening to played the old ballad "Good-bye." The
vocalist opened with the lament, "I'll never forget you." A flash
flood of tears obscured his vision of the roadway. He sobbed.
The sweetly miserable arrangement of violins and oboes under-
mined the lyrics voiced by the seductive baritone. The lyrics were
hopeful but the music behind them told another story: The ties
that bind are weak, memory is unreliable, and the cold universe
has no intention of redeeming the desperate circumstances of
men and women. We lose, the music said—we always have, we
always will—while the baritone made a saccharine argument for
the recovery and retention of joy.

Moss wept helplessly as his car veered to a stop on the freeway's
shoulder. Impatient commuters, unaware of the pointlessness
of their furious travel, honked past. Moss turned his emergency
blinkers on and let his tears flow.

These assaults on the established order of his hard-won
middle-class life made his behavior erratic. The daily routines
that delivered the reliable citizen safely into old age, decrepitude,
and death gave him night sweats.

And so he became reckless. He bought a small Japanese
motorcycle. He thought he might take up skydiving. He considered spelunking. And he began an affair with a coworker, Penny
Cruikshank, an engineer in the Quality Control Department who
studied the failure rates of drop-forged spacers.

Reckless or not, the affair was just another diversion, another
aspect of the predictability he'd come to fear. Corliss had seen
through his weak lies—"unscheduled meetings at the Wichita
plant"—but had forgiven him; even so, the strain on their already
strained marriage increased. They were civil toward each other but
warpages had taken hold. In bed they were still responsive—more
so than ever since Corliss's curiosity over Penny Cruikshank's bed
manners had energized their sex life with an untethered wildness.
Her orgasms, once signaled by comfortable little mews, became
as violent as grand mal seizures. She clawed red stripes into his
back. The mews became growls. She head-butted him once, making
his nose bleed. She left blue incisor prints on his shoulder and

neck. Even after he'd finished and was beginning to withdraw she continued to beat and claw and bite until he had to forcibly restrain her. "I was having multiples," she explained. But Moss believed these violent spasms were not the effects of extended orgasm at all. They were *fury* in the guise of release. Afterward she sulked, and the sulks lasted days.

They'd had a workable marriage—most of the wrinkles, up to now, had been ironed out. They'd made a pact early on to be simple and straightforward with each other. They valued honesty above all else. Without honesty, no other virtue was possible. Marriage without honesty was a recipe for eventual disaster. This is what they believed. But while honesty was the best policy, it was a hard policy to follow. Overnight, it seemed, Moss and Corliss became as secretive and wary as spies in a hostile land.

They tried counseling. They were open and humble in the counselor's faux-oak laminate confessional. But identifying, naming, and analyzing the problem (*the banishment of trust*, the counselor said) did not break its hold. It rubbed at the windows of their marriage like the coarse fur of an impatient scavenger.

Martina was clear about blame. "They like to tell you no one is to blame these days, Moss, but they're wrong. There is always a culprit. In this case, it is you."

He'd already conceded that. But when she located the blame in his physiology rather than in his character, he'd laughed. "Electroshock?" he'd said.

"It's not that simple," Martina said. "Galvanic grace is not primitive shock therapy."

Her wacky ideas made him think about the suspected tumor, the dark intruder rising like a warm ball of yeasted dough in his prostate gland. Perhaps this lethal tumor had triggered the desperate behavior he'd come to believe was a rebellion against the absurdity of a well-managed life. Perhaps the mating instinct, wearing the mask and costume of romance, had been called forth by the proximity of death. Biology plays us for fools—cells endlessly repeating themselves, cells dividing and combining, the busy microscopic world eventually producing the self-deluded macroscopic world of bipedal intelligence. Biology, dealing the cards, worked for the house, not the mark. The mark: a randy goat in the abattoir, knee-deep in the offal of its slaughtered companions, yet still crooning love songs to the sloe-eyed does. A depressing vision of reality, but it made sense to Moss.

Martina had shoved a brochure into his hand: *Disorder Kills*. It was by Dr. Italo Tutta, PhD, DD, EdD. Moss thumbed through the pages—pages full of multisyllabic quackery:

> Osculants in the vagus humor (unidentified as yet by the hidebound techniques of bureaucratic medical science) directly affect the endoplasmic reticulum, hence diverting male galvanic energy to cotqueanistic seep.

Meaningless drivel, Moss thought—the words made up, or, if real, joined in fraudulent syntax. The section about the Logic Battery was illustrated. The machine looked something like a 1950 computer, a Univac, propped up on oil drums. When functioning, panels of festive lights probably blinked on and off in dazzling patterns. There was an accompanying photo of Doctor Italo Tutta—grainy with widely spaced halftone dots—a gaunt, hook-nosed, bespectacled man of fifty who resembled Pope Pius the Twelfth, the pope who cut a deal with Mussolini's fascists to secure the safety of the Vatican and shield it from the untidy moral issues generated by war. Moss read part of the introduction:

> Consider, if you will, the mistletoe vine. We have come to think of it as a beneficent love potion, a facilitator of coital union, but in reality it is a tree-killing parasite, covering branches and leaves alike, shutting off sunlight and thus interdicting the photosynthetic process. This is no love potion, nay, this is the end of love. Is there such a vine choking the vitality from the tree of your life?

Martina herself had been besieged by gathering fears. Fear of breast cancer, fear of weather, fear of large dogs, fear of airborne and touch-borne viruses, fear of strangers. The fears bred like mice in the secret walls of her psyche. She'd become a haunted woman, unable to enjoy life fully on any level. She'd lost her appetite for rich foods, movies appalled her, she slept badly. In vivid dreams she toured the outposts of hell, glimpsed the dark road that led downhill to the smoky gates. Sometimes she woke to the yowl of her neighbor's cats, the smell of sulfur on her pillow.

She had no patience with shrinks and their chemical cures. She had few friends. Corliss and Moss were the best she had. It made sense to her to stay close to Moss now that Corliss was spending more and more time in Tacoma with her salmon-hunting radiologist. It seemed inevitable, then, that Moss and Martina would end up in bed with each other.

Moss was not physically attracted to Martina. Her spine knuckled her back without an intervening cushion of flesh. She was five-feet six-inches tall and weighed less than one hundred pounds. He realized, at one point, that he could actually take hold of her spine in his fingertips as though it were a vestigial dorsal fin. For years she had eaten foods with more fiber than calories. Her thighs had withered under the regimen of a totally fatless diet so that when she stood, naked, the space between them was as wide as the chilling separation between the femurs of a standing skeleton. When they had sex Moss heard her bones rattle and clack. At times he believed they were breaking under his weight. Yet her narrow face remained impassive, from foreplay to orgasm, as if there were no connection between her physical and emotional states. She explained this phenomenon after their first time together: "I don't mean to be insensitive, Moss, but this is merely bifurcated energy drain, not love."

"Thanks for clearing it up for me," Moss said.

Moss worked in a hangar-like building big enough to house Zeppelins. The building was so voluminous that it made its own weather. A wind damp with mist would sometimes brush paperwork off his desk. Moss once thought he saw a blue squib of lightning snap between the arched beams that held up the high ceiling. In this atmosphere hundreds of men and women seated at steel desks thumbed through manuals or worked calculators, identifying and attacking the large and small problems encountered in the design, assembly, and testing of intercontinental ballistic missiles.

Penny Cruikshank was a recent hire out of the University of Washington's school of industrial engineering, a specialist in structural design. Moss had been avoiding her since their brief affair. It had started innocently enough at a Fellini film festival in the University district. A poster had been taped to the wall above a water cooler. One morning, they found themselves looking at the poster together. *La Strada, La Dolce Vita*, and *8½* were playing at an art cinema in the University district. They were both Fellini fans and decided to leave work early to catch the latest addition to Fellini's gallery of grotesques.

Moss hadn't seen *8½* and it took him by surprise. At times he was moved to tears, even though the movie was more comedy than drama, more satirical than sentimental. He identified with Marcello Mastroianni's character, Guido, a film director paralyzed with self-doubt. Guido was at a crossroads in his life. He'd lost faith in himself but found solace in sex. Halfway through the movie, Moss put his arm around Penny's shoulders. She stiffened for a moment, then, as if having made a decision, leaned into him with abandonment.

From time to time, Penny cast reproachful glances across the sea of desks that separated them. Their weekend encounters in a Motel 6, just off the Interstate that skirted the aerospace plant where they worked, seemed to Moss like the fading memory of an embarrassing dream.

Penny was an overweight, near-sighted blonde. Her weight was distributed asymmetrically: her upper body was slim and well proportioned; from the hips down she was obese. It was as if her lightweight upper body had been grafted to a heavyweight lower body as a vicious surgical joke. Her face was lovely but it held a mournful cast that did not lift. When she searched the vast work area for Moss, her large, myopic eyes were often wide of the mark, fixing her reproach on the electrical engineer to his left or on the computer programmer to his right. When her unsure glance fell on him he ducked away from it, hiding behind the large manuals that described his area of responsibility. She had glasses but seldom wore them.

Moss recalled that in bed Penny exhibited the grope-and-feel behavior of the blind, as if committing to memory the contours of his body. This thrilled Moss at first, but when she continued after he had rolled away from her in a state of relaxed indifference, he became annoyed. "Do you have to keep doing that, Penny?" he'd finally asked.

"Structure fascinates me," she'd said, her engineer's fingers exploring his pelvic hollows, the parabolic rise of his chest, the soft undefended area between rib cage and genitals.

She slid out of bed and waddled to the bathroom, her tall neck, narrow shoulders, and lithe torso carried along and humiliated by the elephantine hips and the short thick legs. The tragedy of her body moved him. Better to be fat or thin, but not both. His auditory memory replayed the morose refrain, *I'll never forget you.* Moss sobbed, beginning to hate the ballad and the maudlin baritone who sang it.

Penny heard him cover his sob with a spell of false coughing. "What's *wrong* with you?" she said, suspiciously.

"Allergies," he managed. "Sinus problem. Post nasal drip."

She didn't buy it. "I don't need that from you, Moss. I can live with what I look like. Maybe you think you are flawless. You're not. I think your prostate is swollen. The skin over your perineum is feverish and tight with pressure. I heard you yelp when you climaxed. You may have a lesion. Weep for yourself, Moss. Your instrument, by the way, has serious tensile strength fluctuations. I thought you should know. It might have been a momentary loss of interest, but you should probably see a urologist just the same." Quality control was Penny's job assignment and her specialty within that assignment was structural analysis.

Penny sent him a note: "So, it meant less than nothing to you. Why did I think you had some moral structure to your character?" The note made Moss feel guilty, then angry. He wrote back: "I've got more moral structure than I need. My wife is devastated. Our marriage is on the rocks. Please try to understand. I'll never forget you." But the myopic reproaches searching across the vast gray room, where engineers and programmers grappled with throw-weight equations and the trajectories of multiple reentry vehicles, did not abate.

Moss buried himself in his immediate assignment—calculating the failure probabilities of third-stage guidance systems under severe g-force stress, and the ameliorating effect on these numbers by the use of redundancy in sensitive circuits. The work was important but not difficult, yet his efforts were often emended by his lead engineer, a wall-eyed man in his sixties who had nothing to do beyond second-guessing the work of the people he supervised. "We're making weapons that one day might bring civilization as we know it to its knees, Moss," the lead engineer once lectured. "Try to take your work a little more seriously."

Moss took his work very seriously. The lead engineer, on the other hand, was a sententious nose-picker who took a dozen coffee breaks a day. He was incompetent yet believed he was indispensable to the company. The company seemed to believe it, too. This mutual self-deception fascinated Moss. Incompetence was often rewarded in the aerospace business. At times this disheartened him, and he wondered if this principle of Incompetence Rewarded was universal or confined to the defense industry which was on the receiving end of massively generous cost-plus government contracts. The nameless dread he woke to every morning became focused by this possibility. He began to worry over the fate of the nation as well as the fate of his prostate. The two fates seemed to be related. It was a crazy notion, he knew, but mere logic could not uproot it.

The day Moss and Martina were to see Doctor Italo Tutta, Moss believed he saw streaks of blood in his urine.

"We ate pickled beets last night," Martina reminded him.

"The color was wrong for beets," Moss said.

"You're looking for things to worry about," she said. "I'm on intimate terms with *that* process. Besides, blood in your urine would indicate bladder or kidney cancer, not prostate."

"Thanks for the reassurance," Moss said.

They drove to West Seattle, a part of the city Moss was not familiar with. They turned into a street of narrow houses. The houses were set close together, like brown teeth in a broken jaw. They were old houses, warped out of plumb by decades of rain and hard wind off Puget Sound. The houses seemed to lean against one another, huddled, as if expecting marauders from the sea.

Moss wanted to back out. They'd had dinner at a sea food restaurant near Eliot Bay and steamed clams lay in his stomach like hot stones. In the restaurant, Moss had a vision of his future. An old man, eating alone three tables away, had placed a framed eight-by-ten photograph across the table from himself. He spoke to the photograph as he ate. The sepia-toned picture was of a woman, her clothes and hair-style suggesting the 1940s. At one point the old man raised his voice and pointed an accusing table knife at the woman in the photograph. Moss heard the man say, "You jump to conclusions, Velma, just like always. For once I want to hear you admit—"

Wanting to hear more, Moss heard instead the strains of "Goodbye" on the restaurant's Muzak system. The baritone—Dick Haymes or Vic Damone—crooned "I'll never forget you" above the despairing violins. He gritted his teeth against the tears that were searing his eyes. He strangled back a rising sob. Martina, busy cracking the shell of a large crab, did not notice his condition. Moss was thankful for that.

Martina's appetite had blossomed anew. She'd been eating like a field hand. Along with the crab, she had fish chowder, clams casino, wild rice and mushrooms. Flesh had begun to cover her once visible bones. Her skin glowed with revived health. She was, after all, an attractive woman.

Italo Tutta met them at the door. "Ah," he said. "Miss Benyo and the new supplicant. You are late." He wore a dark suit cut for a larger frame.

"We'll come back another time," Moss said, taking a step back toward the car.

"No, no. Late, but not too late," said Italo Tutta. He raised his gnarled hand as if blessing the air between them. The hand trembled a bit then dropped. He smiled. It was the smile of a man who had come to realize there was little to smile about in this world—the unnerving smile of a saint. Italo Tutta's teeth were long and unevenly spaced—horse teeth in the austere papal face.

Italo Tutta was crippled with rheumatoid arthritis. His hands hung out of his jacket sleeves like paper claws. He wore corrective shoes. His spine had a lateral scoliotic curve. He had to tilt his head against the sideways slant of his shoulders in order to face people directly. His head was long and narrow and seemed too heavy for the flimsy neck that tried to hold it plumb. A panel of thin black hair was lacquered against his skull with a scented gel.

Martina pulled Moss into the house. Half a dozen people sat in heavy wooden chairs facing the Logic Battery. They were wearing hospital smocks, tied in back. Wires were taped to their wrists and ankles, wires that were gathered in a braid and connected to a junction box that had been plugged into the Logic Battery.

The Logic Battery hummed like a hive. Italo Tutta dragged out two more chairs to complete the arc in front of his healing machine. He handed Martina and Moss hospital gowns and instructed them to put them on in the bedroom. He pointed to a door at the far end of the room. "Hurry now," he said. "We must get on with the business of pruning as much parasitic growth as time permits."

In hospital garb, Moss and Martina took their seats. Italo Tutta attached electrodes to their wrists and ankles and then reached under their gowns to tape wires under the collar bones. He apologized to Martina for the impertinence of his fingers on her upper chest. The apology was a formality, Moss realized, since Martina had been coming here for almost two months and knew what to expect.

"You have a disorder?" Italo Tutta asked Moss.

"So she tells me," Moss said, looking at Martina.

The others, six in all, studied him, the dubious newcomer. Four women, two men. The women were middle-aged, the men in their sixties. All of them wasted by chronic disorders. The women smiled, the men did not.

Italo Tutta studied Moss. "What is the nature of your malady?" he said.

"Apparently I'm a son of a bitch," Moss said.

"He's neurotic," Martina said. "He has terminal illness fantasies. He can't control his emotions."

"I see," Italo Tutta said. "And in what way do you wish to control your emotions?"

"His emotions are controlling *him*," Martina said. "It's a matter of balance."

"Ah," Italo Tutta said. "Balance is most important; indeed, it is our goal." He bared his horsey teeth. Moss closed his eyes.

"Let's do it," Moss said.

Italo Tutta hunched out of sight behind his machine and the lights in the panel facing the wired-together supplicants lit up. Just as Moss imagined, the lights began to flash on and off in hypnotic patterns, a science-fiction movie cliché. He saw quick letters form in the lights. MGETH URTBE GERXO. He wanted them to be anagrams. He tried to solve them. He got as far as GET THEM TEX. The effort tired him. He dozed.

The next day Moss was warned of a possible layoff. There was a good chance he would be "surplussed." Such layoffs were routine, but his lead engineer, who did not like Moss, fabricated a reason. "You definitely have an attitude problem, Moss. You're not a team player. It's that simple. The company—the *nation*—needs team players."

It wasn't that simple; it was simpler. Phase One of the contract his department had been working under was coming to an end. The company, in order to economize, had to cut jobs. It happened in predictable cycles. Every job in the aerospace business was temporary, except for the top management jobs, which were secure because they were part of the company's self-protecting political structure. There were other openings within the company and Moss was confident he'd find one, if it came to that. He was still young and his pay was modest—assets, when interviewing for jobs in other departments. Older, well-paid men who lacked political clout were jettisoned without mercy.

"I might as well tell you, Moss," Martina said. "Corliss is dating a medical doctor from Tacoma, a radiologist. He has his own boat. He takes her fishing. It's very good for Corliss, these fishing trips with Dr. Valilis. She looks wonderful."

They were having lunch in a Greek restaurant in the Pike Street Market. Moss shrugged. He knew Corliss was seeing someone. The fact that it was a radiologist, a man of science, a balanced man, was somehow consoling.

"Did you hear what I said?" Martina asked.

He nodded. But he was thinking about something Italo Tutta had said as they left his humble little house in West Seattle: "I have known men like you." It didn't come across as a condemnation. It sounded more like an apology. Maybe a lament. The Logic Battery, whatever it was, had no detectable effect on Moss. The episode was amusing, if anything.

"Men like me?" Moss had said.

"I do nothing for them. They are death in life. Dead, they move on to great things, good and bad. Dead, they continue to succeed. Dead, the world becomes their oyster. They care for nothing. They are loved but they do not love. If they weep their tears are mere abstract gestures—they might weep for humanity but rarely for individuals. You are young for this, but you are progressing."

"In other words, men with attitude problems."

"It is more than attitude. It is grander, you see. It is darker."

"I don't think I can put that on my resume," Moss said.

Italo Tutta smiled sadly. "You see," he said, looking skyward as if addressing an invisible multitude, "even the most serious matters are treated with flippancy."

Martina touched his face, taking him out of his reverie. "The next question," she said, "is what about us."

"Us?"

"You, me. Next week, next month. The future."

"I don't see a future, Martina. Not beyond tonight or tomorrow night."

"Okay," Martina said. "Just thought I'd ask."

She dug hungrily into her bowl of pastitsio.

He loved to see her eat like this. Would the dead appreciate restored appetite? Would the dead be moved by an anorexic turned glutton? She ate without self-consciousness, noisy and fast. He was grateful to her.

"I'll never forget you, Martina," he said, his eyes dry, the song in his head long gone.

Freaks

Moss woke up at 3:00 a.m. with a migraine. He got out of bed and stumbled into the bathroom. When he turned on the light he saw two reflections of himself staring back from the wide mirror. The shock made him reel. The floor under his feet turned. He braced himself on the sink counter and looked down at his four hands. The two-drain sink had four faucets. The number of towel racks on the wall had doubled. Moss felt the nausea of seasickness. He dropped to all fours and crawled to the toilet. He opened the lid of the twin toilets and threw up.

"What's wrong?" Corliss said.

Moss looked up. Two wives in their nightgowns stared at him, their four arms folded against their four breasts.

"I'm seeing double. I've got a splitting headache." He retched again. "Could be food poisoning."

"From my baba ghannooj? I don't think so. It's nerves," she said. "You're very worried. This is what anxiety does to you. You feel sick, like you have the flu, only it isn't the flu. I should know."

"Since when does anxiety make you see double?"

"It's possible," Corliss said. "Leaving your job worries you. The move to California worries you. *I* worry you."

"You don't worry me," Moss said.

"I'm not seeing him anymore, but you worry about it anyway. It gnaws on you. I can tell. You grind your teeth in your sleep. You never used to do that."

Corliss had a brief affair with Dr. Draco Valilis, a Tacoma radiologist. She'd met Valilis in a community college class on

Existentialism. Her affair was in response to Moss's even briefer affair with Penny Cruikshank.

Corliss's affair with Draco Valilis did wonders for her. She'd started exercising, lost twenty pounds, changed hair color, got her teeth fixed, gone deep-sea fishing. She and Valilis studied together. She could quote from *Being and Nothingness*. She could quote from *Being and Time*.

Draco Valilis was a gourmet cook. He taught Corliss the finer points of the culinary arts. Baba ghannooj became her specialty.

Moss's affair didn't improve him much. He gained weight, lost some hair, got a urinary tract infection. At best he learned something about the limitations of romantic adventure. The thrill had a short shelf-life. Penny Cruikshank was bright and often witty, but eventually their conversations got stale. They became circular and repetitive:

—*Fellini's camera work is superior to Bergman's, don't you think?*

—*In color maybe, but not in black-and-white. The Catholic imagination is freed by color, the Lutheran by black-and-white.*

—*I don't think you can call Fellini's imagination Catholic. He obviously hated the Church.*

—*Hate, love—it's obsession either way. His camera work in* La Dolce Vita, *for instance . . .*

And so on.

Their lovemaking became routine too, every caress and sigh predictable. They began to argue like tired veterans of married life. Before long they became anxious to go their separate ways. Reality had taken romance by its swan-like neck and strangled it.

These infidelities were history—side-roads that led to dead ends. Moss and Corliss had gotten past them. Their marriage had survived. Survival became their goal, for the sake of their son, Teller, if for nothing else. Teller was in junior high, a nervous overweight boy who was a natural target for bullies. Teller wouldn't have survived the disintegration of his family.

They confessed these things to a marriage counselor, the third after being disappointed by two others. This marriage counselor congratulated them. "You've matured, both of you," the counselor said. "This is what we hoped to achieve—this transformation from the larval ego to the pupal. Eventually you will achieve the metamorphic. By then you two will have earned your wings!"

The counselor, a large enthusiastic man in caftan and rope sandals shook their hands warmly. As they left his office for the last time, he steepled his long-fingered hands together as if safeguarding their improved attitudes toward each other with prayer. He was New Age before New Age. He burned incense in his office and played Ravi Shankar on his stereo during the counseling sessions. Outside his office Moss and Corliss could not look at each other. They went home, resigned to their familiar routines.

↙

Moss took four aspirins and went back to bed. He dreamed of fire trucks. One slid down an embankment into the fire it was supposed to put out. Other fire trucks stopped and the firemen got out and watched helplessly from a safe promontory as their comrades burned. The first fire truck burned furiously, as if it were made of dry paper.

The headache was gone by morning, but Moss was still seeing double. "Sinus infection," he said to his two faces staring back at him in the bathroom mirror. The two faces were serious, intelligent, trustworthy. They knew what they were talking about. Moss had had severe sinus infections in the past. Not so severe that they caused double vision, but severe enough to make his eyes hurt. The maxillary sinuses alongside the nasal passages were swollen, putting pressure against the eyes. What else could it be?

Moss sat down to breakfast and watched the early news on the kitchen TV. If he tried hard, he could make the twin images of the TV set slide together and merge into one. He was not able to hold them together for very long, but the fact that he could do it heartened him. The affliction could not be all that serious if he could defeat its symptoms through will power alone. He decided not to waste a day of sick leave. He'd go to work in spite of the double vision.

Driving presented a problem. He tried to drive through his suburb but it wasn't possible. The single lane of traffic coming toward him doubled. The lane he was driving in forked. He almost had a head-on collision with a garbage truck. The two garbage trucks he saw confused him. He tried to drive between them. The driver of the garbage truck blew his horn and Moss yanked the wheel and drove up onto the sidewalk. He drove home with one eye closed, his heart pounding. There was no way he could drive on the Interstate. He'd have to deal with sixteen lanes of traffic instead of eight.

Back in his house, he found an old pair of sunglasses. He cut a lens-shaped disc out of a piece of black construction paper and taped it to the inside of the left lens. The makeshift eye patch worked. Using only his right eye, he was at home again in a world on nonrepeating objects. He spent the day at work in his eye-patched sunglasses.

He was preparing a manual that explained reliability mathematics to nontechnical management types. He had to reduce basic probability formulas to simplistic, nonmathematical language. It was easy work, and he didn't strain his right eye very much doing it. Even so, his headache returned by mid afternoon. The headache was accompanied by bright flashes of light at the edge of his vision.

Penny Cruikshank worked thirty desks away. He walked down the aisle to her. "Penny, I need some aspirins," he said.

"Try the dispensary," she said. She'd been cold to him since their breakup. He was a stranger again. Just another coworker in a suit and tie. One of 150. Penny was the only female engineer in this department of drab, gray-suited men.

"You don't have any? I thought your desk was full of pills."

Penny leaned back in her chair and released an irritated sigh. She pulled open a desk drawer and found a bottle of Excedrin. She gave him two.

"Could I have four? I have this pounding headache." He was going for sympathy but wasn't getting any.

Penny shook out two more tablets then put the bottle back into her desk and closed the drawer firmly. Through all this, she hadn't looked at him once.

"Thanks," Moss said. He leaned on her desk. "You didn't ask me why I'm wearing sunglasses."

"Why are you wearing sunglasses," she said without interest. She opened a structural engineering manual and began turning pages.

"Something's wrong with my eye."

"Sorry to hear that," she said. She still didn't look up. She had no curiosity about Moss or his eye trouble. Curiosity, like every other response to his state of being, was a thing of the past. Moss went back to his desk.

↓

"I called Draco," Corliss said. "He said you should see a neurologist."

"I thought you were through with your doctor friend," Moss said. He was lying on the couch, an ice bag on his forehead.

"I am. I wanted his opinion about you seeing double."

"I don't want his opinion. I have a sinus infection."

"Draco said definitely not. You don't have a sinus infection. He said it's something far more serious."

Moss stopped listening to her. He was listening to a voice in his head. The voice said, "Compunction in conjunction with function yields traction by action." The voice was mellifluous, like the voice of a radio announcer. It repeated the same phrase, over and over. The phrase made sense to Moss, but he couldn't paraphrase it. His chest felt odd. He slid his hand under his shirt and felt his nipples. They were larger than usual and sensitive.

"I'm going to make a clinic appointment for you," Corliss said.

"I won't go," Moss said.

"Don't be a baby."

"They're butchers."

Moss was afraid of doctors. This was a fear going back to his childhood. When he was five years old he had chronic ear infections and would have to go to a doctor once a week to have his ears lanced. He was terrified of these visits. He threw tantrums whenever his mother said they were going to the doctor's office. To avoid these outbursts she lied to him. "We're going to the *movies*, honey," she said. "Mickey Mouse, Donald Duck, and the Red Ryder serial." Or, "We're going to the zoo today to see the lions and tigers and giraffes." The deceptions worked until he realized he was climbing the familiar stairs to the ear doctor's office. By then it was too late.

↓

In bed that night, Corliss said, "Are you sure you feel up to it?"

Moss was determined. "Of course I do," he said. "Why wouldn't I feel up to it?"

But Moss had a problem.

"What's wrong with you?" Corliss said.

"I don't know," Moss said.

"Mr. Dingus doesn't seem very interested," Corliss said.

Moss rolled away from her. Corliss threw back the blankets. She knelt over him and studied the situation. "It gets smaller when I touch it," she said. "Like it's trying to hide."

Moss was embarrassed. He got on top of Corliss again and she wrapped her legs around him. She crossed her ankles at the base of his spine. She kissed him hard and he felt her nipples stiffen against his chest, her urgent pelvic thrusts beginning. This usually stimulated him. But now it had no effect. He rolled away again, grinding his teeth.

"It'll be better tomorrow," Corliss said, consoling him. His failure was not as earth-shaking to Corliss as it was to Moss. She turned her back and went to sleep. It always amazed Moss that Corliss could fall into untroubled sleep in seconds. Her small snores proved this.

Moss could not sleep. Double vision and now impotence. What was happening to him? His sinus infection theory was getting thin. He went to sleep listening to the voice in his head. It said, "Basic endeavors need basic levers." This didn't need paraphrasing. "Shut up," he said to the voice.

It occurred to Moss that he was losing his mind.

↓

Moss had been recruited by an aerospace company in northern California. The company, which had just landed a submarine-launched ICBM contract and was in the process of filling its ranks with new hires, wanted Moss to head up a Reliability Engineering group. Moss had been offered a 40 percent increase in salary and a management position.

His son, Teller, an emotional boy, didn't want to go to California. "They're meaner in California. They'll pick on me. They hate fat kids in California."

"Your not exactly *fat*, honey," Moss said. Moss saw two fat Tellers slumped in twin sofas.

"And don't call me *honey*, Dad! Bobby Ebert heard you call me that and he told the other kids. Now they *all* call me "honey," even the goddamned girls."

Teller burst into tears. He was not only fat, he was tall and had a large square head with big velvety ears. Thirteen was an awkward age for any boy but Teller broke the mold. He had no athletic skill and little coordination. Because of his height he slumped when he stood. He was a natural target for the savagery of boys who were savoring the fierce dawn of pubescence. Teller had bushy eyebrows, a wide sensual mouth, and size twelve feet. He was a brainy boy with an impressive vocabulary which he liked to use, and this proved to be another liability. In the prehormonal years of grade school he'd been the star, admired by teachers and students alike. In junior high he was a freak. He'd been first to raise his hand to answer the teacher's questions in sixth grade but soon learned that this eagerness only brought him misery in seventh and eighth.

"Think of it this way, Teller," Moss said. "When we leave here, you'll leave all your troubles behind. We'll all get a new start in California."

Teller thought about this. He brightened for a moment, then darkened. "It'll be the same in California. It'll be *worse* in California."

"It'll be different," Moss said.

His headache pulsed against his skull. Earlier that day, Draco Valilis had told Corliss that Moss might have an aneurysm. When Corliss passed Draco's diagnosis on to Moss, he threw the copy of *Cosmo* he'd been paging through against the wall. "Tell your quack friend to keep his opinions to himself!" he'd said. His voice was pitched high. It warbled in his throat. He almost burst into tears. This hysterical outburst had shocked him and he bit his tongue against the sudden flood of emotion. Corliss looked at him curiously but said nothing. Moss couldn't control his face. He didn't want Corliss to see the spectacle he was making of himself. He'd left the room, hot with anger and shame, tears beginning to well up and spill.

Teller got up. The physical effort made him groan. Two enormous misshapen boys rose up before Moss. He put on his eye-patched sunglasses.

"It'll be different, but the same," Teller whined.

Moss couldn't argue against his son's logic. Teller, like his namesake, Edward Teller, the father of the H-Bomb, was bright and inquisitive. The boy's IQ had not been tested but Moss believed it was easily in the genius range. Moss knew his son would eventually put distance between himself and the mediocre students who bullied and harassed him, but that wouldn't console the boy now. Teller had to get through five more degrading years of public school before he could find refuge in a good technical college. If he survived those years, he'd be fine. It was a big if. Emotional instability ran in the family. The cards were stacked against Teller. Moss didn't know what to tell the boy to make him feel better.

"Tell you what, honey," he said. "Why don't you skip school today and you and I go to a movie?"

"What about tomorrow and the next day?" Teller said.

↓

Moss and Corliss took a shower together. "Let's see what's wrong here," she said, all business. She took his penis and soaped it until it was moderately erect. Then she masturbated him. She observed the ejaculating penis closely. "Ah ha!" she said. "Nothing's coming out of your dingus but puffs of air. You want to tell me that this is also due to a sinus infection? That's one hell of a sinus infection, if you ask me. That's the sinus infection of the century."

After the shower, Moss closed one eye and looked at himself in the steamy mirror. He was changing. He was getting fat. His belly, usually flat, was bulbous. His chest had gotten flabby. His genitalia had shrunk, his penis a pink acorn.

His nipples had darkened and were now large and protruding. He seemed to be growing breasts. He raised up on his toes and came down hard on his heels, making them jiggle. He cupped a hand under one of his breasts and squeezed. Something glistened on the nipple. He looked at it closely. It was transparent but had a whitish coloring.

He went to sleep that night listening to the voice in his head. It was singing "I Dream of Jeannie with the Light Brown Hair." The voice was now an androgynous contralto. Moss found it pleasantly seductive. He fell asleep before the song ended.

↓

The Quality Control group held a going-away party for Moss and Harold Jensen, the department manager. Jensen was a dapper little man who wore custom-tailored suits and expensive Italian shoes. He was on his way to DC to lobby Pentagon brass. Moss liked Jensen. He was a good boss, fair-minded and approachable. Caterers brought a big cake into the office. Bottles of champagne were opened. A quartet of engineers sang "Auld Lang Syne" and "For He's a Jolly Good Fellow," followed by the sentimental "Moonlight on the Wabash." Moss's headache had relented and so he had several glasses of champagne. Someone asked him to give a toast for the departing chief.

Moss raised his glass. "No man can be a leader unless he has a following," he said. "Harold Jensen is a man I for one would follow into a burning outhouse. I'd even follow the little guy to Washington." A few of the gathered engineers chuckled. Moss put down his glass and embraced Jensen.

The embrace lasted several seconds more than was comfortable and Jensen had to break away from it. Moss had held the little man in his arms and at one point lifted him off his feet and swung him back and forth like a rag doll. Jensen pushed Moss away angrily.

"Sorry," Moss said, wiping a tear from his eye. "I got carried away, boss."

The group of engineers laughed. "You're drunk on your patooti, Moss," someone said.

Moss excused himself and went to a restroom. Something astonishing had happened while he was embracing Harold Jensen. It made him burn with shame. He'd been sexually aroused while holding the little manager. He took off his sunglasses and studied himself in the mirror. His face was flushed, his eyes wild—worse than wild, mis*aligned*. His left eye had been pulled into the left corner of its socket. It made Moss look like Jean Paul Sartre on a bad day. "What the Jesus is wrong with you *now*?" he said. Only then did he notice that the mirror reflected a single clear image of himself. A gray shade stood next to his reflection. Moss and a gray almost-Moss stood side by side. A fanciful and terrifying thought occurred to him: His spirit-self had split off from his corporal self. He closed his right eye experimentally. The restroom darkened. His left eye produced a dim shadow world of crudely shaped silhouettes and nothing more. The left eye was blind. Moss drove home in a state of controlled panic, the Interstate packed with cars and spirit cars, trucks and spirit trucks.

↓

"Brain tumor," Corliss said. "Draco's sure of it."

"Sinus infection," Moss said.

"Go ahead, be stubborn. But Draco said it could blind you permanently, or even kill you. I told him you had breasts and they were lactating and that you had become impotent. He said it had to be a hormone-secreting adenoma, in the pituitary area of the brain. It's shut down your testosterone. It's producing prolactin, a female hormone. The good news is that it's probably benign."

"All this over the telephone? He must be clairvoyant. Is your radiologist a follower of Edgar Cayce, the guy who does telepathic diagnoses?"

"You can't make a joke out of it. Draco is disappointed in you, letting these symptoms go this far."

"He's *disappointed* in me?"

"As a man, as someone responsible for his family."

"I'm not a man. I'm half-woman. A freak show could bill me as 'Lacto, the Bearded Wet Nurse.'"

"You're going to see a neurologist. Get used to the idea."

↓

The operation took eight hours, a craniotomy that left the front half of his head bald. A benign tumor big as a golf ball was removed from his brain. A thick horseshoe-shaped scar cabled his skull from the left temple to a point above and between the eyebrows. A piece of his jaw muscle had been removed to make a patch in the floor of the sella turcica, the area on the underside of the brain that housed the pituitary gland. The large tumor had put pressure on the brain and had entered the optic chiasma, stressing the optic nerves. It had also interfered with glandular function—testosterone, thyroid, and cortisol production had almost stopped.

His jaw hurt too much for Moss to chew ordinary food, and so his diet was limited to puddings and soups. But the tumor had been successfully removed, and Moss was himself again, for better or worse. The double vision, the voices in his head, the headaches—gone. He covered his mutilated head with a San Francisco Giants baseball hat.

"We're going to be Giants fans when we move," he told Teller. Teller had been sulking in his room. He'd been called a freak by a quartet of cheerleaders. Teller had tried, heroically, to become part of normal school activities and had volunteered to be equipment manager for the junior high football team. The football players ignored him for the most part, but the cheerleaders, two carefully groomed boys and two conventionally pretty girls, were merciless. "Do *not* ask to hang out with us," one of them said. "It's very uncool for people to see a fat dweeb such as you hanging out with us. Besides, freakiness might be catching." Teller quit his job as equipment manager on the spot, which of course only made things worse. He was not only a freak, he was now a quitter—sealing once and for all his outsider status.

Moss tried in vain to console the boy. "They're morons, Teller. Just remember that."

"They're not morons," Teller said. "They're right. I *am* a freak."

Moss took off his hat and made a Frankenstein growl. "No, Teller. *I'm* a freak," he said, in the voice of Boris Karloff. "They've taken out half my brain." He rolled his eyes and limped back and forth across the living room floor, dragging a leg, tongue hanging out.

Teller laughed a little, then fell back into his blue funk. "Very funny, dad. But I'm the only freak around here."

Moss sat down on the sofa next to Teller. He put his Giants hat back on his head. "Let me tell you something, honey. Everyone's a freak in one way or another."

Teller scoffed. "Even the cool people?"

"Especially them."

Teller's big melancholy eyes regarded Moss skeptically. But Moss saw a flash of hope in them. Teller wanted to believe him, wanted to think the horror of his life was not because of a fault in him, but was a temporary condition that would pass.

Corliss came into the living room. "Come on you two bozos, dinner's on the table," she said.

Moss got up. He took Teller by the hand and pulled the boy off the sofa. "Let's get her," he said, winking.

Dragging their knuckles, Moss and Teller limped toward Corliss, eyes rolling, tongues lolling. They moaned in harmony, giving voice to their wounds, and Corliss shrieked happily and ran from the reach of their needy arms.

Birds of the Mountain West

Kyle DeSmet called at 3:00 a.m.
"Moss, I need you to come straight over here," he said. "I've loaded
the .44. It's on the table in front of me. I can't take my eyes off it.
I feel locked in—I'm going to do it this time."

This was the second time DeSmet had called Moss this week in
the middle of the night. The first time it was about enjambment.
"Can you enjamb on a busted syllable like *to-kay*," DeSmet had
said. "You know, the cheap wino juice, *tokay*—or is that just too
cute for words? And why the hell am I asking *you*?"

DeSmet was a poet. He lived it around the clock. Time had
no meaning to him other than how it pulsed along syllable to
syllable, line to line, stanza to stanza. On the other hand, Moss,
who had once worked for an aerospace company, taught high
school physics, math, and an extracurricular after-hours class in
ornithology. His world was laid out in time-ruled grids.

Moss had gotten out of bed in the early morning dark to
think about DeSmet's question. "It's misleading, I think," he'd
said. "Wouldn't you be bringing a woman into it named 'Kay.' As
in, 'I drink to Kay.' And why the hell *are* you asking me?"

"Moss, you're sharp! That's why I'm asking you. Thanks, bud."

Moss had whispered into the phone and Corliss, his wife, had
not awakened. He was not so lucky this time.

"I'll be there in ten minutes," Moss said.

Moss knew DeSmet had a gun, knew that he could get miserable
enough to jab the barrel into the soft flesh under his jaw and put
pressure on the trigger. Moss had seen him do this in rehearsal.
DeSmet would hold the .44 at an angle that, if fired, would blow
a red tunnel to daylight from his underjaw through the top of

his skull. He'd squeeze the trigger just hard enough to raise the hammer a fraction of an inch.

"You'll be *where* in ten minutes?" Corliss said.

"DeSmet's place. He wants to kill himself again."

"Let him," she said. "Maybe the goddamned drunk will do it this time. Who knows, we might get lucky."

"I know you don't mean that, honey."

She picked up the clock and squinted at the red numbers. "It's 3:00 a.m.," she said.

"I'll make him breakfast," Moss said. "It'll take the edge off the booze."

It was a hot and humid night in July. They had been sleeping naked under a sheet. Corliss kicked at the sheet to free herself of it. She lifted her knees. Her sweat-filmed breasts were silver in the moonlight. Her knees parted.

"Don't," Moss said.

"Don't what?" she said.

"Don't make it a choice."

"But it is a choice," she said. "It's always a choice."

She lay there, damp and silvery and receptive. But Moss just sat on the edge of the bed, yawning and rubbing sleep from his eyes.

"It's blackmail, you know," she said.

"What is?"

"He's blackmailing you. With his life. That's what the repeated suicide threats amount to. You can see that, can't you?"

"That's a stretch, honey."

"Is it?" she said, pulling the sheet over herself again. "You want to know what I think this is about? I think it's about control. He's got you in his pocket. I think DeSmet's got a gay streak half a mile wide."

"Because he writes poetry?"

"No. Because he's over the top with his macho act."

"You've been talking to your shrink."

"Dr. Forester says it's not an uncommon pose."

"You're out of your mind," Moss said, and instantly regretted it.

Corliss turned her back on him and picked up her portable police scanner from the night table. The scanner was her access to the dark outer world of felony and misdemeanor. Chronic agoraphobia kept her housebound most of the time. She shopped on the internet, telephoned for groceries, subscribed to several current events magazines. CNN was her window on the larger world. Dr. Forester kept her supplied with antidepressants, tranqs, and opinions.

"Look, I've got to go," Moss said. "I think he means it this time."

"Would you for once just do what *I* want, please?" she said, her voice small.

She adjusted the dials of the scanner. The few patrol cars that were out were idle. Nothing much of interest was happening. A cop opened his mike and yawned. A second cop belched a reply. A third keyed his mike three times in tacit appreciation.

"DeSmet's a friend," Moss said.

"No, he isn't," Corliss said. She turned off the scanner. "Friends give something back. DeSmet gives back nothing but grief, like any other brain-fried alcoholic."

"I don't expect anything from him."

"That's your problem, Moss. You don't expect anything from anybody. DeSmet's a narcissist. All he does is think about how *he* feels. He's not your friend, you're just handy."

Moss knew there was some truth in this, but he liked DeSmet anyway. DeSmet never worked at jobs that had built-in longevity. He wanted nothing to do with anything that looked like a sensible career. His dedication to his art was unswerving. He'd never published a book and had contempt for the ambitious poets who dominated the national poetry scene, such as it was. "The only thing that matters is the poem," he'd told Moss more than once. "Lose sight of that, you're done."

"Listen to me, Moss," Corliss said, turning to face him. "I may not be here when you come back,"

Moss knew the threat was idle. "You don't have to say that, honey," he said. His tone was solicitous. He could have pointed out the obvious—on her best days she could barely cross the yard to get the mail—but he didn't want to hurt her. She was hurt easily. It took her days to recover from even an accidental slight. Dr. Forester once called her a "hypersensitive bipedal tapeworm—a parasite, stealing its sustenance from its unsuspecting host." Forester, trained in Freudian analysis but a convert to no-nonsense behaviorism, treated his patients with drugs and severe opinions. He'd meant the quip as a stern but illustrative jest. He believed his largely middle-class clientele were stronger than they made themselves out to be and would benefit from his brutal candor. But Corliss took it badly. She stayed in bed for a week after that session with the doctor, refusing solid foods.

"Maybe I mean it this time," she said. "I know you think I'm a basket case. But I *could* call a cab. I *could* get a plane ticket. These things are not totally impossible, you know. I can fly around the goddamned world on Prozac."

Moss leaned down and kissed her forehead. He kissed her eyes. When he tried to kiss her lips she turned her face away. "I won't be long, sweetheart, I promise," he said.

Kyle DeSmet's uncompromising integrity was his doom. Moss saw this as heroic and admired it. He respected it. Once DeSmet got lucky and found a woman of means who had convinced herself that she could put up with him. She inherited her money from her father who'd made his fortune importing rattan furniture when that was all the rage. That affair lasted a few months, but for a time DeSmet was free of want and his poetry flourished. He was now living on unemployment compensation after having worked as a night watchman at a funeral home for half a year. He'd put a manuscript together he called "The Bingo Sonnets," a cycle of poems about working-class Catholics, but the publishers he'd sent it to weren't interested. "The focus here is too narrow," one said. "Depressing," said another. "Insulting to Catholics, irrelevant to Protestants, and pointless to the rest of us."

When Moss arrived DeSmet was at his kitchen table, staring at an empty sheet of lined paper, a bottle of tequila and the .44 next to him. "The muse flew the coop," he said. "I doubt I'll write a true line again."

The table was littered with books, scraps of paper, pencils and pens, and empty glasses. DeSmet was a small, bird-like man but his frail appearance was deceptive. He was tough as saddle leather. He'd worked dangerous jobs most of his life—ranch work, millwork, construction—and had spent a year in a gypsum mine. He was a man of contradictions: He had the broken-nose look of a seasoned brawler along with the generous grin of a good-hearted friendly man. His gray-streaked black hair curled off the back of his neck like a jay's crest. Once, at The Trail's End—a bar frequented by loggers and sawmill workers—DeSmet picked a fight with a loudmouth long-haul trucker twice his size and left the man spitting teeth.

"Listen to this, Moss," he said. DeSmet read three rhyming quatrains and a concluding couplet about a diesel mechanic named Fogarty. He exaggerated the iambs to emphasize the poem's sentiments with ludicrous hammer and anvil rhythms. "Pure cowflop, Moss. The man who wrote that should be inducted into the poetaster's hall of fame."

"You're just depressed, Kyle," Moss said, sitting down opposite DeSmet.

DeSmet's eyes widened with mock wonder. "I guess that's what I love about you, Moss. You've got a death-grip on the obvious." He poured himself another glass of tequila and drank half of it down then offered the bottle to Moss, but Moss waved it off.

"You got any gin?" Moss said.

DeSmet went into his small kitchen and found a half-full fifth of Gordon's. He poured some into a glass and handed it to Moss.

"You're a good soul," DeSmet said gravely. "Drinking with some pain-in-the-ass loser when you'd rather be home in bed with your woman."

"Corliss worries about you, too," he said.

DeSmet laughed. "Thanks for lying. I think I know what Corliss thinks of me." He leaned across the table, his face close to Moss. Under the smoky fumes of tequila, Moss detected the dark fecal stink rising from DeSmet's ruined liver. "She's a winsome girl in many ways, Moss, but she's not able to put up with a lot of nonsense. You know that as well as I. Besides which, she thinks I'm dangerous. What did she say when you told her I was thinking of eating a bullet? 'Let the bastard do it, honey. Let him ventilate his melon and put an end to these midnight phone calls.' Am I right or am I right?"

Moss raised his glass and drank as if it were filled with water. "She's not as bad as all that," he said, hoarse with the scouring gin.

"*Bad?* Hell, I don't blame her a bit, Moss. She's perfectly within her rights."

DeSmet picked up his revolver and studied the fine scrollwork on the dark barrel. "I will do it, you know. You should have no doubt of it, Moss. None at all."

The sky outside had turned gray and birds began to sing in the trees and telephone wires. Moss was drunk enough by now to regard DeSmet and his revolver dispassionately. He said, "I want you to know you will be missed." Moss was gaining steadily on DeSmet—a sober man, he knew, can't talk to a drunk on equal footing. He refilled his glass and drank it down, poured another.

"Kind of you to say so, Moss. I actually believe you might miss me. No one else will."

Moss started to protest, decided not to.

"Will the angels sing me to my rest?"

"God willing, Kyle," Moss said.

DeSmet looked up and regarded Moss with stark red-rimmed eyes. "Jumped on the Jesus bandwagon, have you, Moss?"

He wasn't a churchgoer but Moss never avoided the uncomfortable question, especially when drunk. "I guess I've always been," he said, "In an agnostic nondogmatic blaspheming infidel sort of way. It's the old Jesuit idea: Once immersed, always wet."

The Jesus bandwagon was a favorite topic of DeSmet's. It seemed the entire country had become aggressively pious in the last couple of decades. Watching a football game, DeSmet said, was like witnessing a crusade. Players looking skyward for divine recognition after making a routine catch or sacking a quarterback. Pregame sideline prayer circles, postgame homilies, lay preachers in pads televised from the locker rooms,

"After the meat-grinding twentieth century, you still think there's some abstract scorekeeper in the clouds who gives a shit about us?"

"It'd be nice to think so."

"You're so full of shit, Moss."

DeSmet poured himself another glassful of tequila and gulped it down. "Here's the thing—the twenty-first century is going to make the twentieth look like a Methodist picnic. I don't mean terrorism. That's just a sideshow. Real monsters are on the way. The clever boys in white coats crossed a strawberry with a flounder just to make the strawberry frost resistant. Doesn't that scare the living shit out of you, Moss? If not, it should. And that's just for openers! Those crazy fucking gene splicers are going to turn loose recombinant hell in the name of corporate profits. Remember those flying carnivorous monkeys in *The Wizard of Oz*? They got 'em on the drawing board, along with freshwater sharks and antelope-sized ants and pigs that piss orange juice. Heaven's abstract as algebra, Moss, but hell's just down the road a piece. The new Frankensteins are working out the details now."

"Birds are not abstractions," Moss said, feeling the gin, thinking: DeSmet's gone, the tequila's doing all the work. "People need to watch the birds, Kyle. The birds can teach people a thing or two."

DeSmet filled his glass again. "You're a raving full-of-shit drunk, Moss," he said. "You're drunk on your high-school-teaching ass."

"Ruddy turnstones. King eiders. Marbled godwits," Moss said. "Ever see a marbled godwit? No, you haven't. Nobody sees jackshit anymore. The world is packed with well-defined singularities but people only see the broad categories. Bird, cow, rock, tree."

Moss in middle-age had become an avid bird-watcher. Last winter, during the semester break, he'd gone on an excursion to central Mexico just to photograph the western flycatcher in its winter habitat. Then in February, in a protected wildlife sanctuary near his house where he often walked, he'd come across a mob of drunken waxwings stripping fermented berries from a mountain ash tree. The waxwings trilled bawdily as they zoomed from branch to branch, getting higher and higher on the fermented berries. One knocked itself out by flying into a dead and barkless cottonwood trunk that it must have seen as a patch of white sky in the winter overcast. Moss picked it up and held it in his hand until it came to and flew off in a gray blur of feathers. It went back to its berry-eating binge, a romping stomping airborne merrymaker. At sundown the mob of wasted waxwings settled in the top limbs of a tall tree and faced west, offering long plaintive notes to the dying light—a fine feathered choir of happily pious drunks. It reminded Moss of medieval plainsong chants, offered to a believed-in God. Moss saw this moment as a variety of religious experience.

DeSmet lit a cigarette, went to his picture window that overlooked the dark city. "The world doesn't need another run-of-the-mill poet," he said.

"It doesn't need marbled godwits either," Moss said. "It could get along fine without your marbled godwit."

"Right on the money, Moss. That's exactly what I've been saying."

"But the birds act as if they own the place anyway."

"That's because they're stupid."

"Right. And some people are too smart for their own good."

"You know what I'm thinking, Moss? I'm thinking you're a full-of-shit high school teacher."

"Another arbitrary species?"

DeSmet rubbed the heel of his hand hard against his forehead as if to erase his thoughts. "Sorry, Moss," he said. "You know I love you. You're my only friend. You believe that, don't you?"

"'The world's a hospital,'" Moss quoted. "'Half the people are patients, the other half are nurses,'"

"T. S. fucking Eliot," DeSmet said. "The poet with a paper asshole. What did he know about it?"

"He knew enough to get it right."

Moss made bacon and eggs and toast and a pot of strong coffee. He put a full plate in front of DeSmet. DeSmet studied the plate as if it were a surrealistic painting that needed deciphering, then, having broken the code, grimaced and pushed it away. He lit a cigarette and went to the sofa and fell into it. In another minute he was asleep. Moss took the cigarette from his friend's hand and stubbed it out in an ashtray. He picked up the revolver, opened the loading gate and removed the bullets, which he pocketed. He searched the apartment for the rest of the bullets, found a box of hollowpoints, and pocketed them, too. By that time the sun was coming up.

Moss remembered Corliss's opinion of DeSmet, an opinion no doubt suggested by Dr. Forester. But if DeSmet was a latent gay then what was Moss, looking after DeSmet like a patient wife? What about simple friendship? No room for that in the headshrinkers' hierarchies? Was friendship a simpleton notion, something to wink and cluck at, a smokescreen for the homoerotic impulse? Moss didn't think so. Moss thought such opinions were deliberate subversions of the simple and the pure by people who felt they were too sophisticated, too experienced, too jaded, to believe in the simple and the pure. This made him think of the Jesus bandwagon again. He shrugged—at least he wasn't self-righteous about it. He ate the untouched breakfast, sure now that DeSmet was safe for another day.

On his way home he felt the need to relieve himself. He stopped at the wildlife refuge near his house. He walked a few hundred feet into the dense undergrowth and unzipped.

High in a cottonwood tree, a bird trilled. He looked up. It was a bird he hadn't seen in this part of the state. He ran through his mental catalogue of migratory birds. His excitement grew as he placed it. At first he thought it was a robin, but its white eye-rings and white outer tail feathers identified it as a Townsend's solitaire. A rare sighting in this part of the state. The bird flew to a higher branch and sang its bawdy flute-like song. For no reason he could identify, Moss felt sanctioned by the solitaire's piercing refrain. He went home elated.

When he pulled into his driveway, the sun was up. His house sat on the side of a shallow slope facing east. The windows were a firestorm of reflected sunlight. He liked his house, a two-story early-twentieth-century Craftsman with east-facing dormers and a wide, planked porch. It was a friendly house, an easy house to live in. He thought of it as his nest. His nest, Corliss's cage. In either case it was a refuge—a place to work out your life. He was forty-five now and believed he could separate, at last, the things that had value from the things that had none.

He thought of DeSmet in his small apartment, working out his doomed life syllable by syllable, a bird trapped by its own plaintive voice, and wondered when the next 3:00 a.m. call would come, and if he would once again be moved to answer it. He would, of course, because that's what he did.

He'd traveled to central Mexico to observe the western fly-catcher in its besieged habitat. He knew the habitat of all songbirds was under siege, and he believed that Song—and all its species of singers—made the world endurable.

DEAD MEN

🡇

Hard to salute each other
harder to describe each other
and hardest to look at each other
at our destination

—Amos Tutuola,
The Palm Wine Drinkard

Handyman

"You all right up there, Walter?" I said.

"Sure. No problem," he said.

But he had only one eye and his left leg was shorter than the right and the roof was steep.

"You want me to help you? I could come up there and hand you the bricks."

He looked down over the oak balustrade that surrounded our crumbling chimney. He was bald except for the frizzy straw-colored hair above his ears which he kept long. It had rained during the night and the slate roof of our two-story, nineteenth-century cottage glittered in the morning sun. It was mid-summer and we needed to get the house in shape for the coming winter.

"You go read your newspaper, Coburn," he said. "I'll work on your chimney." He gave me a broad, gap-toothed smile that was benevolent and forgiving. *Angelic*, my wife says. His glass eye glittered like the eye of a toy store doll but his good eye gave direct access to his heart: Walter Endelman was a man without guile.

When he turned to go back to the chimney, he dropped his trowel. It skittered off the roof and hit the ground a few inches from where I'd been standing. I picked it up and tossed it back to him. I had to toss it two more times before I got it high enough. He caught it by the blade. "You got an arm on you, bud," he said, the live eye twinkling.

I went inside and poured myself another cup of coffee. Louise was sitting in our breakfast nook, studying her textbook on hematologic diseases. She'd entered the Licensed Practical

Nurse program at the local community college. She wanted to do something useful with her life.

"I don't know about this guy Walter," I said. "He looks a little shaky up there."

"He picked up a wired baby," Louise said.

"Excuse me?"

Louise sighed impatiently. "In Vietnam. It was a dead baby, booby-trapped with a grenade. There's a piece of bone missing in his leg and he's got some shrapnel in his head. His own impulsive kindness maimed him. His eye—"

"That's not what I mean. It's like he's . . ." I wasn't sure what I meant. "He's in another world," I said finally. But that was too general. Walter Endelman looked like he stepped out of the twelfth century. I could picture him with hay rake or scythe in a golden field. I couldn't have explained that, either.

"Is there a point to this?" Louise said, closing her textbook.

She had found Walter Endelman in Ace Hardware. She'd been thinking out loud about our crumbling chimney, and Walter, clerking for Ace part-time, said "I'm a stone mason. I can fix it for you."

Stone mason, carpenter, plumber, tile man. He said he was qualified in all of these, but tile was his specialty. He loved to make old bathrooms beautiful. I'd asked Louise why he was clerking for minimum wage if he was so multiskilled. "He never misses a meeting," she said.

With Louise you often have to fill in the blanks. I'm used to it and over the years have gotten pretty good at supplying the missing logical links. "You mean he's a recovering alcoholic," I said. "He drank himself out of the good union jobs. Didn't show, or showed up drunk. He lost his ticket."

She looked at me as if I had needlessly restated the obvious. "He hasn't had a drink in almost a year," she said. "Eight months, to be exact."

Her syntactical jumps leave me two steps behind. Working to catch up was borderline fun when we were first married—kind of a cute Gracie Allen thing—but a source of irritation in our middle age.

For example: Louise has two horses, Sisyphus the gelding and Cassandra the small mare. We keep them in a back yard corral. Our neighborhood is no longer zoned for large animals but Louise had her horses before the new zoning laws were put into effect and the "grandfather rule" allowed her to keep them. Once while we were having coffee in our breakfast nook, I looked out the window and saw that the new corral posts were brilliant white when just the day before they had been dull brown. I said, "Louise, honey, did you paint the corral posts?" And she replied, "That's why we keep the mare only during the riding season. Our little corral is too boring for her. Now Sisyphus, he can stand anything."

I worked on that for a while but failed to make the connections. "Are we talking about the same thing?" I said.

She only meant that the bored mare "cribs" on the posts, stripping off the bark, baring the pale wood. It's a horse thing, sort of like deer browsing on the bark of trees. Stripped of bark, the corral posts looked freshly whitewashed.

I could hear Walter limping around on our roof. Now and then a brick hit a slate shingle with a loud crack, followed by the skidding sound as it slid off the roof and dropped into the shrubbery. I looked at Louise, worried.

"We can't afford a regular contractor," she said, anticipating my complaint. I was about to say, Why are we taking a chance with this guy? There are plenty of contractors around town who fix chimneys. "He's charging only ten dollars an hour," Louise said. "You can't get quality people to work that cheap. Besides, he's the sweetest man on the planet."

"Quality," I said. "That's the key word here. 'Sweet' is nice, but sweet doesn't get the job done."

"Burt took money under the table," Louise said.

Her father, Burt—also a sweet man—worked day shift at the Anaconda copper smelter and cut meat every night for nonunion wages at the Blue Hen Café. The Blue Hen paid him off the books, a dollar under union scale. But then there were no deductions for payroll taxes or insurance, so Burt and the Blue Hen came out ahead.

"The Blue Hen didn't have to worry about chimney fires due to Burt trimming their meat," I said.

"Walter lost his certification, not his skill," she said.

Louise had a thing for Walter. Not exactly a romantic thing—more of a brother-sister thing. Burt and Maggie had three girls. "All I had were sisters all my life," she said. "Walter and I just hit it off, like we've known each other from the crib. I've always wanted a brother."

"I see," I said.

"Don't make that face," she said. "You look like you're eating a lemon."

I looked at her over the rim of my glasses. "There's a dark side to every so-called innocent impulse," I said.

"Walter and I are going fishing next Saturday," she said. She had that challenging look she gets when she pushes ahead with a plan she knows I won't like. She still has coltish ways even though she's almost fifty. I would never tell her so, but I often thought this sort of playfulness was more suited to a woman half her age. Her enthusiasms, when displayed in public, sometimes embarrassed me.

"You see a dark side to *fishing*, Coburn?" she said.

I see the dark side of sunshine.

↓

Walter was accident-prone. His third day on the roof, he dropped a brick on his hand. That in itself wouldn't have been so bad, but his hand was resting on a spear-shaped piece of newly installed aluminum flashing sticking up from the base of the chimney. The brick drove the flashing deep into his palm. We had to rush him to the emergency room for a tetanus shot and stitches. The next day he was back on the roof as though he'd just gotten a scratch.

Two days later he fell off the roof. Louise and I were eating lunch when we heard galloping feet overhead, followed by a heavy thud. We both looked at the ceiling. Then Walter appeared in our breakfast nook window that looks out on the backyard garden. He was falling sideways through the branches of our golden willow tree. The branches slowed him down a bit, long enough for us to see his apologetic grin. He had a length of varnished wood in his hand—a broken off piece of the balustrade. He landed on his back in the Japanese barberry bush, which cushioned his fall but scratched him up a bit. I put down my sandwich. Louise was already out the door.

Walter extricated himself from the barberry bush. He patted himself down, looking for broken bones. "Lost my balance for a second there," he said. "The meds sometimes mess up my equilibrium." His face and neck were mapped with scratches from the barberry thorns. There were twigs in his scraggly hair.

"Are you all right, Walter?" Louise said. "My God, you could have been killed!"

He smiled at her, that sweet twelfth-century, gap-toothed smile. "It'll take more than a little fall to kill me, Weezie," he said.

"Weezie?" I said, looking at my wife.

"Walter had an aunt named Louise," she said. "They called her Weezie. It has a kind of old-fashioned charm, don't you think?"

Walter put a foot on the first rung of the ladder. I put my hand on his arm. "Call it a day, Walter," I said. "Wash those scratches and then have some lunch with us. You can finish the job tomorrow."

"I busted your balustrade," he said. "I leaned back on it for a second, but the top rail was cheesy with dry rot. I also took out the bottom rail, which would have lasted you another ten years. I better get that fixed before dark. The shipment of Italian tile will be here early tomorrow morning," he said.

"Italian tile?"

"For your bathroom. Weezie and I decided on plum red with an off-white trim. The insets will have Florentine-style designs.

Fountains, birds, leafy bowers—that type of thing. It's going to knock our eyes out, Coburn." His good eye winked.

I looked at Louise. "You told me we couldn't afford Italian tile."

"Some of the government bonds Maggie left me are too old to draw interest," she said.

". . . so we might as well cash them in," I said, completing the thought that she left hanging. "But Louise, I was thinking we might need a new car this year."

I lusted over her mother's old war bonds, about twenty of them, dating back to 1942 and probably worth thousands by now. Our Chevy was only six years old but I'd been thinking we'd reached that time in life when we should be driving something more substantial—a Buick, maybe. Or even a Caddy.

"We have a perfectly good car," she said. "I'm not going to waste money on another one. A car is not an investment but a new bathroom will add real value to the house."

There was a bright red streak on the side of Walter's neck, partially hidden by his long hair. I decided not to mention it since Louise hadn't seen it yet.

"What I'll do is make some measurements then go to Intermountain Lumber," Walter said. "They've got some finished pieces of oak from remodeling jobs that didn't fly. I think I can get a good discount on something that will work nicely."

"Wait," Louise said, finally noticing the scrape on Walter's neck. "You're *hurt*. Get in the house, Walter, right this minute! The balustrade can wait."

Louise tended to Walter's wound, an abrasion about four inches long, probably from a rain gutter as he rolled off the edge of the roof or from the stub of a pruned willow branch. She doctored the wound with an antibacterial salve and bandaged it with gauze and adhesive tape and then made him a cup of tea. She sat him down on the sofa and brought an afghan from our bedroom and wrapped it around his shoulders.

"Geez, Weezie," he said, grinning. "You're spoiling me rotten."

"I can tell you're in pain, Walter," she said. "I've got almost a full prescription of Vicodin. I got it for a root canal last year but only took two or three of them. The rest should still have their potency."

I watched all this thinking about the time I sprained my ankle going out for the mail on an icy day. She didn't make me tea or wrap me in an afghan or feed me drugs. She said, "If you had put the deicer on the driveway when I asked you to, this wouldn't have happened." We've been married twenty-two years, so you've got to expect a certain amount of tapering off of affection, but thinking back on it while watching her tend to Walter put me in a sour frame of mind for the rest of the day. No doubt she has legitimate complaints about me as well. I went upstairs to the den and played solitaire on my computer.

↓

It was a hot, dry day for a change and Louise and I were sitting in lawn chairs watching Walter finish repairing the balustrade—for which he refused to charge us. ("It was my fault, not yours," he said. "But it was rotten," I said. "We wouldn't have found that out unless I'd gotten careless, right?" he argued. Louise understood this kind of logic; it was natural to her.)

"I love to watch him work, don't you?" Louise said.

"I have a sense of dread," I said.

"You were born with a sense of dread."

I had nothing to say to that, but it irritated me. It irritated me because it was on the mark, though I'd never put it into so many words. I would have called it hypervigilance, a nice euphemism.

I've always been aware of the Worst Case Scenario. That's why I was a good government employee for thirty years. I knew instinctively to keep my fingerprints off situations that had meltdown potential. I learned to distance myself from anyone who had a "bright idea." A superior feels threatened by an underling's bright ideas. The whistle-blowers scared me the most. You never take coffee break with them. If you've worked for the government, you know what I mean. You *never* put your pension at risk.

Walter seemed to be working more slowly than usual. He worked as if he couldn't make up his mind about the simplest decisions. He'd hold a brick in his hand, study it, then lay it aside. He'd pick up another brick and do the same.

"Something's not right," I said.

"In heat like this the horses imagine the freedom of open country," she said.

It didn't take me long to decipher that one. "You think the weather makes Walter work like he's dreaming?"

"He's not dreaming, exactly. He has a rhythm, a certain *inner* quality. He's not being indecisive, he's being deliberate and thoughtful. I swear he's *communing* with the bricks. We're watching a true craftsman work his trade."

"Whatever," I said.

"You only see what you want to see."

"I think he's drinking again."

"Never," she said. "That would never happen. He takes anti-depressants. The two don't mix."

"I think he's drunk."

"You just don't know Walter, that's all."

"I bet there's a flask in his jeans."

"Stop it. You're saying these things just to annoy me."

"Of course I am. Why else would I say them?"

"Very funny," she said.

That night, in bed, she said, "I'd like you to call me Weezie, would you mind?"

"Why would I do that?"

"Is it so dreadful?"

"Weezie," I said.

She pulled me close to her, her breath moist in my ear.

"Say it again," she said.

↓

Louise invited me—halfheartedly, I thought—to go along on the fishing trip. But she intended to go on horseback and we only had

the mare and the gelding. I don't ride, and, in any case, I don't like
to trek into the wilderness area. So it didn't matter.

"If you don't want to ride behind me on the mare, you could
take my mountain bike." she said. "It needs air in the rear tire, but
it's got all those gears. You won't have any trouble at all pedaling
uphill."

"I've got some reading to do," I said.

I wasn't about to ride uphill behind a couple of horses. They
were going to Rattlesnake Lake, up in the mountains. It was eight
miles to the lake and I was in no shape to bicycle up a rocky uphill
trail, stopping every five minutes to pump up the rear tire.

They packed the fishing gear in canvas saddlebags, along with
a picnic lunch. The sky was getting gnarly with thunderheads. I
had a bad feeling about all this.

"Take my pistol," I said. "There've been some cougar attacks up
there. Two kids got mauled last year, remember? It's only a .22 but
the noise should scare them off."

"Cassandra won't spook," Louise said. "And I doubt very much
that Sisyphus will. Besides, they wouldn't attack riders on horseback. In any case, guns aren't allowed in the wilderness area."

I watched them walk the horses to the dead end of our street
and into the woods where the path into to the Rattlesnake
Mountains begins. I spent the rest of the day reading.

I retired from the Forest Service last year and hadn't adjusted
to all the free time I now had. I tried watercolor, but I didn't have
the patience for it, much less the artistic ability. Photography was
next, but after shooting twenty rolls of film with maybe half a
dozen shots worth framing, I got bored with it. So I decided to
catch up on my reading. I hadn't read a book in a year and was
determined to read all the books on the best seller list. It occurred
to me that I might write a book myself: *Telling the Forest from
the Trees: My Thirty Years in the United States Forest Service*—my
tentative title.

I did all my forestry work in a windowless little office, evalu-
ating satellite photographs. "Tree counting" doesn't cover it
all, but that's essentially what I did. "Satellite Evaluation for

Forest Inventory and Analysis" is more to the point. I studied the effect of annual removals and mortalities and the stunting effect of prolonged drought, but I never dealt in a hands-on way with actual trees, just satellite mappings of the forest. They say the real work is done on the ground, in the woods, but this is a throwback notion that undervalues the overview state-of-the-art technology yields.

My job never took me into the woods, which was fine by me. I don't like being in the woods. People might find that odd for someone who wore the Forest Service shoulder patch for thirty years. But I don't mind admitting it. The woods scare me. I got lost for two days in them when I was ten years old and had to be rescued by a search and rescue team. That experience left its mark. The lonely sound of wind in the pines makes my heart quiver. I hear a yapping coyote, I want to bolt.

The storm that had been brewing all day struck in the late afternoon. It was a bad one. A charcoal gray overcast darkened the sky. I counted the seconds between lightning strikes and the thunder they produced and determined that the center of the storm was six miles away and moving from north to south along the mountain front. A tremendous hail rattled against the slate shingles. It was as if a carload of ball bearings had been dumped on the roof.

The sky was black by late afternoon. I had to turn on the lights. The leading edge of the storm blew past and the cold front behind it brought a steady rain. The weather people call it "the August singularity." Every August, about midway through the month, the weather turns from hot and dry to cold and wet. It lasts about a week. The timing of this singularity is so reliable that the County Fair Board changed the dates of the fair in order to avoid it.

About seven o'clock I began to worry. Louise had her cell phone with her but I was determined not to call her. I didn't want to give her the idea that I was lonely and filled with dread. But I *was* lonely and filled with dread. I imagined falling trees taking them by surprise, lions tearing flesh from their broken bodies. At eight o'clock I gave in to my fears. I dialed her number.

"We're having broiled fish—native brookies," she said. "Walter found watercress and wild asparagus, even some edible mushrooms—morels and puffballs. He's cooked up a marvelous feast. He even had some candles in his pack. So you can stop fretting."

"It must be snowing up there," I said. "It's almost cold enough for snow here in the valley." I looked out at the dimly lit driveway. Every window in the house across the road was lit up. Smoke came from the chimney. I could see people moving briskly from room to room, as if preparing for a party.

"There's six inches of snow on the ground, but don't worry. Walter's made this wonderfully extravagant shelter from cedar boughs. It's warm and dry inside. He did it with just his pocketknife. We won't try to get back tonight. That wouldn't make sense."

"Excuse me?" I said. "You're breaking up, Louise. I didn't get that."

"You can just put those thoughts aside."

"*Hello?*" I said. "Louise?"

"Stop being ridiculous. It would be foolish to come back down the trail in this weather and in the dark."

"Should I call Search and Rescue?"

"Stop it. We'll be home by lunchtime tomorrow."

"I'll call Jack Millichap in the Sheriff's office."

"You don't need to call anyone. Have your nightcap and go to bed. We're fine."

I pictured them being fine in the extravagant cedar shelter, eating brook trout, watercress, wild asparagus, and mushrooms by candlelight. I hoped Walter knew morels and puffballs from their poisonous imitators. You've got to look at the caps and gills. The caps and gills of the morel are lighter than the caps and gills of its lethal look-alike, the turbantop. The pink gills of the puffball mimic, the *Amanita phalloides*, aren't attached to the stem, and the spores are white. The deadly mimics will kill you but not before making you suffer extreme gastrointestinal agony.

"Walter says hello," Louise said. "He says you're not to worry. Everything's under control."

"You've got to know what you're doing with wild mushrooms, Louise. You've got to know the *Amanita phalloides* from the common puffball. Remember, Walter is accident-prone."

"Mr. Worst Case Scenario says you're accident-prone," she said to Walter, laughing brightly. I heard Walter's answering guffaw. To me, she said, "Did it hail there? Did you happen to cover my geraniums?"

"No. I had better things to do with my time than cover your geraniums," I said, instantly shamed by my spiteful self-righteousness. "I was worried about *you*, Louise," I amended, "not the geraniums."

"You're being melodramatic," she said.

I didn't call Jack Millichap. I'd look like a fool, calling Search and Rescue for two people who knew where they were and how to survive a stormy night in sheltered comfort. It would only liven up the gossip in the Sheriff's office.

The candles bothered me. Why had Walter packed candles? Just as a precaution? Who packs candles on a fishing trip as a precaution? I had my nightcap but didn't go to bed.

↓

The August singularity passed and the weather warmed up again. Walter finished repairing the chimney and the balustrade and started remodeling the downstairs bathroom. The new bathtub was long and deep and had Jacuzzi jets—wonderful for soaking your bones on a cold winter day. The tile that covered the wall above the tub was stunning. It alone changed the character of the bathroom. The soft wine-red glow of the Italian tile made you feel you were in a another—and somehow warmer—country.

I had to admit that I was wrong about Walter hitting the bottle again. He was a journeyman carpenter and master tile man, and, at only ten dollars an hour, he was creating a bathroom for us that would increase the value of our house by thousands.

Louise told me more about him, things she'd found out on their fishing trip. They'd spent the stormy night talking, like a brother and sister who hadn't seen each other since childhood. She told him about growing up in a smelter town, the long strikes during which her family had to live on donated food, and he told her about his life after Vietnam.

Walter spent six months in a veteran's hospital recovering from his wounds. When he was released he went to work on a carpentry crew, drinking himself into a stupor every night. He lost every job he got, eventually becoming a homeless vagrant, living in shelters when there was room and under bridges when there wasn't. For a period of time, he was lucid and functional enough to get married. His ex-wife and child were now living in Michigan.

He'd been a violent drunk, half-killing a man over a trifle he couldn't afterward remember, and had spent a year in the state prison at Deer Lodge for it. He'd once driven a thousand miles to the West Coast and back but didn't remember leaving home. On his return he found that the back seat of his car was filled with over a hundred army surplus field jackets. He didn't know how he got them but believed they were stolen. He sold them for ten dollars each, the proceeds funding another few months of heavy drinking. His blackouts were long, and even when he was conscious he knew he was not registering his surroundings with any accuracy. Then he started going to AA meetings, and his life changed.

Louise and Walter went to the county fair. Again, I was invited to go along, but I can't endure the dust, the fatigue, and the swelter-ing crowds. They went to look at the 4-H prizes and the exotic livestock—llamas, ostriches, long-haired sheep. They went on the heart-stopping rides only teenagers go on: the Zipper, Whip, Centrifuge, and Cyclone. They went to the quarter-horse races and then to the rodeo and the evening rock concert. They came home late, laughing and teasing like a couple of kids. Louise had a stuffed bunny big as a child in her arms: One-eyed Walter had been deadly accurate tossing plastic rings on a wooden peg. "Say hello to Mr. Wabbit," Louise said, flapping the bunny's ears at me.

None of this made my sense of dread go away. The feeling of impending disaster weighed on me as never before. I tried to dismiss it as nonsense, but it wasn't dismissible. It nagged me like a toothache, holding a place in the foreground of consciousness, never receding. It disturbed my sleep, interfered with my digestion, and preoccupied my thoughts. I went to see a doctor about it and he prescribed pills. The pills let me sleep, but my dreams were still dogged by impending doom.

For distraction, I often logged on to Forest Service websites. I especially liked to keep tabs on the satellite images of western white pine in British Columbia. Reforestation with this fast growing tree with high timber value had been one of my professional interests. Problems with laminated root rot and blister rust cankers were being dealt with intelligently by the Canadians. The blister rust pathogen was under control. Hats off to the Canadians! This bit of good news gave me a better lift than my pills.

One afternoon, while half-dozing at my computer, I heard Louise cry out. It was a disturbing little cry—a mixture of surprise and urgency. I went downstairs, my heart in my throat. I knew instinctively that the worst had happened. The bathroom door was ajar. I was afraid to step inside, afraid of what I might find.

They were on the floor, Walter on his back, Louise straddling him among the stacks of Italian tile. Her mouth was on his. The sounds she made came from her throat. Eager sounds, desperately needy sounds. Her passion had overwhelmed Walter. Fundamentally a decent man, he was helpless against her assault. His arms were unmoving at his sides as he surrendered to the searching intensity of her desire.

"No!" I said. "Absolutely not! I won't have it!"

She didn't budge. An inch of water covered the floor. Walter's jeans were soaked. Louise's wet skirt was hiked up. They didn't care. They were lost in the moment. The room began to turn, as if on a Lazy Susan. I put my hand on the wall to steady myself.

Then rage steadied me. It was as if I'd been injected with it. It was as transforming as a mind-altering drug. I knew that when it subsided I would not be the same man, nor would my life be the same. I put my arms around Louise's waist and lifted her away from Walter. The strength rage gave me seemed limitless. I carried her out to the living room and threw her down on the sofa. She tried to spring back up—the power of love!—but I threw her back down, again and again. She was wet and made dark stains on our beige sofa.

"You damn fool!" she said.

"Oh," I said, calmer now. "*I'm* the fool."

And of course, I *was* the fool. I had completely misread the situation. The old plumbing had sprung a leak while Walter was connecting the new sink to the hot water pipe. The leak was in the wall and there was no way to get to it. It flooded the area behind the sheetrock and then seeped into the bathroom itself. Walter turned off the water main out in the street, and then went to work on the leak. He had to take out an area of sheetrock to get at the old plumbing. He used his reciprocating saw to do it. What Walter didn't know was that the 220-volt line that ran to the water heater in the adjacent utility room was also in that wall. It was the wrong place for such a wire, but the wiring in old houses is often makeshift and doesn't conform to modern building codes.

Walter was accident-prone, but that tired phrase trivializes his life. It robs it of mystery. I saw it another way: Death had been looking for him. It found him at last in our bathroom, where it electrocuted him.

Louise had been giving him mouth-to-mouth when I pulled her away. The EMT crew said the mouth-to-mouth probably wouldn't have been enough and that Louise shouldn't blame herself for failing to revive him. The wet floor, they said, grounded him and he'd taken the full amperage the 220-volt line was capable of delivering.

Louise didn't blame herself, she blamed me. She didn't say so directly, but she didn't have to. She wouldn't look at me, or if she did, it was the look of a stranger. Cool, distant, indifferent. If we spoke, our conversations became more elliptical, so much so that I rarely understood her. If I said, "Louise, why are the horses out in the yard instead of the corral," she would answer, "Doug Mayberry's axle is somewhere between Pocatello and Butte."

I didn't press her for an explanation. I'd eventually remember that Doug Mayberry was the man who brought hay into town for suburban horse owners. His truck had a broken axle and the new axle was being shipped from Salt Lake. The mare and the gelding, in the absence of Doug Mayberry's truckload of hay, were grazing on the lawn.

Other men finished the work Walter had started but Louise treated them with an employer's aloofness. When winter came that year, the house was tight against the hard northern winds. The bathroom, with its deep tub and rich Italian tile, was refuge against the bone-aggravating arctic air, but only for me. Louise would not use it. She used the smaller upstairs bathroom—a cubicle whose ordinary fixtures and white plastic tile had never been touched by the hand of a craftsman.

Bête Noire

Frank Kelso did not sleep well in the desert. He kept his wife Andrea awake with his tossing and turning. His mother, Janelle, snored in the adjoining room. Janelle, afflicted with late-stage Parkinson's, was dying. How long she would take was the question. Frank hoped, for Janelle's sake, it would be sooner rather than later. He and Andrea had come from Seattle to Arizona's high desert country to care for Janelle, which was becoming a nearly impossible job as the old woman's disease worsened.

Andrea said, "What is it *now*?"

"Another dream," he said. "They come like movie trailers, full of color and motion, one after the other. No wonder the prophets went to the desert for their visions. I think I'm having visions."

Andrea got up and went to the bathroom. Frank looked out the window. Somewhere in the starry dark a screech owl made its eerie noise. He turned on the night table lamp. When Andrea came back, he had the pistol in his hand. He said, "I'd been forced to write a confession by the police."

Andrea sighed. "I don't want to hear about it. Your last dream gave *me* nightmares. The buried alive one, you trying to talk with red earth in your mouth. Please put the gun back in the drawer, Frank. You make me nervous."

Frank said, "I told the cop, 'Janelle should have died a year ago, while she was still functional, before Parkinson's got her. Now I have to feed her mush, clean shit off her legs, and put her diapers on. Imagine that, officer. Me, a man of my sensitivities, cleaning shit off his mother's legs and ass.'"

"Sensitivities?" Andrea said.

"It sounds stupid, but that's what I told the cop."

"Cleaning your mother's backside is not a crime," Andrea said.

"The crime's yet to come. I said, 'Officer, she couldn't walk. She had these pressure sores from lying and sitting all the time, craters on her ass and back, and they tunneled. They healed on the surface but not inside, and so they kept tunneling into the meat. She cried out in pain constantly because of these tunneling sores. Then she couldn't swallow, and she couldn't talk. She was so miserable, I had to do something. So I put a pillow over her face. It was a mercy, don't you think, officer? Tell me it wasn't a mercy. Tell me you wouldn't have done the same. Or tell me you *would* have done the same but for fear of the legal consequences.'"

"You dreamed you murdered Janelle and got caught," Andrea said. "The nightmare would have been if you *didn't* get caught. Justified murder is worse than the impulsive kind."

"What's that supposed to mean?"

"I don't know. It's late."

He'd awakened still mumbling to the cop. He remembered his dream confession verbatim. It seemed so real that he'd gotten out of bed to check on Janelle to make sure he hadn't actually smothered her during one of his sleep-walking episodes. She was snoring peacefully in her bed, hugging a pillow as if she were hugging the broad back of her fourth and last husband, Lamar Hayden, dead nine years now. Frank came back to bed and listened to Andrea's light snoring. Then he woke her to tell her about his latest dream.

Frank had become a sleepwalker. It was as if a second self—a puppet self worked by a scatterbrained puppet master—was searching for something in the dark. He'd walked in his sleep a few times when he was in junior high. Janelle, while going through one of her divorces, had parked him with his grandmother for a year. Once during that year he'd found himself digging for something vital in his grandma's garden with his bare hands, wearing only his pajamas. Awake, he couldn't remember what the vital thing was. Another time he fell down a flight of stairs, waking with a bloody nose and broken wrist. These episodes disturbed him. They disturbed him again, fifty years later.

It was 3:00 a.m.—"the hour of the wolf." A poet he once read called it that, called it humanity's most vulnerable hour. He was disturbed not just because of his nocturnal wanderings but of the impulse behind them. What was going on in his brain? What spurious influences was it vulnerable to? He was old now, retired after thirty-five years of making blueprints for Boeing. But retirement did not agree with him. He felt at sea, unmoored.

He sometimes felt that having nowhere to go every day with nothing of importance to do had triggered the sleepwalking episodes. Once he woke up drawing perfect freehand circles at the drafting table he kept in his study. Another time he woke in the garage, in his car, as if ready to drive to work.

Making blueprints anchored him to a narrow reality he had come to depend on. He liked driving Interstate 5 to work every morning. He liked walking across the footbridge over the Duwamish River that connected the parking lot to the factory. He liked the blueprint shop, the smell of it, the solid feel of his chest-high drafting table, the strong crisp paper he worked with, the lovely pencils, the fragrance of ink. He had been an excellent draftsman, a valued employee. He didn't have that anchor anymore. The company had given him a gold watch on his retirement day. He didn't wear the watch; it only reminded him of what he'd once been and no longer was.

He put the gun back into his night table drawer. It struck him that the gun had become an attractive influence, calling to him, appealing to an unknown motive in the busy underworld of his cerebral processes. He liked the gun. He liked holding it. It felt natural in his hand. This affinity puzzled him. He thought: what other affinities lurked in the shadows? He'd never owned a gun and was surprised by the oddly familiar feel of the walnut grips, the smooth workings of its mechanism, the simple thrill of fixing the sights on prospective targets.

He took the gun out of the drawer and unloaded it. He put the bullets in the dresser and the gun under the night table, out of easy reach. Reloading would take time—a deliberate act that would interfere with the impulse to start blasting away at nocturnal intruders. He laughed at himself. "You are one crazy son of a bitch, Frank," he said. Then he reloaded the pistol and put it back into his night table drawer.

The pistol was for protection against javelinas. It was one of Lamar Hayden's guns. Lamar had been a collector of both antique and modern guns. A herd of the wild pigs roamed the acreage behind Janelle's house. Lamar Hayden had killed several javelinas with the big revolver. The wild pigs were aggressive, territorial, and just plain nasty. They were intolerant of human encroachment on their established forage. Frank had shot at one yesterday. He was out in Janelle's orchard watering the apricot trees when he heard a rustling behind a clump of prickly pear. He turned to see an old javelina boar trotting toward him, its little pig eyes hot with rage, its razor-sharp tusks glistening. A collar of gray hair haloed its neck. It was a hermit, Frank decided, separated from the herd because age and disease. But it was big, at least seventy pounds, and rank with musk. Frank unholstered the gun—a Navy Arms .45 caliber revolver—and fired. He missed the javelina but the explosion turned it away. It trotted back into the bushes, grunting moodily.

After that incident Frank became extra vigilant. He imagined javelinas in the house—wild pigs ripping through the flimsy screen doors and flimsier window screens and attacking them in their beds. He wanted wood and double-paned glass between him and the javelinas, but the house had accumulated the day's heat and needed to be cooled by the night air. Janelle, who had lived in this desert for thirty years, liked the dry heat. She couldn't tolerate air conditioning, said it gave her sinus headaches and aggravated her arthritic hips. Except the desert wasn't so dry. The humidity could get up to 50 percent during August—the monsoon season, when damp air from the Pacific coast of Mexico flowed north. It was now mid-July and the humidity had already risen to the discomfort level.

Janelle was almost ninety. Frank had just turned sixty-four. He'd lost most of his hair and he'd let his stomach muscles prolapse. Sometimes when he looked at himself in the bathroom mirror—at the sagging gray-haired chest, the ballooning gut, the dewlaps under chin and jawbone—a surge of panic nauseated him. He couldn't believe he'd allowed this to happen. He felt old age had caught him unawares, like a preoccupied swimmer who realizes too late that a riptide has pulled him out to sea, beyond sight of land.

And his libido was on the wane. Which also depressed him. Andrea at sixty-one was no longer interested in sex but was willing to comply whenever Frank felt ready. He felt ready more often in the desert than he did back home in Seattle. The desert heat made blood flow more readily to his extremities. In Seattle, especially in the rainy season, his extremities were always cold and bloodless. And the Seattle rainy season could last nine months.

After the dream in which he smothered Janelle, he felt a surge of libidinal energy. He didn't question the root cause of this gift. Libido, whatever triggered it, was a gift. He slipped his hand under Andrea's nightgown.

"Oh for Christ's sake, Frank," Andrea said. "It's 3:00 a.m. If I've slept an hour all night I'd be surprised."

"I'll be quick," he said.

Andrea scoffed. "It takes you forever," she said. "Your body is telling you something. Why don't you pay attention to it?"

"I am paying attention to it. It's telling me its horny."

Twenty minutes later he was asleep again and dreaming. He woke some time later, sweating, listening to the screech owls and coyotes and Andrea's steady breathing.

He didn't remember his dream. It involved movement—climbing, running, finding brief respites during which he caught his breath—but there were no visual impressions, no images he could revisit awake. He took the gun out of the night table and roamed the house in his pajamas, checking the screens.

"Three thousand a month," Frank said, tossing the Sagebrush Vistas brochure on the kitchen table.

"What are the choices?" Andrea said.

"Zero and none," he said.

Sagebrush Vistas was a Tucson nursing home. He'd approached Janelle with the idea the day they'd arrived. Janelle wanted no part of it. But it was time. Janelle was practically 100 percent disabled. Frank had been called by Adult Protective Services of Arizona with an ultimatum: "Put Janelle into a nursing home or we'll turn the case over to the Public Fiduciary, who will assume guardianship as well as conservatorship." This came after Janelle had fallen into a glass table, cutting her arm and forehead. A neighbor found her and called an ambulance. Then the Adult Protective people stepped in.

APSA had full authority to take Janelle's property, padlock it, and auction it off to pay for her nursing home care. They'd take Frank out of the loop, make him irrelevant. If there was any of Janelle's estate left after the nursing home expenses, Frank and Andrea would not get a penny of it. Frank decided then to move in with Janelle.

"They've got an available single," he said to Janelle. "You won't have to share."

"I don't care what they have," Janelle said. "I want to stay here, in my own home. I love my home." She was a small woman, made smaller by osteoporosis and general decay. Sparse red hair feathered her white scalp; a thread of silvery drool spilled from her lip.

She sat hunched in her wheelchair, trying to hold a piece of toast in her trembling hand. She dropped it into her lap. Frank picked it up for her. Her eyes were glazed with cataracts but obstinate as ever. She'd always been headstrong, unwilling to give up an eyelash of independence—either to men or to circumstance.

"You can't take care of yourself, Mom," Frank said. "You need around-the-clock care. Andrea and I can't do it."

Frank had registered a Durable Power of Attorney with the Cochise County courthouse and so the choice was his and Adult Protective Services', not Janelle's. Janelle didn't know that. He'd have to tell her sooner or later, but he wanted to avoid it. He wanted her to go into the nursing home of her own free will. He wanted her to believe it was her own idea.

"Besides," Janelle said. "Where am I going to get three thousand dollars every month? I have maybe ten thousand in savings, and there's less than a thousand a month from Social Security. That's nowhere near enough."

"Don't worry about the money," Frank said. He said it as if he were able and willing to take care of the expense. He was not, of course, since he was living on a fixed income himself. He'd have to sell her house and property—worth at least $250,000—but could not tell her that, not yet. To Janelle, selling the house would be unthinkable. She wouldn't be able to see it as an asset that could be converted into cash. She called it her *casita dulce*, and it was worth far more than money to her.

The house was a five-bedroom adobe with a flat roof and real *vigas*. Frank thought the *vigas*—log rafters black with age, the protruding ends of which studded the outside walls of the house just under the roofline—were the most attractive feature of the structure. It had been built in the 1930s, when the builders used actual adobe bricks fired in Mexico. Saltillo tiles, also made in Mexico, covered the floors. The rich burnt sienna squares seemed to glow with internal heat.

Janelle owned the ten acres of desert behind the house. The apricot orchard had been neglected for years and some of the trees were dead; others were surrounded by sage, prickly pear, mesquite, and ironwood—ideal habitat for the javelinas.

After breakfast, Frank strapped on the .45 and he and Andrea went for a walk in the desert. They took a path that led to a low mesa a mile or so from the house. The sun was up and the air was already hot. The javelina bands foraged when it was cooler—in the early mornings before sunup and again after sundown. Unless they stumbled on the dozing herd, they didn't have to worry about being attacked. Even so, Frank kept the holster strap unfastened, his hand close to the gun butt.

It was a steep climb to the top of the mesa, where the view of the surrounding desert was magnificent. In the east, the Chiricahua Mountains bulked the horizon. Andrea had packed a lunch. Frank carried two canteens of water. They sat in the shade of a cylindrical outcropping of basalt rock, sipping water and catching their breaths.

After forty years of marriage, they still liked each other. Frank couldn't imagine life without Andrea. Both of them had grown into their own eccentricities and were comfortable with them and with each other's. The small and large pains of age made them snappish at times, but the marriage had been a good one. They were each other's best friend. They thought alike, kept no secrets, affirmed each other's prejudices, and tolerated each other's small excesses. Their differences were mild. Andrea liked fried liver and onions, Frank did not; Frank watched football, Andrea did not. Frank thought: What more could anyone ask of marriage?

"How are we going to do it?" Andrea said after a long silence.

"Kidnap her, I guess. We'll have to put her into the car, tell her we're taking her on a shopping spree in Tucson, then haul her off to Sagebrush Vistas. Christ, even the name gives me the creeps."

"We could drag her up here on the mesa. Give her some food, a bottle of gin, a baggie of Percoset, and let the wolves, coyotes, or weather take care of the rest."

"That would be the merciful way," Frank said. "No, the law says we have to make the pain last as long as medically possible. We've got to make sure she savors every agonizing moment."

"Promise me something," Andrea said.

Frank knew what she was going to say. They'd both made the promise to each other more than once. But would they—when they reached Janelle's condition—have the courage and will to do it?

"I'll put a pillow over your face," he said.

"No. Put a plastic bag over my head. A gun's messy. Carbon dioxide poisoning is not too unpleasant. I wouldn't want to leave a mess."

Frank thought: I'll do myself with the .45. The mess wouldn't be his to clean up. He wouldn't even hear the snap of the hammer.

A surge of libido surprised him. He kissed Andrea, opened her blouse and felt her sweat-filmed breasts.

Andrea was aging better than he was. Her breasts had fallen a bit, but they were still round and firm, the nipples small and pink. They'd had no children and so her body had never been assaulted by the rigors of pregnancy and birth. Frank's heart sped; he felt like a teenager discovering sex.

"Not here, cowboy," she said. "No way. I don't like ants in my pants."

He persisted but she was adamant.

"What the hell's gotten into you, you ornery old fool?" she said.

When they got back to the house Janelle was on the kitchen floor. She'd managed to get out of her wheelchair and take a few steps toward the bathroom before falling. She was on her side, moaning. She had messed herself.

They picked her up and took her into the bathroom. They stripped off her clothes and checked her for bruises and broken bones. Janelle was incoherent. She tried to speak but only soft ragged sounds came from her mouth.

Andrea filled the tub and Frank picked up his mother and lowered her into the lukewarm water. There wasn't much left of this lusty old woman who'd had four marriages and several lovers in between, and sometimes during. Her old dugs were withered. They hung down on her belly like leather flaps. Her pubic area was almost hairless, and what hair there was encrusted with feces. Frank washed her tenderly, ceremoniously, as if washing a corpse. "We'll take you shopping in Tucson tomorrow, Mom," he said.

That night he had water dreams. He and Andrea and Janelle were on a dark lake, somewhere in the mountains. He was rowing.

Janelle was dressed in what would have been her churchgoing clothes had she been religious. "Your daddy was the best of them all," she said. Frank tried to remember his father, and as he recalled a childhood image, a man stepped into the boat from an island of driftwood. The man didn't look like Frank's father, but he said, "We made our mistakes. You've made yours. Don't confuse the two." Frank said, "I never have, Dad. I wouldn't." This made Janelle laugh. Andrea said, "Show them the poem you wrote." He reached into his pocket for the poem. He tried to read it but the words made no sense. They were ciphers, not words. Andrea pinched him. "Go on," she said. "Read it. It puts you in a good light."

In his next dream he was swimming across a river. He swam easily, but he was afraid. He knew there were undertow currents just below the surface that could pull him down into riverbottom trenches where he would drown. He swam with life-saving fury, but made little progress.

Frank woke up naked in the kitchen, his lungs working hard. The .45 was in his hand, the hammer cocked. He uncocked it and put it on the kitchen counter. He made a cup of instant coffee and went out to the screened back porch and sat in a canvas chair where he held vigil for the rest of the night, the revolver within reach on a wicker table.

He could hear them, out past the orchard, gnawing at the prickly pear, rubbing against mesquite and ironwood, marking their territory—it was redundant marking, but the javelinas were piggish about property rights. He smelled their musk in the night breeze—the sour perfume of the beasts.

He thought about Janelle. There was no easy way: they'd have to take her to the nursing home without further argument. Janelle would never agree to give up her house, her desert refuge, the place where she'd spent the better part of her life. The house and the desert around it were the physical counterparts of her soul; her best memories were embedded here. Putting her into Sagebrush Vistas would finish her off, but not quickly. The nursing home would draw out her death with what passed for compassion, paid for in monthly installments of three thousand dollars.

Andrea said it: justified murder was worse than the impulsive kind. Justice was on his side. Adult Protective assured him of this. "Your mother is a wonderful woman," the A P S A agent had said. "If you love her, you'll do this. We know that if she could reason it out she'd want you to. It shouldn't be up to us."

He went back to bed when the sky turned gray. Andrea was awake, reading a novel. "Touring again?" she said.

When he didn't answer, she said, "I saw you out on the porch. The naked gun himself. I wasn't about to disturb you. Not with that six-shooter next to you."

When he still did not answer, she said, "Hey, you are awake, aren't you? Are you trying to scare me? Goddamnit, *say* something?"

He put the gun back in the night table. "Today," he said. "We take her in today. Then we'll go to a real estate agency and put *casita dulce* up for sale."

"You make it sound like an execution."

"What else is it?"

She reached across the bed and touched his arm. "You're definitions are too broad, hon. This is what people do. Good sons do these things."

"She used to leave me with people and not think twice about it. I spent years with relatives I didn't know while she ran around the country with men I didn't know. She'd lie to me. She'd say, 'I'm going out for a while, honey. I'll be back in a few minutes,' and I wouldn't see her again for a year or two. I always wondered what it would be like to have a real home with a real mom and maybe a full-time dad."

"So you're thinking it's payback time?"

"No. That's exactly what I don't think. It would be a lot easier if I did."

"See? I was right. You've outlived the angry boy you were. You are a good son."

"I don't know what I am. I'm a retired draftsman. I'm a faithful husband."

"Maybe that's good enough."

Taking Janelle to Sagebrush Vistas was not the ordeal Frank thought it would be. He told her they were taking her shopping at the Tucson mall and she seemed to buy it. They dressed her up in her best clothes and put her in the car. She fell asleep on the way. Her sleeps were profound and she didn't wake when Frank put her into the wheelchair and pushed her into the reception area of the nursing home. Attendants took Janelle away while Frank did the required paperwork. Then they went to a real estate office and signed a contract for the sale of Janelle's house.

They spent one more night in the house. Frank had nightmares about Janelle—Janelle locked in a dungeon-like room, alternately screaming with rage and sobbing. Janelle at the kitchen stove trying to lift a cast iron skillet full of hot grease and spilling it on herself, burning her hands and arms. Janelle as a beautiful young woman, sitting on a stone fence somewhere in Florida or California, posing, smirking at the photographer, the photo now coming alive and Janelle saying, "I've seen all this before. It isn't enough."

Frank got out of bed and went into the kitchen. The policeman was sitting at the table. "We're going to extract the truth, one way or the other," the cop said.

Frank said, "You don't understand."

"I understand enough. I understand you."

Frank woke from the dream mumbling. Andrea said, "What?" but she wasn't fully awake. He got out of bed carefully, not wanting to disturb her again, and got dressed.

The room was faint gray with predawn light. He slid the night table drawer open carefully and took out the .45 and went outside.

He walked along the edge of the apricot orchard, thinking: This is the last time I'll see this place. Janelle had been a mystery to him most of his life, and now that her life was over she was still a mystery, one that now would never be solved.

Something moved in the bushes. Frank drew the .45 and stood still. He saw the first javelina moving along the edge of the orchard. He held the gun in both hands to steady it. He sighted down the barrel. A second javelina appeared, following the first, and behind it, a third. Then the stench of the entire herd hit him and he took a step backwards. He was afraid this movement would alert and then enrage the boars—it didn't take much to provoke them. He didn't have enough bullets to protect himself from the entire band. But the boars didn't attack. The javelinas moved steadily, silently, as if on a pilgrimage and couldn't permit themselves a distraction.

When the herd moved out of sight, Frank reholstered the gun. He turned to go back to the house and found himself facing a straggler. But it wasn't a straggler. It was the old loner, the hermit boar.

The gray-collared javelina jerked his head up and down a few times, taking in Frank's scent. It wheezed asthmatically, its little eyes hot with a fury it had been nursing since it first became aware of Frank's intrusions into its forage.

Frank drew his gun. The old boar stood its ground, blocking Frank's way back to the house. Frank yelled obscenities at it. The old boar responded with a lengthy tantrum of grunts and squeals.

"It's my place, you piss-poor excuse for a pig!" Frank yelled.

He raised the pistol. He thumbed the hammer to full cock. It was an easy shot but he didn't fire. The javelina hated him but he did not hate the javelina. He had time and an interval of space should the boar decide to charge. For the moment it was a standoff. Frank and the razor-tusked beast studied each other as the moment expanded.

There was no need to force the issue. A breeze rattled the branches of the apricot trees, then, like held breath, quit. Frank lowered the gun slightly, a peace offering. Maybe things would go another way. He'd wait and see. The decision wasn't completely his.

Dead Men

A man walked into my house without knocking. He began to measure the walls with a measuring tape. He'd make a measurement then make a note of his findings on a legal pad. He hummed Hotel California as he worked. He was short and pot-bellied and walked with his feet splayed out like a duck.

"What are you doing?' I asked.

He dropped his tape measure. He turned and looked at me, mouth open, face turning slack and white. He made a nearly imperceptible sign of the cross and took a step backward. "You're supposed to be dead," he said.

"I wasn't notified," I said.

He sat down heavily on the sofa. "They said you'd been killed. You fell asleep out on the Interstate, rolled your car. They said the house was empty. Your wife is selling it, but she's got to have it fixed it up a little. You know, to bring it up to code."

My house *was* empty except for an old worn out sofa and the kitchen stuff which Janet didn't want. I went into the kitchen and came back with two beers. I gave one to him. He held the bottle up and looked at it against the light. "A dead man has just given me a beer," he said.

"You sure you're in the right house?" I said.

He took a slip of paper out of his shirt pocket. "Six four one, McNutt. That's what they said."

"I think you wanted six four three. I was about to make myself a ham sandwich," I said. "You had your lunch yet?"

The wreck hadn't been bad enough to kill anyone, but then it doesn't take much. Drowsy, then a deer in the headlights, oversteering to miss it, an icy spot, a slide into the median. All this at low speed, the s u v still usable. Wynn Ragdale, who lived next door, left a wife and four kids. No insurance, a load of debt. The house was all Geri Ragdale had. And it wasn't worth much. Maybe twenty, twenty-five. In California it would go for a hundred and fifty. But there's no work here anymore since the mines closed and the smelter moved its business to Mexico and other places where you can get people to defy death working from a catwalk over molten copper for two dollars a day.

I brought the sandwiches out. "It's the guy next door you want, Wynn Ragdale," I said. "He drove his Explorer off the road this side of Bozeman Hill."

I was glad to have company. I'd been more or less alone since Janet took off for California with our son, Bill, and most of the furniture. I'd made a mess of things, no question about it.

"Son of a gun," the guy said. "They told me the wrong address. Said nobody's home. Just go in and take the measurements."

He had a wad of bread and ham in his jaw. His eyes watered from the hot Chinese mustard I liked to use. He gulped down some cold beer. "You looking for a job by any chance?" he said.

I wasn't, but I should have been. I hadn't worked in two months. The flower shop had fired me, and that was okay since the pay sucked. The bereaved don't tip and most of the flowers were sent to them.

Money's scarce in this town. People don't spend what they have on the frills. Before the flower shop I worked on the Arco smelter for union wages. The town thrived back then. You could make a living picking up loose coins outside the bars. We had more bars than churches and more churches than grocery stores. I made good money. Even so I drank and sulked and took it out on Janet and sometimes little Bill. "What's *wrong* with you?" she said more than once, sobbing. I didn't have a clue. Still don't. "Me," I said. "I'm what's wrong with me." I meant it as a wisecrack, not a confession. It was both, I guess.

I never hit her, but I might as well have, if words can bruise. They can do worse than bruise. They can kill off the spirit. They can put you through hell and leave you there. Janet was only saving herself and little Bill. I tried to make it up, but I'd crossed the point of no return.

"What kind of job?" I said.

"This job. Doing shit like this for Lakin Real Estate. Checking foundations, insulation, wiring, measuring square footage, looking for dry rot. Shit-work basically, but they pay fifty cents over minimum wage."

"Why give it up?"

"I'm going fishing. Up in Alaska. Salmon. My cousin Fermin Duran has his own boat. He lost a crew member—washed overboard in a storm. I can make a pile of money in season, then travel in the off. I need to see things. Like Mexico, or Sweden. My wife's a Swede on her father's side." He made a comical face. "Yah, shore, you betcha by golly!" he said. One beer and he was drunk. He got up and hiked his pants and sat down again. He was more fat than muscle and didn't seem too bright. I couldn't see him waddling across the deck of a fishing boat, tossing up and down on the high seas.

"You're not afraid of getting washed overboard in a storm?" I said. "Water's pretty cold up there. A man would die of hypothermia in a few minutes."

"Not something I'd worry about," he said, shrugging. "You can't worry every time an opportunity comes up."

"I guess not," I said.

"You'd never get anywhere," he said.

I brought out two more beers and the liter of Seagrams and two shot glasses. I was using a cardboard box for a coffee table. "What does your wife think about it?" I said.

"Hell! It was Rhonda's idea! My cousin Fermin Duran came through town and mentioned he had a slot to fill, not asking me if I wanted it, or anything. And Rhonda jumps right in and says 'Hire Dickie! Oh Fermin, please hire Dickie! Dickie would love to work on a salmon boat, wouldn't you, Dickie?' What could I say?"

"Sometimes you got to listen to your wife," I said. I filled the two shot glasses with the blended whiskey.

"It embarrassed me, her begging Fermin like that. I tried to hush her up, but then my cousin, Fermin, steps right in and says, You want the job, Dickie, you got it. The rest is history. We're leaving this shit-hole of a town next month." He emptied the shot glass. I emptied mine, then refilled both.

"Who do I talk to?" I asked.

He looked confused. "What?" He stood up again, adjusted his pants, then plopped down hard enough to raise a fog of sofa dust. He was too clumsy to dance around on the deck of a trawler.

"Who do I talk to, about getting your job?"

"Don Lakin. He owns the agency. Come down nine tomorrow morning, I'll introduce you."

"I'll be there."

"Opportunity only knocks once."

"So I've heard."

"You heard right."

He looked kind of dreamy, probably imagining himself on his cousin's boat in the Gulf of Alaska. He'd drown for sure. Anyone could see that. His center of gravity was wrong. The boat would roll into a swell and he'd go dancing off into the ice-cold sea. He belonged indoors, measuring walls, looking for dry rot.

"Fermin Duran," I said. "Isn't that a Mexican name?"

"What of it?" he said, frowning at me through his dream.

"Nothing. Just seems unusual. Up in Alaska and all, fishing for salmon."

"He's from San Diego. They fish in San Diego too, you know. For tuna, mostly. Fermin got tired of the unfair competition. The big tuna companies send out these fucking aircraft carriers dragging nets the size of Rhode Island. They sweep the fucking ocean clean. You'll be lucky to buy a can of tuna, this keeps up. I'm telling you."

He got belligerent with a few drinks in him. He swaggered side to side in the sofa, an old salt, ready to take on the tuna capitalists.

"You got a point," I said.

"Damn betcha I got a point."

I wanted to tell him to forget Alaska. "Dickie, you'll die in Alaska," is what I wanted to say. But it wouldn't stop him. You can't mess with someone else's fate. It doesn't work that way. Also, I wanted the job at Lakin Real Estate. Maybe I could work my way up to agent. Maybe there'd be a revolution in Mexico or wherever and the smelter would come back and the price of housing would rise.

"Good luck, Dickie," I said.

"You make your own luck in this world, buddy," Dickie said. He gave me a grim stare—the look of a man who knew what was what.

He didn't know shit from Shinola, of course, but I nodded in agreement. I filled the shot glasses again, and raised mine in a toast. "North to Alaska," I said.

"Amen to that," Dickie said.

The Life and Times of a Forty-nine-Pound Man

Nick Pitman asked his father to come to West Texas for a visit. Nick's wife, Vasilisa Ivanovna Bikovski, believed the visit would turn out badly. "Big motherfucking mistake," she said. "Bruno thinks you are failure. You know what is to happen, don't you?"

Nick had exposed her to the choice American expletives and Vasilisa used them inventively and with reckless abandon, believing it enhanced her fluency. She was right about Bruno, but Nick hoped that the old man would come to see that his only son hadn't made such a mess of his life after all. Nick taught English composition to techie-wannabees at Western States Institute of Mining and Metallurgy. The English department was small and neglected by the college administration, whose priorities were the engineering and business schools, but Nick was content in spite of the secret life he had to live.

His secret life was his science fiction career, which had just reached a kind of apogee: Cockatrice Special Effects, Inc., had taken an option to make a feature film of his new novel, *The Life and Times of a Forty-nine-Pound Man*. His department chairman regarded science fiction as an unworthy genre, a spurious form completely at odds with the higher goals of literature.

Nick was aware of the higher goals of literature and hoped someday to write a novel that could sit comfortably on the same shelf with the work of Bradbury and Heinlein, perhaps even with the genre-transcending works of Vonnegut and Orwell. But if he wanted tenure—and he wanted it badly—he'd have to keep his science fiction career to himself. His job kept food on the table, paid the rent, and supported his writing. It was a safety net he could not do without.

His father had no respect for teaching as a career for men. He thought it was an occupation originally intended for women. Men who chose teaching over jobs in the competitive workplace were either loafers, incompetents, misfits, or homosexuals. A career in writing, unless it turned out to be lucrative, was even less defensible. And writers who wrote for writing's sake, the *artistes* who lived in willful poverty, were in the same category as street people. Bruno Pitman believed the only reliable indicators of success were the size of a man's bank account and the credit limit of his platinum card.

"Worthless is as worthless does," he was fond of saying.

But at least Nick could show the old man a Xerox of the ten-thousand-dollar check he had received from Cockatrice. If his work meant nothing to his father, maybe the evidence of serious cash would.

Bruno Pitman was a retired bank president who now lived in the Bahamas with his fourth wife, Winona Mufkey, a twenty-three-year-old model. At seventy-four he still bristled with aggressive good health and offensive opinions. He was a big man, over six feet tall, with a great round stomach that pushed out in front of him like blunt warning: move out of the way or get dumped on your keester. He had a big hairless dome pink with blood pressure, a jaw strong enough to carry leaf lard jowls, a nose as thick and as red as a peeled yam. His black unforgiving eyes were as hard and as expressionless as nailheads. He reminded Nick of old photographs of J. P. Morgan, the railroad baron.

"I'm here for five hours, then I fly back to Nassau," he said when Nick picked him up at the airport. "Where's your chubby little red-haired Rooskie?"

"Vasi went ahead to the Weston, to get us a table," Nick said, hoping his father wouldn't refer to Vasilisa's weight problem at the restaurant. Vasilisa was an unashamed eater. She'd nearly starved to death in Soviet Russia years ago, and Nick did not begrudge her occasional self-indulgence. "They wouldn't give us reservations because they've got a union convention this weekend."

"Unions," his father muttered as he lit a cigar. "Blackmailers and extortionists. Featherbedding in the name of social progress. You two got a little Pitman on the way yet, Nick?"

"We'll probably adopt, Dad."

Bruno Pitman narrowed his eyes suspiciously. "*Adopt*? What the hell do you want to do that for? Have your own, like your sister down in Coral Gables. She's got, what—four babies now. She's given me my only grandkids." Bruno Pitman had a proud gleam in his hard little eyes, as if he had sired the four babies himself.

"We can't have kids, Dad. I'm sterile."

"You're *what*? Oh for Chrissakes, you mean you can't . . . ? Bruno's pink dome paled. "Jesus, Nick, they've got this drug now. You've seen the ads. It's called Viagra. I use it myself—makes me want to live forever!"

"I'm not impotent, Dad. Just a disastrously low sperm count. Down in the low millions per milliliter of semen—something like that."

"Sterile, impotent, what's the difference? Bottom line is you can't make babies. It's your mother's fault. I should never have married her. She drank when she was pregnant with you. That's why you've got bandy legs and why your eyes are so far apart. It's probably why you can't get a decent job. Fetal alcohol syndrome. Remember how all the neighbor kids use to call you "Geeko"? Your mother was an airline stewardess when I met her. Breathed too much rarefied air on top of those mickey-sized bottles of Jamaican rum. She came into our marriage with damaged chromosomes. She should have had a warning label pinned on her. 'Impregnate at your own risk.'"

Nick let his father rave on without protest. He was used to this.

Dinner was just as Vasilisa predicted: A nonstop monologue by Bruno that analyzed, mocked, and denounced. His targets were mainly lefty politicians, but he also took on the media—

newspapers, television, Hollywood. He gradually lowered his sights until they came to rest, finally, on Nick.

"So tell me, son," he said. "When are you going to buy yourself some decent clothes and get a real job? You can't expect to spend the rest of your life living from hand to mouth on teacher's pay."

Nick took the opportunity to fish out the Xeroxed check from Cockatrice. "I think my writing career is about to take off, Dad," he said. "This is just for a six-month option. When they make the film, they'll pay me 2 percent of production costs. That could be well up into six figures, maybe seven."

Bruno Pitman was not impressed. "When, when, when," he said. "That's one of the most pathetic words in the English language, along with 'maybe,' 'if,' 'might,' and 'could be.'"

Vasilisa buttered her third dinner roll, looked at it, decided to leave it on her plate. She leaned toward Nick. "Tell old shit-eater to motherfuck himself," she whispered into his ear.

"You shouldn't eat so much starch, Vasi," Bruno said. "It goes straight to your hips. I don't let Winona eat wheat or potato products at all. I limit her diet to fruits, fresh green vegetables, and lamb chops."

"We must take you back to airport, Papa," Vasilisa hissed, her lips compressed to a thin red line.

"You know, Vasi," Bruno said. "If I could have had the time to raise your husband properly, he might have amounted to something. I guess I have to take the blame. The boy's in your hands now. Maybe you can wise him up to the real world."

When Bruno went to pay the check, Vasi whispered furiously to Nick, "I hope fat mother-eating shit-sucker burns up in hell."

Hans Ludens, president of Cockatrice, called Nick at home. He wanted Nick to come to Los Angeles to talk about the script. "This is going to be the first major SF film of the twenty-first century," he said. "I want your script to be hotter than *Blade Runner*. I want to make Kubrick's *2001* look like it was made by Ed Wood. You with me on this, Nick?"

"Script?" he said. "I didn't know you wanted me to do a script."

"Who else if not you? It's your book, dawg. You da *man*, Nick. Don't worry, you'll get help."

Nick kissed Vasilisa goodbye at the airport. "You be good," she said.

"I'd rather be lucky than good," he said, quoting Lefty Gomez, the Yankee southpaw from the 1930s. It was one of his favorite expressions.

"You speak of movie, yes?" she said, raising an eyebrow.

"Honey, that's the only thing on my mind, believe me," he said.

Rodney McQuirk, a cameraman at Cockatrice, picked Nick up at LAX. McQuirk, a lanky, sullen man whose breath was laced with the dark fumes of cirrhosis, said, "Good novel, dude. I'm the one who recommended it to Hans. Looks like we might even shoot the mother, if the money people come across with a real budget."

The Cockatrice studio was located in Van Nuys. Rodney drove an ancient Volvo coupe with no muffler. Conversation during the long ride to Van Nuys was impossible over the sputtering roar. Nick occupied himself by trying to visualize the storyboards for the script he would write.

The Life and Times of a Forty-nine-Pound Man was about a retirement community on Mars. Mars was ideal for old-age homes because gravity on the red planet was one-third that of Earth's. The senior citizens would live under a Sundome, a huge canopy a hundred times bigger than the canopies covering the largest malls on earth. This would be structurally possible because of the low gravity. The steel used for the dome's construction would come from the iron ore mined on Mars. There would be giant lenses built into the canopy which would focus and concentrate sunlight, making the otherwise frigid climate of Mars as mild as south Florida in winter. The weak pull of gravity would also have all sorts of spin-off health benefits. Arthritis, for example, would be a far less painful affliction on Mars. The brittle bones of those suffering from osteoporosis would be less likely to break. The feeblest men or women would be able to move furniture around their condos with relative ease. Little old ladies, palsied and vague and bent with widow's humps, would have strength comparable to an earthbound stevedore's. The aging process itself would slow down: a year on Mars lasts 687 Earth days and time would thus be naturally dilated and slowed, which in turn would retard the deterioration of cells. The appearance of the senior citizens would even begin to change—they'd start growing again because of the lessened gravity. A man who had been five feet ten might discover suddenly that he is six feet three—a dramatic reversal of the geriatric "shrinkage" people suffer on Earth. And as the bodies of the seniors elongated, they'd also slim down. Even the sexual drive would enjoy a renaissance, and the coital positions made possible by the weak pull of gravity would astound the most jaded sex addict. A forty-nine-pound roué would enjoy sexual gymnastics he could only dream about on earth.

Nick pictured the opening scene: the interplanetary shuttle, packed with seniors and their nurses, slipping into orbit around the red planet. He scripted some dialogue in his head:

FRETFUL OLD MAN
Are we there yet, Miss?

ATTRACTIVE YOUNG NURSE
You betcha, Mr. Ainsworthy!
You're just going to *love* Martian Meadows!

Hans Ludens was a big man dressed entirely in black leather. He sat on a motorcycle inside his office. The office looked like it belonged in a meatpacking plant. A bare bulb hung from the ceiling on its twisted cord. The plank floor was worn and splintered. Ludens's desk was gray steel. It was piled high with notebooks and unidentifiable pieces of hi-tech, low-tech, and retro-tech equipment. There were posters on the walls from movies Cockatrice had provided the special effects for: *Red Moon*, *Black Star*, *Water*

Planet, Stone Clone. A papier mâché sculpture—female, wearing camouflage fatigues—clung to the exposed wall studs halfway to the ceiling. Her eyes were wide with adrenaline, and her mouth was open in an exultant cry, the paper teeth white as Chiclets. The sculpture was titled *Fearless Climber.*

"Nick, you're still alive!" Ludens boomed. "That car of El Rodney's is a death trap. I would've sent Lana Faye or Bobbi Jo in the Mercedes, but El Rodney here is your biggest fan. He wanted the honor."

Ludens kick-started the motorcycle—a vintage Harley Electraglide. He twisted the throttle, filling the room with thunder and blue haze, then shut the machine down. He stepped off and shook Nick's hand in a crushing grip. "We're going to make the bitchinest movie out of your bitchin book, have no fear."

Nick knew he was supposed to be impressed. And he was. So here was life in the fast lane! What a fine romantic world Hans Ludens lived in, a world where you could wear black leather and call people "El Rodney" and not feel foolish. It was like an extension of childhood, permitting yourself to dress in costume and play out any game that came to mind. What a great stay against the death grips of responsibility, good behavior, and age.

They toured the studio—"my factory" Ludens called it—before they went to lunch. The tour didn't mean much to Nick—he was technically illiterate. Hans, taking note of Nick's bewilderment, said, "Once you've seen one laser you've seen them all, right?" Now and then Hans would relight his cigar and blow smoke into a ruby red laser beam. He'd study the patterns the smoke made for minutes before moving on to the next machine. Computer-controlled cameras on rails were positioned in front of models of space vehicles, from orbital space stations to interstellar transport ships. Rodney, the cameraman, showed Nick how these cameras worked, how models were photographed against a blue screen, and Nick pretended to grasp the details.

Hans decided lunch would be out on Catalina Island. They drove to Newport Beach in Ludens's Mercedes convertible; Ludens steered with one hand as he wove in and out of light traffic at ninety miles an hour. A woman—Bobbi Jo—sat next to Ludens. She was a blonde with spiked hair and nose rings. Her ears looked like a metal recycling depot. She had a sultry, challenging look that she was evidently unable to turn off. She regarded everything, from her black-glossed fingernails to Nick's elbow-patched sports coat, with the same smoldering hostility. In spite of her demeanor and appearance, she was friendly enough and spoke in the honeysuckle accents of a 1950-ish southern belle.

Nick rode in the back seat with Lana Faye Harmon, a twenty-year-old actress with long black hair that billowed and furled in the eddying wind like thick smoke. She seemed more sophisticated than her years. Nick thought that women like Lana Faye were born sophisticated. He felt over his head just sitting next to her.

At Newport Beach they boarded a seaplane, a converted World War Two PBY search-and-rescue craft. Hans put on an old Army Air Corps cap with a "thirty-mission crush," swiped, he said, from the set of *The Memphis Belle*. The plane belonged to Cockatrice, Inc. The image of a Cockatrice—the mythical snake hatched from a cock's egg—had been painted on the hull of the flying boat. The snake's silver-green scales were big as shingles. The pink mouth with its yellow fangs yawned under the pilot's cabin. The lethal red eyes of the cockatrice stared malevolently.

It made Nick nervous to board an airplane that had as its insignia an image of unrepentant evil, even if it was meant to be playful. It seemed to mock any benevolent forces the universe might be harboring. Flight always made Nick nervous under the best auspices. He seldom flew anywhere, but when he did he'd revert to his grade school Catholicism and recite the Rosary under his breath until the plane was safely in the stratosphere, flying level. Then he'd repeat the ritual as the plane descended.

Nick sat in one of the huge Plexiglas observation blisters built into the side of the hull. A small sofa had been custom-fitted into this area. Lana Faye curled up next to him. Ludens flew the plane and Bobbi Jo sat in the copilot's seat. Ludens started the engines and revved them, and the flying boat began to plow out of its harbor and into the open bay.

They flew low over the gentle green swells. Schools of flying fish broke through the glossy surface as if showing off for the PBY.

Lana Faye scooted close to Nick. "Writers fascinate me," she said. "I mean, how do you come up with all this stuff?" she said.

"I don't know," Nick said. "It just comes to me, like it's in the air."

"You mean like a flu bug. You sort of catch it?"

"Yeah, like that," Nick said. "It's a kind of chronic disease. Incurable." *Bruno would agree*, Nick thought.

A sudden turbulence made Lana Faye roll against Nick. When the air smoothed, she didn't move away. "You're a cute guy, Nick, in a goofy sort of way. You ever mess around?" she asked.

"I'm married," Nick said.

"And your point is?" Lana Faye said.

His mouth went dry. The Plexiglas turret filled with blinding sunlight as the plane leaned into a lazy turn. Nick felt a twinge of disappointment with himself. Here he was, flying over the Pacific in a converted PBY with a beautiful young woman next to him, a movie deal in the works, and all he could do was offer lame excuses. He was not a romantic adventurer like his father. Bruno Pitman demeaned Nick not only because he was an underpaid teacher, but because he had no sense of adventure. Nick was a mild-mannered observer of life, not a reckless participant.

He preferred it that way. He thought his reasons were good. He led a careful and structured existence because he was aware of how delicate the thread was that held things together. You did not risk the things you valued most. It suited him. But it was not the worldview of a Hollywood player.

"I love my wife," he said, shrugging. "She's Russian," he added.

"Well good for you and good for her," Lana Faye said, yawning. Her mouth was pink with animal health. "I respect that in a man. You're a quality guy, Nick. I mean that." She lit a cigarette.

"Actually she's Lithuanian," he said. "Her name is Vasilisa. Her father was shot by the Communists and her grandfather was shot by the Nazis and her great-grandfather was exiled to Siberia by the Romanovs."

"She's got rebel blood," Lana Faye said. "She a wild one, Nick? You able to keep her happy?" She gave Nick a sly sidelong grin.

"She escaped the iron curtain with her mother and two sisters," Nick said. "They rode hundreds of miles in an unheated boxcar in the middle of winter from Vilnius to Kaunas to Riga. They nearly starved to death. Then they hid on a boat that was headed for Sweden. Her little sister died on the way."

"Heavy," Lana Faye said, blowing a cloud of blue smoke into the lasering sun.

"I'm loyal as a spaniel," he said. "If anyone deserves loyalty, it's Vasi."

"Stay cool, Nick. I'm not going to pull your chubby out of your Dockers. I'm with someone anyway. An actor. His agent calls him the next Brad Pitt."

"The *next* Brad Pitt?"

"They come and they go, Nick. Everyone's a temp."

Bobbi Jo staggered toward them, her hands gripping the exposed ribs of the fuselage struts. "He wants you up front," she said.

Nick poked himself in the chest. "Me?"

"You. He needs you."

Nick crawled past Bobbi Jo and into the front cabin of the PBY. Crash dummies dressed in flight suits and wearing old Army Air Corps sheepskin caps were seated at the radio operator's console and at the navigator's desk.

"Hey, Nick," Ludens said. "Sit down."

Nick sat in the copilot's seat.

"You want to fly this crate for a while? I'm going back to take a piss."

"I'm not a pilot, Hans."

"No sweat. We're flying by wire. You got the wheel, but you won't have to horse it around. No primitive hydraulic servo mechanisms to do your bidding. You fuck up, cause a pilot-induced oscillation, the computer will put the damper on it. I paid a cool five mil to upgrade the old Cockatrice. Go on, Ace, take the yoke."

Ludens pointed at an instrument. "That's a level-flight indicator. All you got to do is keep the nose on the horizon and that bubble on the line. The horizon moves up into your view, you know you're descending. If you're in doubt, check the bubble. Take your cue from the engines, they'll talk to you." Ludens lit a cigar. "Keep us out of the drink, Nick. The only tough thing about a flying boat is putting her down in chop."

"Chop?" Nick asked, as if that was the only part of Ludens's monologue he did not understand.

"Gnarly water. Like putting down in a potato patch."

Ludens climbed out of his seat and put his Memphis Belle cap on Nick's head. "Enjoy," he said. He left Nick alone with his terror and the roar of the flying boat's twin radial engines. The Cockatrice was still low, less than a thousand feet above the Pacific. Nick pulled the yoke back slightly and the horizon fell away. The engines began to labor and Nick moved the yoke forward. The horizon came back, but now it began to rise up into the windshield, like water filling a glass tank. The engines gained rpm's. The roar rose in pitch. Nick moved the yoke back again and finally settled the PBY into level flight.

He was thrilled. He felt adventure in the tingling vibrations the engines produced in the yoke. The tingle traveled up his arms and across his chest and back to his spine. He felt it in his crotch, in his tailbone. He pushed the yoke forward and leveled off a hundred feet above the ocean's glossy swells. A school of flying fish rose out of the water off the starboard wing like aquatic angels. Every creature on earth loved to play. Why not Nick Pitman?

He eased the yoke back and started a slow climb into the afternoon sun. The ocean became smooth as oilcloth, a silver arm of sunlight bisecting it all the way to the western horizon. Nick listened to the heavy throb of the lugging engines, watched the altimeter tick off the increasing altitude. His ears popped.

At nine thousand feet he pushed the yoke forward. He felt himself rise off the seat, his thighs straining against the lap belt. He felt the insignificant weight of his presence on the planet. He sensed the canard gravity had imposed on the world: Gravity was the mother and father of all restraint, even the self-imposed kind. The world was heavy and the things of the world had real weight.

Weight was the key: you had weighty thoughts, you made weighty decisions, you weighed carefully your every move, and there were so many things that weighed on your mind. What was the sound bite that had surfaced during the recent national elections? *Gravitas.* A man without gravitas was not fit to shoulder the weight of leadership. Nick wanted no part of gravitas. He wanted to be lighthearted, unburdened, a blithe spirit skimming weightlessly through the vast and intricate world, knowing there was nothing to lose. Was it possible? Had it ever been possible?

When the Cockatrice reached the top of the parabolic arc, just before it began its shallow dive, Nick started laughing hysterically. Truth hit him like a pie in the face. He thought: *The forty-nine-pound man, c'est moi!* His novel, ostensibly science fiction, was really about him, about his longing to free himself of all artificial restraint. He was not even forty years old, but he could see how the rest of his life would go. No adventures, no surprises, but plenty of dependable security—tenure, generous annuities provided by his college, and then Social Security and Medicare. Nothing ever to worry about again, except that he was locking himself in a very narrow space, cozy as a coffin. "Jesus Christ!" he yelled into the roar of the engines, "I've even got burial insurance!"

The horizon rose in the windshield and disappeared above it. The engines raced. They howled like twin banshees. The airspeed indicator trembled at 165. Nick thought: *I could fly this old crate straight into the ocean, straight into instant nothingness. What would be lost? Where would this pint-size ego go? Why should it matter to anyone?* Terrifying thoughts, but also exhilarating, and Nick could not account for the impulse behind them. Then he remembered something his biology teacher told him in high school: The human skeleton, stripped of flesh, blood, and marrow, weighs about forty-nine pounds. The unconscious source of his novel? The ultimate lightness of being was death.

He didn't want to die. But hadn't he *been* comfortably dead and hoping to secure it with tenure? Dazzled, confused, he reminded himself that there were others aboard the Cockatrice who might want to hold onto their lives. He eased the yoke back and the plane flew low over the dark swells of the Pacific. Nick's heart was pounding like a bass drum.

Hans Ludens stumbled into the cabin. "What the fuck are you doing to my airplane, Nick?" he said. "You made me piss all over myself! The girls are screaming! Ease up, cowboy, you're going to tear the wings off my bird!" Ludens slid into the pilot's seat and took over the controls. He flew the PBY the rest of the way to Catalina and put it down in the smooth waters of Avalon Bay.

They hiked up the hill above the bay to an Andalusian restaurant. They sat in a narrow booth and ordered margaritas and paella. Nick had three margaritas before the paella came. At one point, Lana Faye put her hand on Nick's thigh and squeezed. "I think you're some kind of crazy man," she said, her breath sultry and close. "Are you some type of intellectual adrenaline freak, Nick?"

"This cowboy's a stone cold troublemaker," Hans Ludens said, winking, and they all saluted Nick with their margaritas.

Nick never made trouble for anyone. He avoided trouble. Now he saw that trouble was a way to break out of the box. Without trouble you stayed safe in your homemade prison. Where you eventually shriveled. He felt drunk with this idea and its remedy, which continued to frighten him. He left the table and found a telephone booth and called Vasilisa.

"Vasi, I'm quitting my job," he said. "We're moving to L.A."

Nick misinterpreted the silence on the other end of the line. "It'll be okay, honey," he assured her. "We'll be fine. I'm going to make it. And you know what? It won't matter if I don't."

"Nicky," Vasilisa said. "Sit down, take deep breath. Your papa, he has passed."

It seemed like a rebuttal rather than bad news. It didn't fully register. "Vasi, listen to me. I'm through playing it safe." Then it hit him. "Passed? You mean Bruno is *dead*?"

"I am so sorry, my dear. It was heart attack, this morning."

Vasilisa's use of the old fashioned "my dear" touched him. His eyes welled up.

"Your papa, he forgot to take nitroglycerin pill. His heart could not breathe. Poor skinny cocksucker Mufkey, trapped under big dead body, feeling big dead body get cold."

Bruno dead? How could that be? He was a monument, a colossus.

"You are free, Nikita," Vasilisa said. She was crying, too. "No more you must kiss papa's big fat ass."

Nick brushed his tears away. He went back to the table and finished his fourth margarita. Bruno, the old risk-taker, dead. Died atop the bimbo. Nick smiled, thinking of the skinny model stuck under Bruno's cooling bulk, but it was not a cruel smile.

It wasn't the worst way to go. You could live to be a hundred, tied to tubes and respirators in the impersonal white walls of a nursing home on Mars, Martian nurses probing your almost nonexistent forty-nine-pound body with their long clammy fingers, the sun in the glass ceiling thin as a dime.

Nick didn't love Bruno, he could admit that easily and without guilt, but he felt sorrow anyway. Sorrow was a prepackaged feature of the human psyche, one of the weights built into the genetic code.

Nick looked at the faces of the people around him. Strangers, strangers to him and probably to themselves. It didn't matter. They were all temps, but having a very good time anyway. He wouldn't mention Bruno. There would be no point in adding unnecessary weight to the splendid afternoon. He ordered another round of margaritas.

Hell's Cartoonist

"Why me?" I said.

"Why not you?" Billie Blood said.

That's how it started, three months ago. Billie had a place downtown, a little studio apartment with a pull-down bed. I was like a kid with a new toy.

My wife, Ursula, noticed the change but it took her a while to make the connection. Why shouldn't it have? I'd been faithful as a dog for almost five years.

"You've lost weight," Ursula said, fingering my neck suspiciously. She worked in Denny's. We were in a booth next to the kitchen, having a 3:00 p.m. lunch. She went back to the unbusy kitchen and brought out another basket of steak fries for me. "You're not feeling well?"

I was eating more these days but weighed less. I was energized, the atoms of my body buzzed. I felt translucent, weightless, electrified.

Ursula saw the change. "Tell me her name," she said.

"Billie," I said. Lying is not my strong suit. Better to own up to it now than later.

"You love her, then?" she said. She was calm, steady. Tears rolled down her long face. She kept her hair dark. It looked black as wet tar against her pale skin. Her grave Bavarian eyes looked past me to our compromised future.

"Love is a strong word," I said, guilt-stricken. "The strongest, maybe. This thing with Billie Blood is just . . ."

I didn't know what it was. It was something I'd never experienced before even though Ursula was my third wife. I'd married women clueless as myself. I always thought it was love, but after a year or two I had no name for the thing that brought us together, held us for a while, then let us go. I was almost fifty and still feeling my way in the dark. It wasn't just women who mystified me. Everyone did.

"Billie *Blood*?" Ursula found some dismal comedy in the odd name.

"A *nom de peinture* she calls it."

She uttered a small dry laugh. "You think you're trading up again. You are going to be a wretched old man, all alone, full of regret. It's very simple. Anyone can see it."

"You're wrong about this, honey. Really."

"What would you like me to say? How nice for you, how wonderful you've found someone who stimulates you so much that you lose weight?"

I had put it all in jeopardy—wife, home, stability. And I needed stability. I couldn't work without it. What had I been thinking? But I hadn't been thinking. Thinking's got nothing to do with it. It was electrical, a surge, hidden amperes electrocuting good judgment.

Women don't hit on me. I'm not great looking, I don't radiate masculinity. I'm a little unkempt, even seedy. I don't send out flirtatious signals. And I'm preoccupied—mostly with my work.

I never expected it. I didn't see it coming, and when it came I had no defense. An image of Billie Blood on her queen-size Murphy pull-down came to me. Graceful even in supine repose, sturdy igloo breasts refusing to slump, curves and planes tapering into each other, flaming masses of kinked red hair consuming the white pillow. More woman than a man like me has a right to expect.

She was magnetic north. The iron in my blood danced for her. "A true artist needs an active love life," she said. I didn't know whose state of need she meant, hers or mine.

We'd met at a gallery. We both had paintings on the back wall, next to the restrooms. Billie did levees, cotton fields, and badlands. Sunlight like blood clots thrombosed the flat brown skin of her West Texas skies. I do downtown decay—buildings, warehouses, the plaza with its fractured humanity: whores, transvestites, glue sniffers. Maids and gardeners waiting for the bus. Loafing pederasts, panhandlers, undercover cops. Cartoonist in Hell, Billie once said. "Not that that's a *bad* thing," she amended.

"No way I'm finishing my shift," Ursula said, lighting a tear-dampened cigarette.

I was between jobs. The free lunch I got at Denny's was my food for the day. I'd get the garlic-mushroom-Swissburger, and Ursula would pile on the fries until they spilled off the plate. Then two slices of French silk pie for desert. Unlimited coffee. It was like a date, and—I realized too late—not a good time to discuss Billie. As if there could be a good time.

Ursula slid out of the booth and took off her apron. The day manager, Derek Hubble, came over to us. "Please put out your cigarette, Ursula," he said. Derek Hubble is a suave black man. Tall and lean, goateed, manicured. He looked like one of the dark-suited Modern Jazz Quartet guys, elegant. I could picture him wearing shades behind a vibroharp, mallets poised, confidently cool.

"I'm sick, Derek," she said.

Derek Hubble looked at her, looked at me. "Uh-huh," he said. "Enjoy your lunch?" he said to me. He knew Ursula was feeding me gratis but let it go—another patron of the arts.

"Always," I said. "Thank you."

We both looked at Ursula as she moved careful as a drunk down the aisle and pushed her way through the double doors out to the parking lot.

"She coming in tomorrow?" Derek Hubble said.

"I don't know, Mr. Hubble," I said.

"She don't, could be her job."

"I'll smooth this over, Derek."

He looked offended by the uninvited familiarity.

↓

Ursula is a UFO freak. Not crazy enough to claim abductions or encounters of any kind, but crazy enough to believe in them to the point of spending hours in Internet chat-rooms with other UFO freaks. I took a generous position on it from the beginning and looked at her obsession as a kind of harmless hobby.

When we first met I mentioned my UFO experience, which was really not my experience at all. It was Henry Russo's experience. It turned her on. It lit her up. I couldn't tell the story enough. She combed through it, pressing for details I might have left out or forgotten. When we got married I had the feeling that she had found, in me, someone to validate her life. I was living proof that UFOs were not a national joke.

Henry Russo and I were stationed at an Air Defense Command radar base in northern Montana years ago. I was working swing shift at the blockhouse—the concrete bunker where the radar scopes were kept. Henry was a radio technician. Before going on duty most of us "scope dopes" stopped by the chow hall for hot roast beef sandwiches and peach cobbler. Orson McCabe, the squadron psycho, was being a pain in the ass. He liked to stuff raisins up his fat red nose then pull them out with a disgustingly elaborate nose-picking gesture and toss them at other tables. Someone was yelling at Orson to knock it off but not in an "or else" way since Orson was a big mean bastard, when Henry Russo came stumbling in yelling Oh my God, Oh Jesus.

Henry was quiet and uncomplaining, the kind of guy who gets fast promotions because the air force needed to keep uncomplaining people who took their work seriously. He'd made Airman First Class in only two years and was squadron pinochle champ. Unlike most of us, Henry was goal-oriented. He knew computers were the coming thing and wanted to be on the ground floor when he got back to civilian life.

So when he said a flying saucer wide as a parking lot had hovered over the radio tower for maybe a minute, it was hard to laugh it off. Everyone in the chow hall looked at him in silence for a few seconds, trying to process what couldn't be processed, then started giving him a hard time. Henry never lived it down. But that night reports of UFO sightings came in from Yellowstone south to the Rio Grande. Casper, Fort Collins, Raton, Albuquerque, El Paso, all night long. Nothing appeared on our radar screens. That was my UFO experience. And now it was Ursula's UFO experience, which gave her prestige in chat-room freakdom.

When I first told her the story she was married to an army lifer but considering divorce. We were at a Halloween party in northeast El Paso, near the Fort Bliss artillery range. I was drunk enough to give up the UFO story, embellished a little with fictitious squadrons of Air Defense Command F-102s making Combat Air Patrol orbits in the general vicinity where the visitors from planet X had been sighted. Ursula Klock—her married name then—pulled me into the kitchen of the party giver's house and made me tell it again. Rum punch in hand, she backed me against the sink and leaned in recklessly—thigh to thigh, nose to nose, chest to chest, her excited blue eyes ferreting details. She shuddered orgasmically when I said the dark gray disk was big as a stadium and made no noise other than a windy whisper that Airman Russo would never be able to forget. I took her home and we made out in her driveway for half an hour while her soon-to-be ex-husband, drink in hand, stood on the porch trying to peer into the heavily tinted windows of my '73 Monte Carlo.

We eloped to Mexico, to Chihuahua City, took the train through the Copper Canyon down to Los Mochis on Mexico's Pacific coast. I was happy, I knew this was it, and when we got back to El Paso I found work at a greenhouse nursery and painted pictures mornings and weekends. Ursula took a waitressing job, which was all she'd ever done since coming to the U.S. from Stuttgart with her clueless lifer husband, Sergeant Major Maynard Klock.

↓

After lunch at Denny's, I went downtown and crossed the Paso del Norte bridge into Mexico and had a fifty-cent shot of tequila in the Kentucky Club. I had my sketch pad with me. My idea was to go over to Boys' Town, the whorehouse district between Calles Ocampo and Mariscal, and do some sketches. I wanted a drink to loosen up. Sketching in Juárez made me a little self-conscious.

I didn't want my sketches to be tight with strained intent. I had no point to make, no agenda. I just wanted to catch the unfiltered kinetics of doomed life.

Boys' Town was a mistake. The whores and pimps were off the streets and helmeted cops on horseback looked at me through their tinted visors as if they needed a gringo to walk on, so I took my pad and pencil over to Avenida Diez y Seis de Septiembre to the three-hundred-year-old cathedral and made some quick contour sketches of the beggars who sat or were otherwise propped up against the short walls of the old church's plaza, looking for turista coins. A man with no feet moved toward me on homemade crutches. He swung wildly between the crooked sticks like a suspended wind-up toy, grinning. He made almost no progress. I gave him two quarters, a dime, and a cigarette.

Midwestern tourists took digital pictures of him. One posed with him, then the other. They gave him paper dollars and everyone was happy. I sketched the tourists large and serene, Ray-Bans hard as turtle shells against the relentless Mexican sun. A fast unpremeditated sketch: Ordinary doom surfaced in these transactions under my moving hand.

I thought: How were these people going to explain their photos back in Eau Claire? *Here's the grinning Indian with leather pads instead of feet. Those are his uneven crutches. Here is Georgette standing next to the Indian with no feet and uneven crutches.*

UFOs aren't the mystery. We are.

↓

"We give birth to ourselves," Billie Blood said. "Over and over until we almost get it right, or we go wrong beyond help—either way."

We were out at the Hueco Tanks. She was painting the huge rock formations, I was sketching the rock climbers. The Tigua Indians were trying to put the rocks off-limits to the climbers but had not yet succeeded. The rock climbers claimed to have as much respect for the sacred rocks as the Indians, which severely annoyed the Tiguas. The dispute was going to the courts.

Billie's rocks, assembled on canvas, looked like a reclining Venus figure. Pregnant stone: milk rising in the pocked sandstone breasts; full, red stone belly tight with its stone child. She'd named it already. *Bloodstone Madonna.*

We took a break, walked up to the tanks where water collects under stone shelves in shallow depressions. Godsend water for thirsty travelers, Indians then whites, in this treeless West Texas *llano.*

We crawled in and sat next to the pool. "How you handle rebirth is the thing," she said.

For Billie there were no trivial aspects to life. She found intensity where most found stupefying dullness. She wore me out but she liked to have fun, too. But even fun had its risky nontrivial side. Once, on the roller coaster at Six Flags Over Texas, she screamed, "Gravity is God!" Later, at a hot dog stand she adjusted that. "Gravity is God's muscle. This is how we come to fear God, through gravity. Fear of falling. Everyone should be shot into space at least once, or take a roller coaster ride, to acquaint themselves with their center of fear by temporarily losing their center of gravity."

She made gravity visible in her landscapes. Light fell like lead bullets. Sky had density and weight, the sun always iterated as a string of blood clots—Billie's signature image.

The important galleries had begun to show her work. She sold *Blood Moon* for two thousand dollars. Fame began to tease her. It made her cautious. "Fame's another kind of rebirth," she said. "A dangerous kind."

"I'll try to remember that," I said. She ignored the irony.

She knelt by the water. She cupped her hands and drank. She crafted a ceremony, her thirst not physical but spiritual.

"Drink," she said. "These waters have power. They might begin your transformation."

I went along with it. It was hard not to. To doubt Billie in the smallest things was to doubt her loftier ideas. She was fragile that way, and I didn't want to lose what I had. The water was slimy but sweet.

Before we crawled out of the crevice I found the graffiti some nineteenth-century adventurers had chiseled into a narrow shelf of stone:

Thomas and Ondine Holland
August 12, 1851

Thomas and Ondine drank the ceremonial waters of the Hueco Tanks then headed for California transformed, ready for rebirth in the promised land.

↓

"It's over, honey," I said. "Billie's gone. I don't know what came over me—temporary insanity, maybe. I take full blame, but honestly, I was swept up. I couldn't fight it. I finally realized what I was risking. I came to my senses."

This lie was not an adequate explanation of my two weeks in Santa Fe with Billie Blood. I made it seem as if breaking off with Billie had been my idea—a man realizing what was truly valuable to him. In fact, I never gave up hope of seeing Billie again.

When she said she was moving north I took it hard. A major Santa Fe gallery wanted to feature her work. She couldn't say no. She was headed for the big time. She asked me to help her move her stuff. She rented the U-Haul truck and I drove it north to the foothills of the snow-capped Sangre de Cristos. It took two weeks to move her into a tiny cabin that leaned into the wind on a blue mesa.

I said: "It's pretty small for two people."

Billie said: "It's fine for just one."

The silence between us held volumes of meaning. Even so she said, "It's time for both of us to move on, don't you think?"

"To new births," I said.

"You're learning," she said.

"You're right," Ursula said. "It's over."

There was another man at Denny's. Ursula had let him into our booth. He was a dark little man wearing a nice houndstooth jacket. He had perfectly combed hair, parted almost in the center. The part looked as if it had been made with the help of a carpenter's straightedge. His groomed mustache looked like a third eyebrow. Ursula brought him a bacon Swissburger stuffed with onions, tomatoes, lettuce, and sprouts. He had very small hands and he held the Swissburger in his napkin so that the makings wouldn't fall out.

"This is Basil Taks, originally from London," Ursula said. She sat down next to him. "Basil was abducted in 1988. Tell him about it, Basil."

Basil cleared his throat apologetically. He touched his skimpy mustache. "Perhaps he does not wish to hear it," he said.

"It doesn't matter what he wishes to hear," Ursula said. "Tell him."

Basil cleared his throat again. "I was in my vintage Saab Turbo, driving from Ithaca to the Saranac Lakes. I am a computer engineer. I say this to prove my seriousness as a person."

He waited for me to acknowledge his seriousness as a person. He was too small, too delicate, too politely British to coldcock with the ketchup bottle. I nodded, assenting to his seriousness.

"An extremely bright light appeared in the sky above the expressway," he said. "Then my usually reliable Saab ceased to function. My mind became blank for minutes—perhaps it was hours. Then I found myself within a closed area, as in a shell of some sort. Small men—I call them *men* but in truth I did not have any way to determine their gender—examined me, head to foot. They probed my flesh. It was intensely painful. Then it was over and I was back in my Saab. I have told this story under the polygraph to prove its verity."

"There you have it," Ursula said. "Firsthand experience, not secondhand." She sneered. The sneer was meant for me and Henry Russo and the entire United States Air Defense Command.

Ursula and Basil faced me like a triumphant debating team.

"Did you experience rebirth?" I asked.

Basil looked at me, puzzled. "I do not quite grasp your meaning, my friend."

"You know—did the experience change you in some fundamental way. Your outlook on things, I mean." I was actually interested in his answer.

He laughed, a musical little laugh that went well with his perfectly combed hair, his houndstooth jacket, and his small hands. "No, no! Not at all! I went back to my job, fit as ever!" His eyes widened with bemused merriment. He smiled and nodded his small head. "Oh, I see what you mean. Well, yes, it changed my perception in that I now know as a certainty that we have alien brethren. We are not alone. It is a very warm and comforting message. This is what I came to understand about our place in this grand universe."

"You, on the other hand, *are* alone," Ursula said. "I've packed your clothes. You'll find them on the front porch along with your paintings. I've never really liked your paintings. I tolerated them. But they are warped. They spill over with negative energy."

"I absolutely concur," said Basil jovially. "Ursula showed them to me. They are full of horror and misguided mockery as well as vulgarities of a distinctly sexual nature."

"Our alien brethren wouldn't approve," I suggested.

"Quite so," Basil said. "The galactic visitors are emissaries of good will, orderliness, and common decency."

Ursula put her long arm around his narrow shoulders. "Basil has invited me to his U F O abductee support group," she said. "It's a weeklong session, up in Roswell."

"You're not an abductee," I said.

"No matter!" Basil said with full enthusiasm. "We are a very democratic! Abductees and friends of abductees! Ursula would be most welcome!"

"I take it then," I said, "that you two are . . ."

"*Lovers?*" Basil said. "No, no, not at all! We are just excellent companions who share mutual interests!" He looked shyly at Ursula. Ursula looked shyly back. Her neck flushed red. His hands fluttered toward her, fluttered back. Lovers make bad liars. I should know.

Basil released a dainty burp and pushed his nibbled bacon Swissburger to the middle of the table. Ursula stood up and pulled Basil out of the booth after her. They left Denny's together, arm in arm.

Derek Hubble appeared. "He didn't pay," he said.

"Wasn't it a freebie from Ursula?" I asked.

"Ursula quit . . ." he glanced at his watch, "as of twenty minutes ago. No freebies since then." He dropped the check on the table in front of me.

I hadn't eaten that day and I saw no point in wasting three-quarters of a perfectly good bacon Swissburger. Basil had left most of the steak fries, too.

I paid the cashier with my last seven dollars, bought a newspaper with the change, then stepped out into the grinding city.

Life would be harder now without Ursula. But Hell's Cartoonist had work to do. It was dirty work, full of horror, misguided mockery, and vulgarities of a distinctly sexual nature. But someone had to do it.

Desperado

They were the only two people in the kiosk waiting for the airport shuttle that would take them to the Radisson in downtown Minneapolis. They had arrived early and the shuttle was now ten minutes late. He didn't like to initiate small talk, but he didn't like the pressure of silence either. Silence could be uncivil, a confession of indifference, an implicit denial of the other's existence. He said, "I had to stay overnight in Wichita because of a missed connection, and now this."

She smiled. "I used to work for Northwest but I hate to fly. You don't know who they're letting on the planes these days. I wish they'd give Amtrak more western routes. Don't tell anyone I said that, they might not let me fly out of here." She laughed then, a bright sound that rose in pitch then stopped short, as if she needed to rein it in.

"I sat next to a Saudi on this last leg," he said. "He was wearing the customary stuff—white throbe and ghutra—big bushy beard you could hide a machine gun in and three-hundred-dollar Italian shades. The woman next to him, his wife I figured, was all in black, head to ankles. It was hard not to profile them. The guy was tall, too, like Osama. Everybody was jumpy, especially the flight attendants. Christ. The poor bastard must have thought he was traveling with a psycho lynch mob."

She was definitely pretty, he saw that now. He hadn't thought she was—airline passengers are too fatigued and short-tempered to be seen as attractive—but when she smiled and laughed he saw that his first impression had been typical and wrong. She had hooded eyes, cool Scandinavian gray, and she smiled in a way that made him think he'd known her for years.

It was a humid day in early June and he was eager to get home to Seattle. This stop in Minneapolis was unnecessary, but he wanted to see his brother who worked at Honeywell. He hadn't seen his brother in almost ten years.

"So what brings you to Minneapolis?" he said.

"Work, I'm afraid," she said.

He liked the inflection she gave to "work"—a weary but upbeat acknowledgment that life was more than slavish routines. He worked for an aerospace company, a technical editor in the Missile Development division, a good but undemanding job. He did most of his work in the morning before his lunch break and spent the rest of the day visiting the cubicles of his colleagues or going out to a favorite bar near the plant. His boss had so little to do himself that he was away most of the day, allowing his people all the freedom they wanted. They worked under generous cost-plus contracts with forgiving default clauses and ample lead-times.

"You're staying at the Radisson?" she said.

"For a few days. My brother lives here. I haven't seen the old desperado for years."

He almost laughed, calling his straight-laced brother a desperado. His brother was anything but that. He was a no-nonsense, nose-to-the-grindstone type. A systems analyst with degrees from Stanford and Cal Tech. What had he been thinking? Did he expect this woman to believe he belonged to a family that produced desperados? Would she think that maybe *he* was a desperado himself, a carefree type looking for adventure, a born-to-be-wild risk taker? If the word meant something to her, she gave no sign.

By the time the shuttle came there were enough people waiting in the kiosk to fill all the seats. He sat next to her on the bench behind the driver. They were wedged between two sweating heavyweights in three-piece suits. "Sardines again," she murmured, and he grunted in agreement, but he welcomed the pressure of her thigh against his.

At the hotel, the check-in line was long and the clerks and bellhops were overwhelmed. The stressed and impatient travelers, dragging their luggage behind them, grumbled at yet one more bottleneck in a world increasingly clogged by bottlenecks.

She checked in ahead of him, speaking to the clerk in confidential tones. He leaned forward but could not hear her name. When she took her keycard and picked up her bag, she turned to him. "God, a nice long shower is going to do absolute wonders for me," she said.

Only one side of her face smiled. Her left upper lip curled in a friendly sneer—a character trait, he saw, not an affliction. The smile was conspiratorial and tough. It included him in a rebellion of two against the indignities of mass travel. He was momentarily dazed by her smile. He watched her walk to the elevators, imagined her in the shower, her drenched hair, her glistening skin, the half-smile that promoted him from victim to rebel. Her hooded eyes fascinated him, too. They had a subtle Asian quality common to some Scandinavians, Norwegians in particular. The clerk jarred him out of this reverie. "Sir? Are you checking in?"

He saw her again a few hours later in the hotel restaurant. It was too early for dinner, and the restaurant was almost empty. The maitre d' led him to a table close to hers. When she looked up from her menu she saw him watching her. "Hello there," she said. She had changed into casual clothes—cream-colored sleeveless blouse, silky teal slacks, white strapless sandals.

He waved, struck again by her odd smile.

"Why don't you sit with me?" she said. She pushed the chair next to her away from the table with her sandaled foot. "They're still serving lunch."

He carried his menu to her table. "I never liked eating alone," he said.

"You can get used to anything."

It was a coded remark. There was a history behind it, but he didn't try to decipher it. He filed it away, studied his menu.

"Did they give you a room over the street," she said, "or one of those that look out into the alley?"

He put the menu down. "You know, I didn't notice. I didn't even open the drapes. I turned on the air conditioner, called my sister-in-law, took a nap, then came down here."

"A man of simple needs," she said. And there was that smile again—conspiratorial, rebellious, worldly. "I've got a glorious view of the alley. Although, as back alleys go it isn't half bad."

The waiter took their orders. When their food came she said, "So, tell me about your family—back in *Seattle*, is it?"

"It's that obvious?"

"You said it yourself. You don't like to eat alone. You're used to others at the table, a wife anyway."

He laughed. "Wife, two kids, big dog."

"Let me guess," she said. "A big old retriever named Pal or Dudley."

"Close. We call him Buddy."

"The demographic ideal," she said. "The recipe for a happy ending."

He couldn't argue with that. He had a decent enough job, his wife was still young and pretty and relatively content with life in a suburb of what was arguably one of the nicest cities in the country. The kids, a boy and a girl, were high-achievers and reasonably well behaved. He hardly ever felt trapped anymore; he'd outgrown that early claustrophobic sense that all the escape hatches had been welded shut. Happy? Of course he was happy. He'd be a damned fool to argue otherwise.

Having a motorcycle in the garage helped him through that early sense of domestic confinement. He'd bought a Harley Sportster seven years ago but he hadn't taken it out on the road in months. His wife hated that machine, believing it represented needless risk. "The way the streets get when it rains," she'd said, tearful—but angry, too—"one miscalculation, by you or by some idiot driving a Suburban, and you're *dead*. Then what would we do? You've got to think of *us*."

And she was right. The Sportster was a young man's machine, a young man without responsibilities. He was almost forty. He knew he'd sell it soon and use the money to put a brick patio in the back yard, something his wife had wanted for several years now—and to be fair, he wanted it, too.

"Family life can be fulfilling," she said, "but sometimes the rewards don't compensate for the sheer drudgery."

"I get the feeling you've been there," he said.

"Four years. One child. A jackass of a husband who couldn't deal with ordinary domestic boredom. He took off with his secretary and now he's got two more kids and enough domestic boredom to anesthetize the continent. Turned out, he did me a big favor. I've been footloose and fancy free ever since. Revenge is sweet." She laughed, and he laughed too but cut it off when he realized his laugh had the thin sound of regret in it. She studied him for a long moment. "So, tell me the big secret," she said.

He shrugged. "No secret. You find the right person, you make the commitment, you live out your life. Sure, boredom comes with the package, but there are plenty of high points too. End of story."

"And that's enough? That keeps you from swallowing the rat poison?"

"What else is there?" he said, annoyed. "It's a big lonely world with no mercy for the loner."

"You're right about that. On the other hand, the snipers are on the loose and we're in the crosshairs. Live it up while you're still up."

"Sorry, I flunked Existentialism 101," he said.

"Okay, I deserved that. I've always been a loner, though. Marriage didn't change that. My parents split when I was two and I lived around the country with different relatives until my mom married again. By then I was sixteen, no longer a virgin, and ready to fly the coop after my stepfather came into my bedroom and tried to make me his girlfriend."

"I'm sorry," he said.

"I am too. But hey, most people have a checkered history." She raised her water glass. He clinked glasses with her and she smiled in that lopsided way, the sly rictus sneer that made them old pals and conspirators.

She dug into her purse and took out a small note pad. "Listen," she said. "I've got things to do this evening, but if you're in by, say, ten or eleven, why don't you come up for a nightcap? I need more enlightenment on the rewards of domestication. We'll call it research and make it a tax write-off."

She jotted down her room number and gave it to him. He folded the note carefully and put it into his wallet. His mouth felt dry and he drank some water. She was studying him again, her gray eyes cool, analytical. He had no idea what she was thinking. He was sure it wasn't about the pros and cons of domestic life.

His brother picked him up that evening and they drove out to the upper-middle-class suburb where his brother had put down roots fifteen years ago. The house was a two-story brick with a steeply pitched roof, set in a manicured landscape. The broad lawn was edged with juniper and dogwood and fenced by a tall privacy hedge. A replica of a Civil War cannon sat on a bark-covered knoll menacing the neighborhood. Off to one side of the knoll there was a twenty-foot flagpole. The spot-lit flag was tangled in the ropes. A soft breeze raised one ragged corner of the flag. Even though Christmas was six months past and six months in the future, strings of festive lights dotted the eaves and peaks of the house. He remembered calling his brother a desperado and almost laughed out loud again.

They were greeted at the door by his sister-in-law, a heavy, nervous woman in an A-line dress that hid her bulges in a starched pyramid of blue denim. He recognized her from recent snapshots his brother had sent to him, but she looked nothing like the slender girl his brother had married twelve years ago.

The children were paraded out for his inspection, two girls and a boy, pink as their parents and already tending toward obesity. A family of unabashed heavyweights. He made the appropriately flattering remarks, shook hands with the boy, whose grip was firm and manly, patted the blond heads of the giggling girls.

His brother led them into the formal dining room and they all sat down to dinner. To his surprise, his brother said grace.

They hadn't grown up in a family that observed any kind of religious formality, but now here was his brother praying at length over the food. He prayed with his head bowed, his voice pulpit-clear. It was obviously an established ritual, and he realized his brother was more of a stranger to him now than when they were growing up.

He wasn't hungry at all but managed to force down a wedge of meatloaf, a scoop of mashed potatoes, and spears of asparagus in a white sauce. He gave his sister-in-law the expected after-dinner compliments and she seemed pleased, even though he'd turned down her dessert specialty—a black square of mud pie the size of a paving stone.

He and his brother retired to the rec room and talked about their jobs, the little annoyances and the petty personalities they had to deal with. It was clear that between them his brother had the more prestigious job, a job that had a real effect on Honeywell's prosperity.

His job, on the other hand, was routine and could have been done by almost anyone with a modest education. He'd always played second fiddle to his brother, who'd been the star of the family, and so he felt compelled to inflate the importance of his work at his company's missiles division with exaggerations and outright lies. Which didn't matter much, since his brother showed no interest at all in his work as a technical editor other than saying, "We call them 'liberal arts hacks' in my department. They're generally clueless, but useful now and then."

They switched to world politics, the future of capitalism, the threats of embargoes and bombs from the Middle East. His brother seemed heroically amused about it all, as if he were personally invulnerable. His wife, however, was another story. She had developed unreasonable fears since the World Trade towers came down. Anthrax and other biological weapons terrified her. "She microwaves the mail before she opens it," his brother said, chuckling. "She won't open the door to strangers. She won't set foot in an airport, much less a plane."

By the time he was ready to leave, it was after eleven. For

whatever reason, he hadn't been asked to stay at his brother's house and was glad of it. Three days of meatloaf, mud pie, and prayers, along with his brother's casually issued insults, would have been hard to take.

His brother didn't want to drive all the way back into the city and offered to give him a car to use for the few days he'd be in town. He understood then that his presence here was an inconvenience. He didn't feel unwelcome exactly but knew his surprise visit complicated a life that had been made simple by unchanging routines.

His brother had a new Mercedes, a vintage Cadillac, and a ten-year-old Volvo wagon. "You can't have the Caddy," he said. "It's almost a collector's item. And the Merc is my go-to-work car. So you get the boat. It's the wife's, so do *not* ding it up. Consider that fair warning."

He drove back to the Radisson in a rage, thinking it would be just fine if he wrapped the old Volvo around a light pole.

She answered the first ring. "Still offering nightcaps to strange men?" he said.

"Give me a minute, stranger. You like gin? I've got a bottle of Bombay Sapphire on ice."

He took a shower, shaved, splashed on some cologne. He looked at himself in the bathroom mirror, his image haloed by steam. He'd gotten pudgy in the last few years. Not like his brother, who was getting to look like a sumo wrestler, but he didn't like what he saw. He vowed to get in shape when he got back to Seattle. A few months in Gold's Gym would flatten his gut and put some steel in his chest and arms.

She answered the door in silk pajamas and robe. "I'm beat," she said. "I think I signed two hundred books tonight."

He didn't know if he was supposed to understand what she meant. He said nothing. She picked a book up from her dresser and held it so that he could see the jacket cover. *Sins of the Mother*, by Valerie LaSalle. "That's me," she said, "Valerie LaSalle. Except that's not my name. I write romances, so the name on the cover's got to have a romantic ring to it, you know? I write for the Torrid Zone imprint, a hardback lust-or-bust series. We tweak the old material a few degrees hotter than the competition. It's a good living, but these signing tours are a drag."

She handed him the book. He read the jacket copy, looked for her picture but there was none. Valerie LaSalle. He was reminded then that he didn't know her name just as she didn't know his and that neither of them had been forthcoming. If there was a time to identify themselves, this would be it, but mutual self-restraint kept them from speaking—a tacit agreement to remain anonymous. It excited him, knowing that they were both on the same page. Conspirators.

"You're a celebrity," he said, stating a fact. "You disguise it pretty well. I mean that as a compliment."

"Thank you. But no, I'm no celebrity. It's a job, a damn good one. I deliver masturbation fantasies to housewives who haven't given themselves permission to invent them on their own."

He laughed because she expected him to, but his mouth felt dry again.

She made drinks and they sat down on the small sofa opposite the T V.

"I've learned to go directly to the chase," she said. "I'm forty-five and don't like to play footsie. I've had breast cancer, I take meds for superventricular arrythmias, and my doctor doesn't like the sonogram of my uterus. He's put a hysterectomy on my calendar. Time is not on my side."

He swallowed some gin, felt the cold heat sear his throat. "Why are you telling me this?"

"Oh please Mr. X. Are you going to make me spell it out? I'm not asking for commiseration."

It was a line he hadn't crossed in eight years of marriage and he didn't think he'd cross it now. It was enough to approach it. The thrill of possibility was an adventure in itself. But when she touched his thigh and said, "I want to do nice things for you," he knew he'd crossed the line earlier that day in the kiosk, when she first smiled at him.

He composed a gin-inspired justification: Anonymity made it easier. Stripped of names they were fragments of a vast population of bodies. Some of the bodies would be dead by morning, others more alive than ever. Planes full of bodies would fall from the sky, buildings packed with bodies might collapse and burn. Gun-toting bodies would kill other gun-toting bodies—for grievances ancient and new, or for the simple joy of it, or because God in his sacred texts willed it. New bodies would be squeezed into the world and old bodies would be fed to the worms. None of them had a name that would stick. The fetus and the corpse are nameless. Names are baggage, dead weight, figments. Names die, bodies go on forever. He found these notions erotic.

"You have to think it over?" she said.

"No," he said.

They stayed in bed through the next morning. Room service brought them lunch in the early afternoon. They ate ravenously. "Fuck fuel," she said—that smile, that laugh, capturing him again. And he was willing prey, happy in the net. He kissed her reconstructed breasts, the pale flesh above her afflicted womb, her fierce mortality.

He watched a baseball game on TV while she sat at a small table working with her laptop computer. In the early afternoon they took a shower together and then he went back to his room, changed his clothes, and drove out to his brother's house.

"What happened?" his brother said, frowning.

"Happened? Nothing happened. Why do you ask?"

His brother studied him, a sidelong glance, suspicion creasing his forehead. "Did you ding the Volvo? Is that it, you *dinged* the damned Volvo?"

His brother inspected his wife's forest green station wagon, kneeling at the wheel-wells and bumpers, looking for nicks. He opened the driver's side door and felt the seats and headrests. He checked the odometer. He opened the hood and pulled the dipstick out, brought it close to his face, then slid it back in, unsatisfied.

Dinner was ham, mashed potatoes and red gravy, buttered green beans, and slabs of homemade bread. *Cardiac city*, he thought. In fact it was the kind of food he loved. But he ate too much and had to refuse dessert—German chocolate cake and ice cream. This time his sister-in-law seemed hurt by his refusal. He asked if he could take a piece of the cake back to the hotel with him. This mollified her somewhat and she gave him enough cake for two, her generosity innocent, no implication that he would have help eating it. She packed the cake into a Tupperware box and he thanked her, said she was too good to him, she was a wonderful cook, and he kissed her warm fleshy cheek, and got the hell out of there before his brother could make him eat humble pie again in the rec room, another kind of dessert he wouldn't be able to stomach.

He got back to the hotel early. He called her room but she wasn't back yet from her second signing gig in a downtown bookstore. She called her signings "gigs," and he felt like an insider to the life of a celebrity. He watched a movie, *The Asphalt Jungle*, a classic noir, then fell asleep.

He woke to a tapping sound. The sound had entered his dreams. He dreamt he was driving his brother's car, the Mercedes, on a freeway. The car was stuck in low gear but he was traveling at freeway speeds. The engine was roaring, the tachometer needle deep into the red zone, and then the engine began to tear itself apart but he couldn't take his foot off the gas pedal. He finally managed to steer the car off the freeway and bring it to a stop. A policeman dragged him out of the car, cuffed him, and slapped him hard enough to knock him down. He didn't know what city he was in, but in the distance skyscrapers were burning. He woke up, a sob stuck in his throat, his heart pounding.

Someone was knocking at his door. Not "someone," of course, it could only be *her*, and he went to the door naked, without bothering to cover himself. She smiled, weary now, but that smile was all he needed and maybe all he'd ever need.

In bed she said, "Tell me your secret. Tell me the thing you don't want anyone to know. I want to know your blackest sins."

She was playing with him, her lips on his neck, his face, his chest and belly, rousing him again.

"I'm afraid my sins are trivial," he said.

"How unlucky," she said. "Then tell me something you've done that you're proud of." Her nails dug into him, mock torture urging confession.

He thought about it, but in fact he wasn't really proud of anything he'd done. Not proud. Not ashamed, either.

"My life story would make dull reading," he said. "I'm pretty ordinary."

"I think you're deluded," she said. "I think you're a desperado—dangerous in your modest way. A man the feds should keep tabs on. You're pure possibility waiting for a triggering event."

He laughed, flattered in spite of himself. "And you?" he said. "What are you?"

"A chronicler of boredom. Boredom is bomb fuel. It can reach critical mass. The explosion can be spectacular. Go to any supermarket—you can hear the hausfraus ticking."

On their third day together she said, "Don't go to your brother's house tonight. Come with me to St. Paul. I'm doing a reading there before I sign books. Then I'll take you out to the best restaurant in the Twin Cities. How about it, chum?"

"That's a no-brainer," he said, tickled by her use of the word *chum*, because that's what they'd become. Chums. "If I never see my fat-ass sibling and his neurotic jumbo wife again, it'll be too soon."

They went to the bookstore in the Volvo. She sat close to him on the long drive that took them across the Mississippi and into St. Paul.

The bookstore was crowded with women. A table had been stacked with the books of Valerie LaSalle. The manager of the bookstore tapped a wine glass with a pencil, quieting the crowd. "We are delighted," she said, "to have Valerie LaSalle with us tonight. Valerie, as you know, is a rising star of the Torrid Zone series, and she has consented to read a chapter of her new novel to us." The crowd applauded and Valerie LaSalle took her place behind a podium that had been set up next to the signing table. He lingered at the back of the crowd, the only man in the bookstore.

"I'm going to read something new," she said. "Something I'm working on. And yes, I'm using you ladies as a test audience." The women tittered, pleased to be literary guinea pigs. "As you might know, I take my work whenever I can from real life. The following scenes are more or less true, with some embellishments." She held her hand out flat and titled it one way then another, suggesting the digressions from fact that fiction required. She smiled then, that cordial sneer he knew he'd never be able to forget, and he became erect between islands of travel books.

He picked up a book on Tahiti and thumbed through the color photographs. He imagined them together in a grass hut, one day like another, no clocks or calendars, no seasons, just the simple cycles of day and night, sex and food, sleep and wakefulness. Time would be nameless here, the days unnumbered—which was the original condition of human life.

Her reading voice was not like her speaking voice. She delivered her lines with practiced ease, modulating the differences between narrative and speech, acting out each role. The sound of her voice was hypnotic as a lullaby, and it wasn't until he heard her say: *". . . the stranger kissed her wounded breasts, kissed his way down to her damaged womb, his lips hot, his tongue a searching flame that ignited her, and her back arched with a pleasure she hadn't known but had longed for, a pleasure her husband would not provide, and she moaned the helpless moan of release, wanting to call out his name—but she did not know his name, just as he did not know hers . . ."* that he realized she was writing about *them*.

There were scenes of them dining together—the words they'd spoken, the silent communication of gestures, the quick meaningful glances. She was a skilled writer, her talent shaped and muted by the genre she worked in: The housewives got their masturbation fantasies at twenty-five dollars a copy; she got her royalties. One or two of the women in the audience turned around in their chairs to look at him and he hid behind the Tahiti book. The island seemed less like a real place now and more like a setting for a fantasy.

In the car, on the way back to the Radisson, he said, "You've been using me."

"Chum, you're only half-right. I don't think you've got much to complain about."

"Grist," he said. "I've been grist. I should get a cut of the profits."

"You want me to send you a check?"

He laughed at the idea, a "consulting fee" from her publisher coming in the mail. His wife studying the check, looking at him, puzzled: *Consulting? What consulting, honey?*

"What the fuck is grist, anyway," he said.

"Wheat. Grain. A Middle English word, I think."

"Now I'm a character out of Chaucer."

"Hey, there's nothing wrong with Chaucer." She touched his face. "You've been good grist. Likeable grist. Grist of high quality. You've even transcended grist, if that means anything to you. Tell me you haven't had a good time."

He stopped in a dark neighborhood and kissed her hard. She resisted—it was over now, her work done—then she relented and they got into the back seat. He was rough with her but she didn't complain. Her reconstructed breasts, which he had treated like wounded children, were just breasts, her damaged womb just one of countless damaged wombs.

Back at the hotel he said, "Tell me your real name. I want to know who you are."

"I can't."

"You *can't?*"

"It's protected."

"Meaning what exactly?"

"It's a contractual thing. I write serious books under my real name. I'm actually taken seriously in some quarters."

"Serious books. What kind of serious books?"

"Muckraking stuff. Social criticism. Some neogeopolitics. Blurbs from the big boys, some of those very public intellectuals you see on Charlie Rose. But I've developed a high-maintenance lifestyle and muckraking doesn't pay the bills."

"And you don't want to let people know you write fuck books for the hausfraus. That explains the absence of a photo on your dust jacket."

"I give you my name, you might find a buyer. The tabloids pony up for gossip."

"I don't believe you," he said. "You're lying."

"And you? You're a fountain of undiluted truth?"

She was goading him on purpose, looking for a clean break, a getaway.

"I want to write to you," he said. "I don't want this to be just another one of your tax-deductible fucks, goddamnit." He gripped her arm hard enough to leave bruises, but she wouldn't wince.

"Write to Valerie LaSalle, in care of my publisher. They send me all my fan mail."

"Fuck you, lady."

"Yes, and wasn't it fun."

And there was that lopsided smile again, not so conspiratorial now, and the Asian Scandinavian eyes were arctic cold. He knew he might not survive that smile. It would haunt him in Seattle, it would hollow out his life, his marriage.

He drove the Volvo back to his brother's house early the next morning. "What's up with you?" his brother said. "You look terrible. Have you been drinking? It's a little early for that, don't you think?"

His brother, still in his robe and slippers, inspected the Volvo.

"What's that stain on the back seat?"

"I don't know. It must have been there."

"No, no. I'm sure it wasn't. Did you leave the door unlocked at any time?"

"Maybe. I don't remember."

"I can't believe you'd be so irresponsible. A bum might have spent the night in the car doing God knows what."

After a breakfast of Canadian bacon, eggs, and English muffins, his brother drove him to the airport. The subject of conversation at the breakfast table had been job security.

"You'll never have it," his brother said, "as long as you work for a company that depends on government contracts for half its capital. The government compensates companies like yours for every man they hire, x dollars for every warm body they put on the payroll, more dollars by at least 50 percent than the company pays out in salaries. Your company makes money on body count. So they hire, excessively by any standard, until the contract terminates. Then they surplus the unneeded bodies, which have now become a liability rather than a source of revenue. It amounts to fiscal pornography."

You son of a bitch, he thought, but didn't argue the point, which might have been close to the truth. He was too hung over to defend his company from "fiscal pornography," a lurid notion coming from his pious brother.

He was still a little drunk from an evening spent in the Radisson's piano bar, alone, where a gray old man in a purple tuxedo played melancholy favorites including "One More for the Road," a maudlin piece of synchronicity that made him laugh out loud hard enough to cause some late-night drinkers to look at him with fleeting interest. She had checked out early, before he got up. He'd called her room, let it ring ten times or more before admitting to himself that she was gone.

His brother dropped him at the airport. "I want you to apply for work here, at Honeywell," he said. "They usually don't like to hire people out of the aerospace business—they tend to have poor work habits—but I can put in a good word for you. I have garnered some leverage in the past ten years or so."

He wanted to tell his brother off, puncture his inflated view of himself, but didn't have the energy. His brother, as if trying to get a rise out of him, brought up the stained back seat of the Volvo again. "It wasn't there," he said. "It got there while you had the car. I'd like to know how it got there. I don't think it was a bum."

"It's jism," he said.

"*What?*"

"It's jism, ordinary gonad spew. You remember having some yourself, don't you?"

"You're disgusting."

"I think maybe your wife's got a secret. Maybe she's got a backseat thing going with her butcher. She must spend a lot of time with him, the amount of meat you people eat. I wouldn't be too hard on her though. She puts out a damn fine meal."

His brother took the insult calmly. "I don't know you," he said. "I don't think I ever knew you. And you know what? I don't want to know you. Do us all a favor and don't come back." And then his brother slapped him. The slap didn't have much force but it made him catch his breath. He cocked his fist, then laughed.

"Desperado," he said. "You fat fucking desperado." He got his luggage out of the trunk and entered the terminal.

His flight was delayed because of a security problem involving the metal detectors, which weren't working properly. The boarding areas had to be evacuated and every passenger would have to be rescreened. It was going to take several hours and he'd miss his flight. The next plane to Seattle wouldn't leave until late that afternoon. He spent the time in one of the bars in the unsecured mall. When he was finally able to board a plane he was drunk.

↙

She was pretty, and he had caught her glancing at him as he took the seat next to her, saw her hesitant smile. The world was teeming with possibilities.

After they'd exchanged the usual complaints about the inconvenience of air travel, he said, "Some people need killing, don't you think? I mean, the world would benefit by their absence." His tone was confidential but also jovial. He thought she'd be amused. "I'm not just talking about Osama types. It's not just the religious fanatics that need killing. You know what I mean? I bet there are a few people in your life you'd be better off without."

The flight attendant came by with the refreshment cart and he ordered a bourbon and soda. The woman next to him asked for water. She was pretty in a wounded way, a way he found appealing—probably a legal secretary or maybe a dental assistant. Not a professional, in any case. She seemed self-conscious and unsure of herself, even self-abasing. These deficiencies were not what you'd expect in a lawyer or upper-tier executive. He thought: She'll be grateful for the attention. She was in her mid-thirties, slightly overweight, wearing gray slacks and a black silk blouse that accented her cropped red hair.

"I'm talking theoretically, of course," he said. "I just spent a few days with my self-important brother. I'm glad I wasn't carrying a gun. I might have shot the whole goddamned family. Five well-placed shots to their smug heads." He downed his drink, signaled for another. "They probably wouldn't have noticed they were dead."

He was presenting himself as a risk taker, thinking it touched something in women who were weary of predictable men who lived in a world of bar graphs, flow charts, and bottom lines. From now on, he told himself, he'd be ready for adventure—and take his lumps if it came to that. He'd buy another Harley. A big one, a *hog*.

The woman next to him said, "Please don't speak to me," and leaned away from him.

This surprised him. Please don't *speak* to me? What had he said to her? She reached up and rang for the flight attendant. He understood then that the woman was terrified. God, how easily people frighten these days, he thought. He touched her wrist, wanting to put her fears to rest and to make human contact. "I bet you microwave your mail," he said.

"I asked you not to speak to me," she said, pulling away from his touch.

When the flight attendant came, the woman said, "He's violent. He said he wants to kill his family. I think he's armed. The metal detector at the terminal wasn't working very well."

"Jesus Christ, don't be ridiculous," he said, forcing a chuckle. He looked up at the flight attendant. She looked frightened, too. "It was just *conversation*, you know? People *talking* to each other. Is that a fucking crime? She's blowing it up way out of proportion!"

"Blowing *what* up?" the passenger in the seat in front of him said. A commotion had started in the seats surrounding him.

"Sir, you'll have to come with me," the flight attendant said.

He unbuckled his seat belt and stood. He felt very warm. His pulse tapped against his shirt collar and he broke a sweat. He shouldered past the flight attendant and went down the aisle to the restroom. Two male flight attendants followed him, their faces stiff with fear and duty. He locked himself in the restroom and waited.

He felt strange. He'd suffered a mild concussion once playing a rough version of flag football. The blow left him lightheaded, the sense of reality diluted. This was how he felt now. He washed his face but the cold water did not shock away the strangeness. He was locked in a narrow cubicle, thirty thousand feet above mid-west America. He looked at himself in the polished steel mirror, and the brooding, stubbled face that looked back at him was not familiar.

His life, all the things he'd ever done and all the places he'd ever been, flattened out into two-dimensional unreality. He tried to think of his wife, his kids, his job, but he couldn't bring them into focus. His past was fading, a snapshot left in the sun. He only had a future now. When he opened the restroom door it would begin.

Nightwork, 1973

The man who castrated himself was watching a late-night repeat of *The Brady Bunch* on a small black-and-white T V in the lobby of the Barker House, an old Market Street hotel. He was seated with a group of the permanent residents, all elderly. There was a massive bulge in the crotch of his pants.

"I'm in a schizophrenic state," he said.

My partner, Bob Eckstrom, took off his hat. Cops in hats intimidate the citizens. Take off the hat and right away things get less tense. What you lose in authority you gain in trust. This is Bob's theory. It makes you more human to the fringe people, he says.

"The E M T van is almost here," Bob said to the man. I got the man's room key from the night clerk. The room was on the fourth floor. The old hotel didn't have an elevator and I was winded by the time we got to the man's room.

"Good Christ almighty," Bob said.

I'd never heard Bob use off-color language in the six months we'd been partners. "Good Christ almighty" was about as loose as he got. I tend to uncap the whole available vocabulary, but I tried to keep a lid on it when I was working with Bob. Not that he was religious or anything, it just wasn't in him to cuss. He'd been with the First Marines in Vietnam and had seen a lot of things, things that would make you want to use the whole available vocabulary. I had to smile when I thought of Bob saying, Holy mackerel! Gosh all fishhooks! while the V C were lobbing 120 millimeter mortars on his bunker. That's Bob, that's how he is. I respect that.

"Damn," I said, holding back. *What a fucking shit storm!* would have been a justified reaction to what we saw in that room.

The gore trail went from the blood-soaked bed to the bathroom. Red blobs littered the bathroom floor. A pair of dark plums floated in the pink water of the toilet bowl.

"I'm going to puke," I said.

"Hold off, Charlie," Bob said. "We don't know for sure what happened here. If you toss your cookies you'll contaminate the scene. Stick your head out the window if you feel it coming on." Bob was new to the job and felt obligated to go by the book. As if in nutcase scenes like this it mattered.

I went back to the bed. This is where he'd done it. Red castration tools were scattered on the blood-soaked sheets. Scissors, single-edge safety razor, hunting knife. He'd worked at it for a while.

On the wall opposite the bed was a bookshelf. Most of the books were highbrow stuff. Wittgenstein, Korzybski, Nietzsche, Kierkegaard, which surprised me. The other books didn't—picture books showing middle-aged men sodomizing boys and girls, all under ten years old. The kids were someone's babies once—fat and happy, maybe even loved.

We went back downstairs. The man was still watching *The Brady Bunch*. He was really watching it, too, even though he was probably bleeding to death.

"How you doing, sir?" Bob said.

"I dreamed I cut my nads off," the man said. He made a distracted finger-on-wrist sawing motion, his eyes still glued to the TV.

"Yes sir," Bob said. "You did."

"I didn't feel a thing. It was a dream."

"It was and it wasn't," Bob said.

Bob wrote down the man's name and went out to the car.

He came back in. "I ran a check on him," Bob said to me. "He's two months out of Atascadero."

"Three months next Friday," the man said. He grinned shyly at Bob. He looked sixty but was probably in his late thirties. Streaked black hair, faded skin, the usual tattoos.

"Have you behaved yourself?" Bob said.

"Oh yes sir. I certainly have."

"Fucking baby-raper," I said.

I couldn't help myself. I've seen too many of them and they keep on coming, like there's a production line direct from hell. They get a year or two in Atascadero and when they come out they pick up where they left off. I say poison their food while they're still locked up.

Bob gave me a sharp glance.

I shrugged it off.

The man was shaking now, as if the room temperature had dropped to zero. It was early October, and even though it was past midnight the outside temperature was still ninety. The Santa Ana winds were blowing in from the desert. The old hotel didn't have air-conditioning. It creaked in the wind, like a derelict ship. I heard the EMT siren, probably ten blocks away.

The man stood up to adjust the bulge in his pants. Blood spotted his shoes now as well as the floor in front of his chair.

"You have something in there?" Bob said, pointing to the man's crotch.

"A towel," the man said.

"He wants to live," I said. "Even fucking baby-rapers want to live."

"Take it easy, Charlie," Bob said. "The man's a human being."

"Really?" I said. "Based on what?"

Bob and I have different takes on life. He was still in his twenties, and I had just turned forty. Maybe when he got to be my age he'd see things differently. I became a cop in 1954, nineteen years ago. We didn't put up with a lot back then. We were the law, and the law had teeth.

The ambulance arrived and the crew put the man on a gurney and hauled him off. I think he was already dead. His eyes were open but had the unfocused glazed-over stare you come to recognize. He wouldn't make it to the hospital, at any rate. A couple of pony-tailed narcs came in to kill some time. We filled them in on the details, which they found amusing. Bob and I went out to our car.

"The baby-raper did the world a favor," I said.

"You're right about that, Charlie," Bob said. "That's exactly what he meant to do."

"I'll nominate him for a humanitarian award. He'll give that Mother Teresa woman a run for her money."

"You know something, Charlie? You've been a cop too long."

"Stay with the job ten more years, Bobby, then tell me that."

Our shift ended. I drove home, tired and pissed off. Pissed off at Bob, pissed off at the baby-raper, and especially pissed off at the system that keeps turning them loose.

Peg was in bed but awake. "Jesus," she said, "you got some kind of awful stink on you, Charlie."

I took off my shoes and put them on the back porch. I guess I'd walked in the mess. Then I took a long shower. When I got into bed, Peg was asleep. Which was fine. It was a dangerous time of the month. Peg was on the pill but she often forgot to take it. Eager for family, she sometimes forgot on purpose. She was thirty-six. Now and then she'd mention her biological clock. "It's ticking," she'd say.

It had been a nontypical shift. Most of the time you sit in coffee shops half the night bullshitting the waitresses, but now and then you run from snake pit to snake pit. The night started with a biker shooting dogs in North Park. We didn't find the biker but we looked at a few dead dogs, talked to the weeping raging owners.

An Eagle Scout in Kensington had whacked his family with a double-bladed axe. Mom, Dad, sister—skulls split, brains on the walls. We didn't have to cover that one, but we picked up some details from radio chatter.

A sailor from Iowa—gut cut open with a Bowie knife on Horton Plaza. We found him spread out on the hood of a car, tunic pulled up. A gray intestine ballooned out of his belly. He'd challenged a hippie, wanted the hippie's girl, made some ornate karate moves. Trouble was, the guy wasn't a hippie. He was a dealer. He stepped through the karate crap, his big blade out. The farmboy didn't know what planet he was on. Horton Plaza was San Diego's central marketplace for the dope trade.

The Plaza was also favored by the Hare Krishnas. They were out in force that night, chanting and waving their tambourines. They worked a crowd of simple-minded tourists who flashed peace signs and gyrated along with the Krishnas. Which made it easy for the one-legged pickpocket, Isaiah "Oldtown" Jukes, to score big. A downtown beat cop collared Jukes after first enjoying the performance. "Oldtown" was more colorful character than criminal. Judges went easy on him. He never did more than a month in the county lockup.

I watched a wino running from another wino. The running wino raised his knees high in a herky jerky sprint, but his feet came down in the same place. He ran like a mime, making no progress. The other wino caught him, threw him down hard, then dragged him off by the arm. Love comes in all shapes, most of them sad or laughable.

We did some follow-up work on two break-ins, one at a Payless drugstore, where a desperate hype took everything he could find that looked like prescription medicine. We found him in Mercy Hospital, on a respirator. The inhalation therapist took the respirator off, just to see if the guy had started breathing on his own. His chest sunk, then sunk again, concave, and didn't rise. The therapist put him back on the respirator, then shrugged. "The moron ate everything—downers, thrusters, poppers, plus all the codeine cough syrup he could find. We gave him Narcan but he didn't respond. My humble opinion? He's brain dead."

"The world has lost another genius," I said. Bob didn't bother to adjust my attitude this time.

The other break-in was an apartment. The girl tenant tied up and gagged but not raped. Found by her landlord. She was hysterical. Bob calmed her down, even got her to laugh a little. He wiped her tears with his handkerchief. Blonde, quick blue eyes, nice build. After we took inventory of her missing goods, Bob made a date to see her on the weekend. Dinner at Anthony's Sea Grotto, maybe a movie.

Bob is a piece of work. To him people are just people, serial killers to saints, a spectrum linked by blood. More time on the job would change that. But I respect him too much to get on his case. He got a Purple Heart in Nam plus a bronze star.

I couldn't sleep. Peg was awake now, too. She stroked my thigh but I got up and went out to the backyard. The air was still hot, as if a black sun burned overhead with noonday heat. Tomorrow or the next day, wildfire would char the hills. We live far out in the east county, past Santee. Without irrigation it would all go back to desert.

Bored twelve-year-old arsonists set these fires every year during the Santa Ana season when the grass is dry and the wind is dryer. Borate bombers, old World War II Neptunes, would attack the flames. It was always fun to watch them come and go, making their runs. Now and then a house on the ridge would burst into flames, as if napalmed. I had a ringside seat on the action.

I sat in a patio chair and lit a cigarette and listened to the crickets. In the blue halo of a streetlight, long-eared bats feasted on swarms of moths. Hunger and feeding the hunger. That's all there is. Maybe I'd get some sleep before morning. Maybe not. I was glad I had no children. I pitied those that did.

The Horse Dealer's Lovers

Magda Belascu said she knew what
I liked even if I didn't because it was what all men liked and you
are a man, aren't you?

I asked her, "Do I sit or lie down or what?" She undid my
belt.

"Was it bad, the war?" she said. She unbuttoned my pants. She
reached in. We were in her kitchen, bacon in the pan. Muffins and
jam. The coffee perked. It was windy outside. The dry fronds of
the palm tree out her window clicked in the breeze. We were on
the second floor, so I could look out at the top of the palm. It was
familiar—all of it and none of it. She took it in her hand and moved
it until it was ready. "You *are* a man, aren't you?" she said.

The paint on her windowsill was peeling. The screen loose
enough to let flies in. It tapped against the window frame. Someone out back was throwing garbage into an incinerator. White
smoke like a long finger rose out of the chimney. Her hand was
strong on me and fast. The urge came on and I tried to hold back
by watching the wind riffle through the palm tree. Her hand was
hot and slick with sweat. "Was it bad, the war?" she said.

It was my first time with a woman, not counting the Texas girl,
RonniLee Jenks, who I had to pay two dollars for it, and so did
not count. Anyways, the two dollars I paid to RonniLee didn't
get me what I was about to get from Magda, which I had only
heard about from some of the guys in my squadron, and then
you need to take those stories with a grain of salt because there
are braggers everywhere.

Magda said, "You're going to like it this way, honey."

"What way is that?" I said.

She squatted down. Her tight dress was hiked up so the seams wouldn't split. I saw the tops of her nylons and the garter belts that held them up and the girdle the belts were attached to and the darkness. She was all business. Like a nurse fixing to stick you a dose of sulfa. Her warm wet pull made my knees unlock. I stood there jaws agape like the village fool while she went to work on me. Things were different here in California, I could see that much.

My brains got sucked down my neck. I saw red stars in the wallpaper. She quit for a second, looked up at me and said, "You ever had it like this, corporal? Your girlfriends ever do you this good?"

"Uh-uh," I said. I didn't tell her I never had a regular girlfriend.

"Did you get a medal in the war, Clarence?"

"I got some," I said.

"Was it bad?"

I felt like a wind-up toy in her hands. I stood rock still while she turned the key to tighten the spring. I felt like I might explode and burn. I told myself, "Hang on, Clarence! Don't faint on her floor. You'd look pretty stupid out cold on the linoleum."

It wasn't as if I'd never heard of this type of thing, I just never believed a girl would actually do it. Some fellows in the Air Corps who had been around spoke of it like a joke you whisper, elbow in your ribs. They called it "Frenching." So I had a picture in my head of what it would be like, but here it was, the real McCoy. The picture in my head didn't hold up against the real McCoy.

This is when Hell feels like Heaven. I hoped Martin wasn't present in that kitchen and being forced by the Devil to watch his wife "French" me, her head moving so fast her hair lifted and fell in the wind she made.

Martin's dead, but I don't rule out ghosts. The Devil can make a ghost do most anything he wants if the ghost is not already protected by angels in Heaven, and I knew the ghost of Martin Belascu was not protected in Heaven. It doesn't work that way. Only the innocents are protected—babies, idiots, virgin girls, and the righteous. You couldn't say Martin Belascu was in any of these categories. None of us was. You can't set fire to a country and claim innocence.

She poured six whipped eggs into the hot skillet. She chopped up an onion. She sliced these green things she called "alligator pears" and spread them and the onions over the bubbling eggs. Then she grated up some black market cheese and sprinkled it on top. When it melted, she crumbled bacon over all of it then folded it over on itself. Coffee and muffins, real butter and three kinds of jam. She was one heck of a cook. My stomach ulcer hurt from the excitement though it all seemed familiar to me.

She was experienced and I was a babe in the woods. I was barely twenty years old and she was thirty going on ten thousand and one. She knew more than I did, more than I ever would. I was just back from overseas, where I served two years in the Army Air Corps. I was two and a half years off the sharecrop outside of Slaughterville, Oklahoma, and had seen some things, but I had seen nothing like Magda Belascu.

I was stationed with the 484th bomb group that operated out of Toretta on the Adriatic side of Italy. Martin and I were waist-gunners in a B-24 "Liberator." He was older than me by ten years.

"She could give lessons to Mae West," Martin Belascu said.

Martin was her husband. "Martin was the love of my life," she said, wiping her chin.

Martin said this about Magda and Mae West the night he died. He said Magda could make the Pope flog his mule. He died in my arms eighteen thousand feet above Romania. We'd been at twenty thousand but were now coming down. Our bomb run over the oil fields of Ploesti was finished.

"Maybe I'll go to hell for saying that about Pope Pius," he said.

I said, "I believe we're already on the inside of Hell, Martin," which made him chuckle up some blood. There was nothing funny about it.

Martin was a Catholic. We were three miles above Romania, a Catholic country. His parents were born in Romania. He still had relatives in Romania. He said maybe they were burning or buried under the wreck of a house that had collapsed because of our bombs. He was smiling when he said this, so I guess it didn't really bother him all that much. I don't think he believed in Hell. It was his big mistake. Many good folks make this mistake, as if what we're here for is to enjoy the weather, the food, the pretty sights, and to get "Frenched" now and then. There is more to it than that.

Martin's last words before he was gutshot were "Bogies four o'clock low!" but he never got them in the ring-sight. They got him first. He was the left waist-gunner, I was the right. After the German fighters let up on us I tended to Martin, but there was nothing I could do to save him. He was shot up pretty bad. I held him in my arms. His blood fell out of his flight suit. It pooled then got stiff then turned into red ice there on the waist deck of "The Grim Reaper." That's what we called our plane. I have this artistic streak, and Lieutenant Fred Mahoney, our nineteen-year-old pilot, had me paint "Death Holding the Scythe" on the front end of the plane, just back of the Plexiglas nose behind the front gun turret and the bombardier's crib. I painted the words "The Grim Reaper" under it and dead Hitlers stacked like cordwood under that.

At our altitude the temperature had been below zero, and Martin's blood froze solid quick. No one ever said for sure that Hell had to be *hot*. We were waist-gunners in Hell. I always enjoyed the rapid *dududududu* of the big fifty-caliber Browning. I was good with it. I had top scores at the Blanchard Field gunnery school in Texas, where I learned to use it. The gunnery sergeant said, "Nail one of them bastards for me, Clarence." He had been in the first war and now was too old for combat. I dedicated my first confirmed kill to him. I hope he got the letter I sent him. "One dead bastard for Sergeant Kramer." I drew a picture of a Focke Wulfe 190 burning in the sky, the dead bastard in the cockpit blood spilling from his mouth. "I gave them the whole nine yards, Sergeant Kramer," I wrote. The whole nine yards meant the length of the ammo belt that fed into the gun. Twenty-seven feet of .50

caliber bullets, enough to turn a brick outhouse into red dust and flying shit.

We got caught in the German searchlights. The Ploesti oil fields had good protection. Flak popped and flashed all around us in the black sky. I thought we'd never get out of the flak. When we did, the JU-388 night-fighters came after us. We couldn't see them. All we saw was the tracer stream from their 13-millimeter guns, and by then it was too late to return fire with the idea of hitting anything.

"Bogies four o'clock low!" Martin yelled, but he was just guessing. He was a dead man talking, for he would take a couple of those 13-millimeter slugs in his belly before he even felt them. "Bogies four o'clock low!" dead Martin Belascu said. He was the left waist-gunner. I was the right.

His words still echo around inside my head like an iron ball in a steel drum. It was like he might still be blasting away at the invisible thing that killed him. When the night fighters came out under my side of the ship I gave them a long burst, but they were long gone and I can't say I ever saw them. I watched other B-24s from our squadron break up, the burning wrecks caught in the searchlights, dead crews windmilling into Romania.

"You're a good kid, Clarence," Martin said as he lay dying in my arms. "Promise me something."

"Sure thing, Martin," I said. I didn't think I'd get back alive, so I could promise him anything he wanted.

"When you get back home, take care of Magda."

"Count on it, Martin," I said.

"Go to college, Clarence. Make something of yourself. The world is going to be a wonderful place after this lousy war."

"I'll do it, Martin." I didn't want to tell him that he was dead wrong about the world after the war. Nothing was going to change, it was only going to get worse, because that's the way it works in Hell.

Martin kissed my gloved hand and crossed himself. A question trembled on his lips. Then he died.

ↆ

"Was it bad, the war?" Magda said. We were at her breakfast nook, eating black market omelets with onions, cheese, and alligator pears, drinking warm Mexican beer. She liked warm beer, like the English. I felt I knew her.

"I guess so," I said. "Hell, some called it."

I'd been in Hell but I was still there—every "where" is Hell—but this had to be the best part of Hell. You carry Hell with you once you've seen it. It's like a special pair of glasses you put on that show you how the world really is no matter how clean or pure it seemed to you at one time. It also has a smell, which you recognize first. Parts of it are pretty horrible, other parts will give you pleasure. Nobody gets off light. It smells of sulfur and dung, it smells of food and perfume. It gave me ulcers.

Magda had twenty jars of marmalade sitting in her cupboard like a squad of fat, jaundiced soldiers. She had sixteen pounds of butter and twelve one-pound bricks of cheddar cheese in her icebox, all from the Challenge Dairy. She had eight pints of Challenge Dairy cream, also in her icebox. She had thirteen pounds of Farmer Brother's coffee and five pounds of Lipton tea. She had filet mignon steaks and Canadian bacon and lean pork roasts in her big fridge. Sausages hung in her larder. I drank a pint of cream now and then to ease my stomach pains. She didn't mind.

The war had been good to her. She was fat while most were lean. Not too fat or ugly fat, but fat. She had big round breasts and thighs like drums. Her jowls tended to hide her jawline. Her arms jiggled when she reached to put canned goods on the top shelf of her larder. Her rump was generous but not flabby. Strong with muscle, not just dead weight she hauled along behind her.

She smelled good. The smell of food surrounded her like an invisible shawl. Even when she had put on her sandalwood perfume, you could smell bacon under the sweetness. First thing I noticed when she opened her door was her smell. It seemed like I had smelled it before.

My first night in her apartment we had lamb chops for dinner. She was determined to put meat on my bones. "Skinny men make trouble, one way or another," she said. She didn't explain this, but I thought I understood. Martin, for a waist-gunner on a B-24, was pretty hefty, two hundred pounds at least.

I was six feet tall but only weighed 137. I'd flown thirty-one missions, four short of the regulation thirty-five, and came back to the USA with a bleeding ulcer and a so-called mental disorder the army medicos called dementia praecox, a fancy name for crazy. They gave me some medals and an honorable discharge, but they could just as soon have given me a Section-8, the discharge they give to mental cases.

I froze up after Martin died. I couldn't get out of my bunk. I weighed eight hundred pounds. That's what it felt like. My legs were lead. Steel straps held me to my cot. Even on the days I was able to move, I couldn't get into the bomber. I tried to explain: The plane won't be able to take off with me in it, lieutenant. I'm too heavy. I cannot fit through the hatch, lieutenant.

I'd approach the plane, pushed along by my new partner in the waist-gun spot, a seventeen-year-old Dago kid from New Jersey named Carmine Ruggio. But when I tried to climb into the plane, I could not fit through the hatch. I could not lift myself. Help me, Ruggio. But Ruggio, the new waist-gunner on the left side, wasn't strong enough. No one was strong enough. I was too big and they were too weak. I think I knew better. I think I knew it was all in my head. But what isn't all in your head? If it's not all in your head, where is it? You can't answer that! They put me into the field hospital strapped to a cot. They didn't need straps, I already was strapped. In my head.

Major McPherson, the squadron operations officer, was a good ole boy. He visited me. He wanted to talk to me. "We need you, son," he said, gentle as a priest, "but if you can't do the job for a while, I'll understand. We'll get you some help. You're our top waist-gunner. I've looked at the squadron records. I've looked at your gunnery school records. Some of the best scores on the books. You've got three confirmed kills—two Focke Wulfes and

a Messerschmitt. We need eagle-eye gunners like you. You're not
going to let us down, are you, son?"

"No sir," I said. It was a lie—what could I say?

"You're a good boy from good stock no doubt," he said. "You'll
come through this."

That's the kind of man he was. He'd give you a kindly lie to live
by. I did not come from good stock. I didn't even know what good
stock was. Fat rich people who mind their manners? There was
no good stock anywhere near where I came from.

Major McPherson took care of his men like a daddy. He knew
us all by our first names. He cheered us on. I liked him. I admired
him. He was a brave pilot, with fifty missions under his belt. He's
the one who helped flatten the monastery at Monte Cassino, which
was being held at the time by the Germans. He was flying B-26s
out of Foggia back then. Likely killed a hundred monks. He was
handsome and straight as a nail. You want a daddy? He's the one
you would pick.

He was also Satan. I told him this. I couldn't help myself. I felt
I owed it to him. I did not blame him for it and told him so. Satan
has a right to know who he is.

I said: "Sometimes you can't help being the Devil. It's an assignment they give you. You can't turn it down. Any assignment they
give you have to take on. It just happens that way through no fault
of your own. And there's nothing you can do about it. Before you
can figure it out, you are obeying some dark thing that had taken up
residence in your brain without your knowledge or say-so. I didn't
make this up, sir. I'm telling you something I know is fact, sir."

When the major left my bedside I heard him say to the doctor,
"Some of them are so damned simple. It breaks my heart to see
them go down like this. If they don't get tagged upstairs, they
come apart downstairs." He made a plane with his hand then
crumpled it in his other hand. The doctor nodded.

Major McPherson was a good man from Wyoming ranch
country. He and his daddy raised Black Angus. His mom was
a schoolteacher. Do people get any better than that? You know
they don't.

Major McPherson attended services every Sunday and did not go to the whores. He had a wife and three children back in Cody. But he sent men to their deaths, and the men he sent to their deaths sent other men to their deaths. This is how the Devil works. The dead men are all conscripted back into Hell because they do not usually die in a state of righteousness or grace. How can they when they are killing and being killed?

In the hospital they gave me the "Blue 88" treatment. The "Blue 88" was the name of the Sodium Pentathol tablet they gave to people like me to get them back on their feet. They called the pills "Blue 88s" after the German 88-millimeter anti-aircraft shell. This was because the pills were so potent and so feared. I'd take a pill and a little later get to feeling strangely. Then a head-shrinker would come in to talk to me while a bright light flooded my eyes. He'd ask about what it was like bombing the oil fields day after day or night after night. He held the light closer to my face and made me think I was firing the .50 caliber gun at the German night fighters. I could hear the gun stutter. I could see the long white arms of the searchlights. I caught a glimpse of a JU-388 as it sliced through slabs of light. I was screaming but I couldn't hear myself over the roar of our four engines and the rapid *dudududu* of my gun.

The doc made me believe I was holding Martin Belascu in my arms while his blood thickened and froze on my boots and on the waist deck. "He's the left side waist-gunner!" I screamed. "I am the right!" The doc brought the light so close I could feel my eyes burning. "Easy does it, son," he said. "Can you see sergeant Belascu's face? Did he take his oxygen mask off? Is that his blood on your hand? Can you remember his exact words?"

All this was supposed to help me. They figured if I could get back into the airplane in my *mind*, then I could face another mission in real life, because they needed good gunners. Not everyone can be a good gunner. If they could get one more mission out of me it would be worth the trouble they'd gone to. But it didn't work out like they wanted. It backfired. I threw up blood like *I'd* been gutshot. The "Blue 88" treatment made me crazier.

↓

I didn't ask Magda where she got all the food. She had more food than you could get with ration coupons. I figured she'd made a deal with crooked officials.

Her neighbor, Arno Railchalk, was a fifty-year-old milkman. He had no trouble trading butter and cream for gas coupons. His thirty-year-old wife, though, stepped out on him. He had his gas coupons but someone had his wife.

Magda had gas coupons, too. She had enough gasoline for us to drive down to Mexico every other week. All the way from West L.A. to Ensenada in her 1936 Ford coupe. We'd spend a day or so in Ensenada. She'd go shopping and I would go out on the beach and pick up shells. I kept the big ones for ashtrays. There was a whorehouse down by the beach. The fat madam would come out to greet me in her housecoat and slippers every time I passed, but I would ignore her. Finally she yelled, Mary Cone! or Man Floor! Which I figured were some kind of Spanish insults, but it didn't bother me none, even when she spit on me.

I wanted to ask Magda what she did in Ensenada since all she took home was a package wrapped in brown paper which she hid in the trunk of the Ford under rags and such. I also wanted to ask her where she got all the food and gas coupons from. But I didn't really want to know. I think I was afraid of what she might say. And I had promised Martin that I would take care of her. I promised him I would go to college. This was a source of amusement to me. College? I hadn't even finished high school! And Magda? She was taking care of *me*, not vice versa.

Here is an example of what I mean: In bed when I tried to crawl atop of her proper like a husband, she would push me off. "It's for your own good, Clarence," she said. "I don't want you thinking you have rights. You don't need that kind of distraction at your young age. You are more like a son to me than a husband with rights. Furthermore, I intend, as much as it is possible, to remain true to the memory of Martin. He was the love of my life." Then she went down under the sheets and I was plenty satisfied with the "French" job and decided that I would settle for it, at least for the time being.

She took real good care of me. But I wanted to take real good care of her. I promised Martin. I like to keep my promises even when it seemed I wouldn't have to because of dire circumstances.

I would put my hand on her belly and let it slide downhill and she would slap it away. "*That* place you're messing with young man belongs to Martin Belascu, you just remember that!" After a while you get the message, though I had nothing to complain about.

I warned her that black marketeers went to federal prison. But it wasn't my place to ask questions or give advice. Martin Belascu said Magda knew her way around the block. "She'll be good to you as long as you take good care of her, Clarence." Before that final Ploesti mission he showed me her picture, a snapshot taken at the Santa Monica Pier in Los Angeles, California. "If I don't get out of this alive, kid," he said. "I want you to look up Magda and tell her what happened to me. I want you to tell her that no matter what, I always loved her."

We were in a half-wrecked cantina in Cerignola, a town thirty miles from the airfield. We hitched a ride there with some MPs. We were drinking spumante. I got drunk on three glasses of it. I stared at Magda's picture and almost believed she was staring back at me. Because I was drunk the picture seemed alive. I understand now that I was more than just drunk at that point. Things don't just come alive because you've had three glasses of spumante. Maybe I've been a little crazy all my life. I did not come from good stock. My mama used the word "tetched" once when discussing something I had done to hurt some other kid pretty bad. "The boy gets a little *tetched* when something riles him." No one noticed I was "tetched" until I got heavy in Toretta and could no longer fly because of fat and the loss of strength. In the snapshot, the sky behind Magda was white and the sea was whiter.

I got hard staring at that picture of Magda standing on the Santa Monica Pier. The white sky, the whiter sea, her shining hair, her wide round breasts, her strong legs, her big bare feet gray with sand from a day of beachcombing. Martin jerked the picture back, sensing that it had aroused me. He could see the workings of my dirty mind on my face. I was an open book.

"Sorry," I said.

"For what?" he said. "What were you thinking that you should be sorry for?"

He was mad at me. I could tell he wanted to hit me. His fists clenched and unclenched. He knew what I was thinking. I was thinking of her breasts, how they seemed to rise out of the glossy photo as though they wanted you to put your worries and woes between them. I was thinking of her legs, how the wind had blown her dress into them, showing the heft of her thighs and the vee they held. I could almost smell that rich smell she has as if I knew it. I was guilty as charged and would not have hit him back.

↓

I mustered out of the Army Air Corps in Texas. When I showed up at Magda Belascu's apartment door in West Los Angeles a week later, she said, "They've already been here. Thanks anyway, but I already know Marty is dead."

I was in my Class A uniform, medals and all, my shoes spit-shined hard as dark brown glass. I wasn't a war hero but I looked like one.

She was tall and fat and her breasts filled out her dress. She was very sure of herself. Her dark eyes looked at you, they looked into you, they looked straight through to the back of your skull. She had a thick nose. Her breathing was noisy as if her nose had an obstruction in it. Her black hair was piled high in shining waves. She looked Indian—American Indian, not Hindu. She was a beacon for men who needed direction and guidance in Hell.

"I'm not here for that, ma'am," I said. I showed her my empty hands, palms up, so that she could see they did not hold a telegram from the War Department.

"Then what are you here for?" she said. There was more in this question than I could ever hope to answer.

She said, "You look tired. Come inside, hon, I'll fix you some breakfast."

"I was Martin's friend," I said, entering her small second-floor apartment that had a view of the date palm and the row of incinerators where the tenants burned garbage. "He was the left waist-gunner, I was the right."

"No lie?" she said. "I didn't think Marty had any friends. He was a loner. He wrote poetry, you know."

I didn't know.

"'O sun thou art a dead candle next to her smile,'" she quoted, sing-songy.

"That's really something," I said.

"Martin was the love of my life," she said.

I tried to picture Martin writing poetry. It seemed unlikely. In civilian life he'd been the manager of a Piggly Wiggly grocery store. Even though he was in Italy, he'd still carry a pencil behind his ear now and then. "Once the green grocer, always the green grocer," he once said, making fun of himself. He was the kind of man who could make fun of himself, but not when it came to his wife. I could see him, now, taking that pencil from behind his ear to write a poem to her.

That first day was when Magda "Frenched" me. That's all she would ever allow. When I kept nagging her for more, or for the proper way that men and women do it, she said, "Let's keep it clean, Clarence. The other thing is messy and complicates things. Husbands and Wives is not a game we're going to play. Get used to it. I'm a grieving war widow. It would be very unseemly to have marital relations with a boy young as yourself so soon after Martin's death. I understand you have pressing certain needs. It's only normal. But let's see where we stand after you turn twenty-one."

"That's six months away," I said.

"Good. Six months is good. You'll have something to look forward to."

⥥

I got a job at the Douglas plant in Santa Monica. It was summer, 1944, and the war was in full swing. Douglas made the S B D dive-bomber which was sinking Jap ships in the Pacific Ocean. I was a "bucker" on a riveting crew, tacking the aluminum skins of the Dauntless dive-bombers to the frames. I got my own apartment in Santa Monica. A one-room efficiency with a pull-down bed and a view of Ocean Park Boulevard. I had a two-burner hot plate for a stove, but I didn't use it much. I ate at Magda's two or three times a week. She would call me and say, "How does roast pork loin sound to you, Clarence?"

"How do you think it sounds?" I'd say and hurry over.

After work one day I walked out onto the Santa Monica pier to watch the people enjoy the rides. I had some beers and even rode the roller coaster and the tethered planes that were hooked to a tower at the end of the pier. These planes flew out over the water then back over the pier in a wide circle. I would look at the kids in the plane behind me and turn my fingers into twin .50s like the top turret gunner had and shoot them. *Dudududud.* The kids shot back. They were killers and the mothers and fathers of killers for our future wars.

After that I took the train to West L.A. and got off at Washington Boulevard and walked from there to the Ridgely Drive Apartments, where Magda lived. She wasn't expecting me. I'd bought some flowers and thought I'd surprise her.

I tiptoed up to her second floor apartment and tried the door. It was locked but I knew she kept a spare key under the doormat. I got it and opened the door slowly, so it wouldn't squeak.

She wasn't home. I set the flowers in a jar and put some water in the jar, then set the jar with its flowers on her kitchen table. She'd come in and see the flowers and know who it was. I expected it would melt her heart, and since I was just a month short of my twenty-first birthday I figured she'd go easy on me and take me to her bed proper.

Then I heard her on the stairs. I'd come to recognize her slow stomping way of coming up. She never went out that she didn't come back with a load of goods, and that made coming up the stairs hard work. I wanted to go out and help her, but I wanted to surprise her more.

She was talking to someone. A neighbor I figured, but she kept talking even as she approached the door. I'd been sitting at the kitchen table but now that I realized she had someone with her, I ducked into her bedroom taking the flowers with me. They were for her alone not her company.

It was a man, but it wasn't Arno Railchalk the milkman or anyone else whose voice I could recognize. I left the bedroom door open a crack so I could see them. They sat at the kitchen table and the man, a tall strong-looking fellow with thin blond hair and gold-rimmed eyeglasses, lit a cigarette. He had a grocery bag with him. It was filled with cartons of Lucky Strikes. Lucky Strike "greens," which meant they were pre-'43. ("*Lucky Strike green has gone to war!*") Magda didn't smoke, so I figured she was taking the Luckies in black market trade and then she'd trade them off for something else later on. Arno the milkman was a smoker, and he was smoking more now that his wife had left him, and so I figured she would trade the Luckies for more butter or cream.

They weren't talking much. He'd take a puff of his cigarette and say something like, "You got a nice place here, Mrs. Belascu," formal like that, so I guessed they were not friends but had some kind of business between them. She got up and went to her larder and came back with one of the brown packages she got in Ensenada. It was all sealed up with tape and she cut it open carefully with her kitchen scissors. She lifted a corner of the opened paper and the man wet his finger and dipped it into the package. His finger came out grayish white and he licked it clean. "Not bad, Mrs. Belascu," he said. "They didn't step on it but once, which I appreciate." Eventually he took some money out of his wallet and handed it to her. She squinted through his cigarette smoke as she counted it.

"You're my most dependable horse dealer, the best in town, Mrs. Belascu," he said. He reached over and touched her shoulder and she tilted her head so that her cheek lay on his hand. What was *that* all about? And horses? What did Magda have to do with horses?

Then they got up and headed toward the bedroom. I jumped away from the door and got into the closet at the foot of the bed with my jar of flowers. I left the door open a crack. They came in and the tall man sat on her bed as if he owned it. He took off his shoes and socks and then his suit jacket. I saw him take a police badge in its leather holder out of his shirt pocket and put it on the night table. He had a pistol in a shoulder holster, and he unstrapped that and set it next to his badge. Then he finished undressing. Magda took off her dress and underwear. I realized then that I had never seen her completely undressed and I wanted to step out of that closet and make them stop.

But I watched like I was under the spell of a Blue 88, because all at once I remembered something from childhood that I had forgotten about. A man—not my pa, he left us a year earlier—came home with my mama and he took her down hard to the living room floor and fit himself on top of her. I think I was only five or six and I remember crying because I thought he meant to kill her. I remember running through the living room in front of them but they didn't notice me and kept at it, his loose suspenders slapping against the linoleum. She was wearing her best yellow-flowered dress and her white high heel shoes and didn't seem to mind that the dress was up on her hips and getting wrinkled or that she was getting killed. The man went at her hard, face clenched like a fist. They scooted across the floor and she got her nice dress dirty. They knocked over a table that had a vase of flowers on it and the water spilled. I remember her whimpering all through it, and then her screams, and then I also screamed because if she died I would have no one to take care of me. Her screams, I realized all those many years later, were not from pain.

Neither were Magda's. I laid down in the closet and bit my hand to stop the pain in my stomach. I should have gone in there and accused her of betraying Martin, the love of her life. I would remind her of Martin's poem, *"O sun thou art a dead candle..."* but my stomach hurt too much just then. I listened to Magda's breath hiss out of her obstructed nostrils as she calmed down and her breathing slowed. The man lit a Lucky Strike. "The cigarettes, Mrs. Belascu. They're yours. Gratis, of course," he said.

They left together. I set the flowers back on the kitchen table, glad I had not spilled them in the closet. I followed them down Ridgely toward Adams Boulevard. They walked along holding hands. They bought tickets at the Variety Theater. *The Flying Tigers* with John Wayne was playing. I sat two rows back. That John Wayne is something. He makes it look easy. You know *he* never got ulcers.

When the movie let out, the air raid sirens were screaming and a hundred searchlights with their five-mile beams combed the sky for Jap bombers. Air raid wardens were on the sidewalk yelling at people to go home and close their drapes, we're having a blackout. I imagined the Jap gunners clearing their guns, their ulcers flaring up, as the man patted Magda on the rump and walked away. Magda walked back to her apartment.

I knocked on her door after she'd been home fifteen minutes. "Clarence!" she said. "What are you doing here?"

"I was just out for a walk and thought I would drop in to see you."

"Out for a walk? All the way from Santa Monica?" She could spot a lie as if it was printed on your face in bold letters.

"Well actually I rode the train over. I wanted to see you about something. I came over earlier but you weren't home so I let myself in with the spare key. Then I went for a long walk up Adams."

"Really," she said. She looked suspicious, finding lies written all over me. "I guess that explains the flowers. Thank you, Clarence, but do not come into my home again without an express invitation."

"Yes, ma'am," I said. I was still mad but also a little embarrassed. I said, "It's my birthday next month, and I was wondering . . ."

"Oh my. You are *such* a pest!" she said. She unbuttoned my pants. She found it small and uninterested. She worked on it though, and it got hard in spite of the fact that I wished it would not because I did not want it this way anymore.

I gripped her wrist and removed her hand from me. "I do not appreciate being treated like a child," I said.

Her eyes got hard. "I think you'd better go now, Clarence," she said. "We'll talk about this some other time. You're in a very strange mood and I don't think I like it."

I admit I was agitated. "You're in the black market and you also sell horses," I said. "Why *horses* when you can get all the black market beef you want which you can turn around and sell off? No one likes to eat horsemeat if they can get real beef. I ate it once because we were poor after my pa left us. It is very tough. It also tastes sweet but not a good kind of sweet. You don't like your steak sweet or tough as leather. But you need your protein, even poor people need protein. Maybe they need it more since they have to work hard all the time."

She looked at me like I was crazy. I guess maybe I felt a little crazy at that point, like my head was getting light. There was a rushing sound in my ears, like wind roaring past the gun bay. "You're a good kid," Martin said, his blood icing the gun deck.

"You don't know what you're talking about," she said. "Where did you hear this nonsense about horses?"

I told her. I was sick of lying.

"You sneaky little voyeuristic son of a bitch!" she said. "You blab one word about me dealing horse, I'll feed your nuts to the squirrels!" She slapped me hard. I'll tell you something maybe you don't know—when a woman big as Magda Belascu slaps you, you feel it. In fact, it knocked me down. I saw stars. While I was down she kicked me. I rolled away from her as best I could, but I could not avoid all the kicks. Her shoes were pointed and she put the heels to me, too. She broke a rib.

When I was able to get up, I punched her gut. If she had a soft spot, it was the gut. She went down on her rump, trying to get air. Then I did her the favor she did me. I kicked her some. One kick caught her neck and she choked. She wanted air but couldn't find any. I stepped on her neck for a while. She turned blue. I knelt down atop of her and we finally got to doing it like a man and a wife, proper I mean, the way it was intended. I figured I had rights and meant to claim them, busted rib or not.

I wasn't finished yet but her eyes rolled up and the fight went out of them before I pulled myself away from her. She was dead. Right there on the same kitchen floor where a few months ago she had "Frenched" me. I got myself a Coca-Cola from her ice box and rested. I was tired out. I felt like I'd hauled an eighty-pound bale of hay on my back half a mile uphill from the lowboy trailer to the hay barn.

I thought I was in the best part of Hell when she fed me like a king and then "Frenched" me, but I was wrong. The best part was yet to come.

She was cooling off pretty fast and I figured I'd better hurry while she was still soft. I claimed my rights again. I was almost twenty-one. I liked it that she didn't scream out like she had with the Lucky Strike man. It was more normal—more husband and wife–like, calm and peaceful. This last part is why they put me here, in the state mental hospital at Napa instead of the gas chamber at San Quentin. Figure that out.

I try to remember Magda Belascu by drawing pictures of her every day, but she is fading from my memory. Was she pretty? Was she as big as I remember? Did she betray Martin, the love of her life, or me, the other gunner? Or did she think it was all right to lie with the Lucky Strike man since Martin was gone and I didn't count?

What does not fade is the memory of Martin Belascu, dying. He said, Take care of my wife, Clarence. (*O sun thou art a dead candle next to her smile!*—solid proof that love is blind.) He didn't know her like I did or like the Lucky Strike man did. Magda didn't need anyone to take care of her. She was at home in Hell.

Martin looked at me before he died, his eyes focusing hard like he needed to see more than what was there. "Who are you?" he said. I guess he forgot for a minute due to shock from the loss of blood.

"I am Clarence, your friend," I said. "The left gunner."

He shook his head. "No," he said. "You're mixed up. You're the right gunner. I am the left."

I thought it over. I saw the truth in my mistake. I wasn't mixed up at all. "Now I'm both," I said.

I triggered his gun to make the point. He wanted to ask me something else but the light in his eyes went out, replaced by dull confusion. He died.

But death is nothing. It's no escape. You're here for keeps as somebody or other. It won't end. It can't. Hell is forever. It's here, it's only here, it's always here.

I felt Martin's familiar grin draw up the corners of my mouth. Sometimes everything is familiar for a reason.

You've seen it all before. You know you have. The cut of a stranger's jaw. Sun on a brick wall. Ants on a sill. A pond rippled by small fish feeding.

Wait a minute. I almost forgot. That bleeding ulcer? Gone.

Palochky

December, and suddenly it's
winter in the high desert. Snow falling fast, mercury sinking, air
from the arctic tundra rolling down America's steppes and into
El Paso, Texas. But Norton in his overheated apartment is boiling
with sweat after an evening of tequila, grifa, and garage-lab crystal.
A twist of memory-tweaking blues from the remnants of Canned
Heat throbs in his brain. *(My dear mama left me when I was quite
young / She said Lord have mercy on my wicked son . . .)* Canned Heat:
The original heart of the band, Blind Owl and The Bear, both dosed
to death, but the band still lives and remains Norton's favorite
blues band after all the crazed years since Nam.

Canned Heat getting gigged at Papa's on the west side of El
Paso—the relatively well-behaved side—was a major surprise
to Norton and thus a major treat. And now, after the evening's
festivities, a major *blur*. He smoked much reefer, drank much Her-
radura Gold, and got into it with a gnarly crank-dealing biker from
Las Cruces. Over a woman? Over price gouging? Maybe Nam?
The biker was a marine, Norton with the 196th Light Infantry
Brigade. No, never over Nam. Only the suits in DC whose sons
were safe in Ivy League schools thought it was a holy war. Norton
doesn't remember *what* the beef with the biker was over. Clarity,
just now, is a problem. His left cheek under the eye is swollen, his
knuckles raw. Norton, who has just turned fifty-two, thinks: I'm
too old for this kind of merriment. But he had a good time, he's
almost positive he did.

Why is he not in his bed? Heat. Not Canned Heat, but the
endless busted-thermostat blast from the heat registers in his
apartment. It's hot as a sauna in the windowless bedroom, and

he's staggered naked and feverish to the front room of his tiny flat and curled up on the sofa, which is a foot shorter than his bed and hard. The small oscillating fan he'd turned on in the bedroom sent weak zephyrs across the leviathan expanse of his body irritating the sciatic nerve in his bad leg, but it did not cool him. The bedroom *has* a window, but Norton's three floor-to-ceiling bookcases block it.

Little drifts of snow have formed on the sill of the opened front room window, but the icy breeze does not reach him where he lies in a fetal curl on the sofa, and he remains glazed with fever and sweat. I must be sick, he says to himself. Flu, late onset malaria, dengue fever. He feels he's back in the bush, thirty-some years ago, on patrol, pissed off, scared, sick, but mostly scared, because Norton, at six-five and two-fifty, was an easy target, even for an incompetent v c sniper, and most of them were not incompetent. He'd spent a month in the l b j—the Long Binh Jail, the famous stockade—for ending a brawl he didn't start. He felt safe there, dealing only with stoned m p s, and offered to stay on as resident recidivist.

Norton's internal heat could be due to his medications—antidepressants and painkillers—as well as to the apartment's furnace and its inept thermostat. His hangover doesn't help. He steps out to the landing in front of his apartment, savors the icy wind and the snowflakes that seem to sizzle when they settle on his hot skin. He leans on the railing, looking out at the parking lot two floors down. Under the sodium vapor lamps the asphalt is dusted with yellow snow, as are the parked cars. *Piss-yellow snow*, Norton thinks, filing the image away for future use. The title of a possible painting. Winter scene: *Jaundice Snow*.

A gust of wind moves his door. Norton hears the lock click behind him. The click has a finality to it, a punctuation mark that signifies both an end and a beginning. Norton has come to see his life in that bleak way—a string of unconnected episodes with distinct beginnings and abrupt endings. A segmented life with no hope of sustaining what seemed good and beneficial, but also with no fear of long-term commitments to entanglements that enervate and depress. He married a few years after the war—Jolene, a made-over country girl from the steep arroyos of Manhattan. She was determined to stick it out, but there was no *out*. Norton climbed deeper and deeper into the hole his life was becoming. Jolene traded up, found herself a Mormon cowboy from Salt Lake, and had a brace of Mormon babies. Norton seldom thinks of her anymore, cannot recall her face. He knows she does not recall his.

Norton is neither happy nor unhappy—he sits on the fence between the two untrustworthy states of being. He has survived. He has survived two tours in Vietnam, jobs that required neckties and white shirts, a head-on collision that has left him with a steel plate in his head and short-term memory glitches, but most of all he has survived himself. In bad times he's been a public nuisance, a querulous drunk, a barroom orator, and in better times a dependable laborer, careful reader, and gentle lover. Slowed now by medicine and age, he lives comfortably within sensible limits. Physical pain is an old companion. "I hurt, therefore I am," he likes to say. He thinks of himself as a neo-Cartesian: Pain, the mother of Being. Without pain all phenomena would coalesce into one giant self-satisfied protoplasmic glob. He reads Schopenhauer and Nietzsche, and at times feels he almost has a grip on things.

Norton is a painter. He paints signs for his daily bread, and landscapes for what he laughingly calls his soul. He is a mystical atheist who believes the world is a dream with no wake-up call, a dream without a dreamer. Beautiful and ugly, architecturally splendid yet chaotic as a schizoid's nightmare. It is one hell of a dream, endless and perfectly imperfect.

His paintings reflect this view. His deserts, mountains, cityscapes, and portraits are tainted with it. He is reckless with color and form, he treats perspective as illusion. These earnest distortions raise eyebrows but not cash. He has never sold a painting.

And now Norton stands naked on the outdoor catwalk landing, locked out of his apartment. He stands there amused for a few minutes before the seriousness of his situation dawns on him. He knocks on his neighbors' doors but no one answers. This is a high-crime neighborhood and no tenant here would risk opening his door to insistent knocking this late at night. They would look into their peepholes and see a large naked man standing in the wind, a maniac.

The apartment building is an old motel that has been converted for the benefit of low-income citizens. A murder was committed in a first-floor apartment only a month ago. Robberies are common. This is the heart of gangland, on the edge of the Segundo Barrio. On a pleasant evening, one can sit on the steps and hear the distant call of gunfire. Sometimes the gunfire is not so distant.

It's dangerous to pound on these doors in the middle of the night. People, frightened or enraged, have been known to send bullets through their doors and walls at random disturbances. Poor people live here, and the rage of the poor is not to be tested.

Norton is no longer sweating. His sweat has frozen. A thin sheet of ice has formed across his broad shoulders and on his big feet. His nose hairs are becoming tiny icicles. He feels them stiffen with each intake of breath.

Out of desperation he goes to the apartment of a Russian woman he's been friendly with, Svetlana Redmond. She's in her late thirties or early forties, and lovely in that big-boned workhouse Slavic way. She has been flirtatious with him in the past, has even invited him for coffee and special Russian confections. ("You have eaten palochky? No? Yes? You have *never* eaten palochky until you eat *my* palochky." It seemed to mean more than pastry when she said it.)

Svetlana Redmond opens the door a crack, then a bit wider. She eyes him up and down, amused. Norton, a naked tower of shaking white flesh, his long gray-blond hair lifting and twisting in the breeze—doesn't intimidate or scare her. "You go for walk naked in such weather?" she says, eyebrows arched.

Norton clears his throat sonorously and creates a plausible fiction: "I was very hot in my apartment after taking a hot bath. I stepped outside to cool off and the door slammed behind me, locking me out. I need to come in because if I stay out here much longer I'll most likely freeze to death. I need to call management to let me back into my apartment."

"I can't let you in now," she says. "My husband, Charles, is here. Come back in five minutes. He will be gone to get video then. He wants to see *Dumb and Dumber* again. He has seen *Dumb and Dumber* four times. I find it most dreadful annoying picture show I never want to see again."

It takes a few seconds for Norton to process this. But by then she's closed the door. "Call management!" Norton yells at the door. "I'm freezing to death! I'll be dead in five minutes! Call them now!"

Svetlana comes back with a bathrobe. It's a woman's robe, pink chenille with a feathery boa at the collar. Norton puts it on but cannot close it around his chest and stomach. Even so, it gives some protection from the wind, which has stepped up its ferocity. He stands with his back to the gale. It is probably twenty degrees, maybe even into the teens, and the wind chill factor is considerably below that. Five minutes! He can feel the burning pain preliminary to frostbite in his toes. *I feel pain; I exist.*

Norton is not a genius, but he is far from stupid. Even so, he sometimes finds the obvious elusive. It occurs to him finally that he can find refuge in the laundry room. It would be empty now, but some heat would be piped into it, even at this time of night. He goes downstairs holding Svetlana's robe close against the wind only to find the laundry room locked. Winos have been taking pry bars to the washers and dryers to get at the quarter-choked coin boxes, and so management has started locking it after dark. Next to the laundry room there is an alcove for the soft-drink dispensers, which have also been attacked by vandals. There is no way to protect these machines, and so the soft-drink company has declared its intention to remove them permanently. It is cold in this alcove, but at least Norton is safe from the wind's cruel reach.

From this alcove he can see the second floor landing and the door and front windows of Svetlana's apartment. He knows something about her. She is a mail-order bride, brought to this country by Charles Redmond, a seventy-year-old widower. It amuses Norton to think that a fine-looking woman like Svetlana would accept Charles Redmond's offer. What offer? Not love or money. Redmond was a poor retiree, living on Social Security and a military pension. He'd been an army lifer, a thirty-year motor pool sergeant. What can explain this? But Norton is not fond of explanations. People are what they are and need no explanation. Thrill killers, saints, and child prodigies are born, not made. Environments only turn up or moderate the annealing heat.

Norton has a nodding acquaintance with Redmond. Redmond is tall and stooped and wears a thick black beard streaked yellow and gray. His eyes, always searching for focus, float like black oysters behind fishbowl glasses. Though tall he is narrow and light-boned, this flimsiness mocked by a tumorous belly. He's had two heart attacks in less than four years. He wears work clothes exclusively—baggy dungarees held up with wide, colorful suspenders, denim shirts, logger boots, a billed cap perched on his bushy gray head. Svetlana clearly did not come to America for romance. Norton believes she was running from something or someone and wanted a quick way to find haven in this wide, safe continent, so abundant in all things.

Norton, his feet burning with cold, watches Charles Redmond emerge from his apartment, watches him take long spidery strides down the open staircase and head for his car, a twenty-five-year-old Chrysler Cordoba, its Corinthian leather seats eruptive with white spongiform cushioning material. The side panels of the old Cordoba are rusted out, the fenders spooned by huge dents, the glassless taillights covered with Saran Wrap held on with duct tape. Redmond pulls the reluctant door open with both hands, making the bent and rusted hinges groan, but the door only opens a foot and Redmond has to negotiate his entry. When he is finally behind the wheel it takes him several tries to reclose the door. The car's battery is already affected by the cold air and barely turns the engine over in its thickening oil. Norton, mystical atheist, aims a small prayer at the ignition system of the Cordoba, visualizes strong sparks igniting vaporized gasoline—and, *gracias a Díos*—the car starts with an unmuffled roar that rattles all the windows in the apartment building. Both hands in a death-grip on the wheel, his bearded face and goggled eyes close to the fogged windshield, Redmond eases the geriatric Cordoba out of the parking lot and drives off to get *Dumb and Dumber.* Norton heads back upstairs, shaking with cold.

Svetlana meets him at the door. "Crazy man," she says cheerfully. "Idiot."

"I've been called worse," Norton manages.

"I am sure of this."

She leads him into the kitchen, then goes into the bedroom. She comes back with Redmond's ratty terry cloth bathrobe and a pair of leather slippers with almost enough room for Norton's big feet.

"Why did you make me wait outside?" he says. "I could have gotten frostbite. Maybe I did."

"If I let you in, Charles would not go to Blockbuster. He *sees* you, he would be jealous and not go. Charles is suspicious. He is crazy with jealousy. He thinks men come to me when he is not here. Sit down. You need drink."

Norton pulls an iron chair out from an iron table. It's patio furniture, black filigreed iron, the furniture of poor people.

"I didn't come here to make trouble," Norton says.

Svetlana gives him a sidelong smirking smile. She is beautiful, in that Russian-Asiatic way—high Mongol cheekbones, the slightly epicanthic eyelids, the full lips and the wide, hungry mouth. She is blonde, but her eyes are hard Asiatic black. A descendant of the Golden Horde. He pictures her in iron beanie with buffalo horns, carrying a hind-quarter of elk over her shoulder.

Charles Redmond is no match for her, Norton thinks. Men come to her, in their dreams at least, Redmond is right about that. Norton feels her sexual magnetic field, is drawn to it, and, looking at his skinned knuckles, reminds himself he's had his fill of trouble tonight.

She opens a cupboard and takes down a bottle of Stoli. "Here, you need this to fight cold." She fills a juice glass within an inch of its rim, then pours one for herself.

Norton knows it's a little early to be looking at the hair of the dog. On the other hand, he is grateful to her for letting him in and feels he owes her the courtesy.

"Your health," she says, raising her glass.

"And yours," Norton says, raising his.

Norton, not interested in small talk, cuts to the chase, "Why did you marry that old man? You're a beautiful woman. You could've had your pick."

Svetlana gets a long ago and far away look in her eyes, visiting sad landscapes, sad people. *"Ya robotayet na zavodya,"* she says.

"Uh huh," Norton says.

"It means I work in factory, in Novosibirsk. In tractor factory, for nothing, for bread, but little more. I wear rags. I live in one cold room. My husband, Yevgeny, he go away with teenage whore slut. What am I to do? So I go to bride broker."

"You're young, you're beautiful—" Norton feels the Stoli. Its warmth descends to his feet. He reaches across the table and touches the arm of this woman from the Novosibirsk tractor factory.

"No, not so young," she says. "I am forty. These men, they do not want middle-age bride. I am lucky to take Charles. Love? No, I do not love Charles, no one could love Charles, yet I owe to him. I am American citizen. For this I owe to Charles." She looks directly into Norton's eyes. "Anyway, it comes to nothing. Charles is not able. In two years, not once has he been able. He cannot—what is word?—consummate."

"There's medicine for that," Norton says.

"For Charles, no, there is not. He has heart medicine. If also he has consummate medicine, then, boom, heart attack."

Norton feels the tropical fever coming back. His neck feels hot. He is sure his face is red. He feels beads of sweat tickling his upper lip. Dengue, it could be that. There's plenty of it across the

Rio Grande, in the *colonias* of Juárez. But is this the right season for Dengue? He thinks not.

Impulsively, he leans across the small iron table and kisses Svetlana. Svetlana kisses him back, her mouth working against his, their tongues becoming acquainted. He feels this is a dream, that he's not fully awake, then remembers his notion that it's all dream anyway, a dream cut loose from the dreamer, and the way things spin out is never going to make sense, be predictable, or matter. Shit happens, as Schopenhauer said.

"I want to eat your palochky," he says, rakishly, riding the tidal wave of lust to the promised shore.

"Come then," Svetlana says, taking his hand. "I have been thinking of you, many times. I need more than citizenship. Charles will not come home for half-hour. He goes to Blockbuster on North Mesa street. They have better selection. We enjoy each other, *da*? I have strong appetite for enjoy."

Norton hesitates. This is happening too easily. Where are the doubts, the second thoughts, the perfunctory argument that overrides guilt? Where in fact is the guilt?

He feels as though he's being led into a situation he will later regret. Svetlana is *acting*, he feels, overacting, in fact. Stagey, making him feel he's been given a supporting role. But these thoughts dissolve in the libidinal flood as she takes him into the bedroom and into her bed, Redmond's shabby robe tenting the choreography of sex. Norton finishes too quickly; then, after a few minutes, they're at it again, Svetlana on her knees this time, Norton behind her on his, driving furiously, making thick noises in his throat, Svetlana muttering dark Cyrillic syllables to the headboard.

↓

"I have plan."

"Plan?" Norton feels the tab for the bedroom feast has arrived.

"Charles has weak heart, as I have said. We will make it to fail. It is so easy."

"Whoa," Norton says. "You want me to clip him? That's a high price for a piece of palochky."

"You speak crudely. You have insulting manner. I deplore this."

"Oh, I'm terribly sorry. We were speaking politely about murder. Thoughtless of me."

"*Nyet*, not murder." There is steel in her black slanty eyes. In spite of the turn the conversation has taken, Norton wants her again.

"I have plan," she repeats.

"You have plan," Norton says.

"Charles is fisherman. We go together, to Elephant Butte reservoir, three of us. Charles likes to fish. He has smoker in back of car. We go up to reservoir. It is winter, no one will be there."

"Then we cut him up and use him for bait. Good plan."

"*Nyet*. You speak like fool. We push him into cold water in early morning, make him stay in cold water. He is not strong, he cannot make strong fight."

"We drown him."

"No, not to *drown*—" she laughs with excessive gaiety, as if drowning her husband is an insanely farcical idea, "—*nyet, nyet*, my dear, we push him into lake to make him *cold*, like *you*, locked from apartment, naked. He is now in hypothermia, his heart fails. He goes unconscious. He slips away. He dies. This is not murder. He *wants* to die, you must understand this. It will be favor to him. He cannot make it stand up anymore, this makes Charles sad. He cries in bed because it will not stand up like good soldier."

"He's seventy years old," Norton says.

"And so death will be his friend, you see."

Norton wants to turn the conversation away from this crazy talk of impotence and murder, but she's caught him by the persuader, reawakening it. "Charles has insurance policy from American army," she says. "Ten thousand dollars."

She takes him into her again and establishes the rhythm, vigorous at first, her factory-strong hands on his buttocks directing the timing and force of his efforts, slapping him smartly to quicken the pace, pinching to slow it down, muttering *da! da! da!* taking her cue from television, the shampoo commercial in which the actress fakes orgasm—yes! yes! *yes!*—as she lathers her hair. Norton, the pony, feels used, a dildo with legs, and that's fine with him. He hasn't been with a woman in months, almost a year, and he's not about to refuse this gift on fussy moral grounds. Besides, sex isn't commitment: the last thing he'd do is murder Charles for an evening with the old lifer's orgasm-faking wife. Norton recalls *The Postman Always Rings Twice* and thinks what an idiot that guy Frank was, killing the old Greek for nothing, for the old man's greedy bitch of a wife, Cora, who also, truth be known, faked. Norton thinks, I am not Frank. No way.

"You loving me now, yes?" Svetlana whispers into his burning ear.

"Why not?" Norton says. It's not exactly an evasion.

"You loving me so much nothing is bigger than love you have for me?"

And Norton realizes then that she has also read *Postman*, or saw the film, and that she sees him as Frank, the bum, the stupid killer—his role in her murderous fantasy.

Svetlana's shuddering convulsions as he thrusts harder don't stop her from talking. "Ten thousand dollars—is enough for new start—we go to San Francisco—I have cousin there—Mikhail Boronowski—in import market—you will drive truck for Mikhail—you and I—we make new life—we have child—we buy house in Petaluma—we have American dream—you see? You *see* this now?"

Petaluma? Norton thinks. Meaning, of course, that she's had a scheme cooked up for some time now, a detailed fantasy that needed an accomplice. Exhausted, he lies heavy on Svetlana, nose in the tangles of her yellow hair, thinking *Petaluma, north of San Francisco, a beautiful place, but expensive. Ten thousand dollars doesn't buy patio furniture in Petaluma.*

"I'll think about it," he says, getting up. He pulls Redmond's bathrobe around his overheated bulk and limps to the door, the sciatic nerve in his right leg suddenly awake and throbbing.

"You will *think* about it?" Svetlana says, following him, snatching at the bathrobe. "You will not *think* about it! It is past time for thinking!"

"Never past time for thinking," Norton says.

"Please, we will talk tomorrow of this. It is good plan. We have wonderful future."

"In Petaluma. Sure. We'll talk tomorrow. Thanks for the palochky."

"Tomorrow I give you real palochky."

Norton is out in the cold again, welcoming, for the moment, the icy air. He still has Redmond's bathrobe but is tempted to take it off. The north wind still moans in the ironwork of the outdoor catwalk that rings the upper floors of the apartment complex, but he is full of fever and thirst. He'd give ten dollars for a frosted bottle of Negra Modelo, his favorite summertime beer. I'm sick, he tells himself again. Dengue? Malaria? Maybe the beginnings of cholera, another bordertown disease on the rise. But he doesn't feel sick, just hot. He takes off Redmond's robe and drapes it on the rail of the catwalk just as Redmond turns his flaking Cordoba into the parking lot, the unmuffled V-8 bellowing.

Norton watches Redmond squeeze through the rust-pinched door, holding *Dumb and Dumber* high, as if he's stepping out into a hip-deep swamp.

Norton suddenly remembers Lowell Pickering, a fellow grunt wading through a monsoon-flooded paddy, holding his M-16 high then dropping it, then sitting down to retrieve it, sitting until the water was over his helmet. Redmond reminds Norton of Lowell Pickering, wading through muck, unsuspecting, not happy, not unhappy, his fate lying in wait like a dozing cobra. A VC sniper blew a 7.62 millimeter hole through Pickering's neck, severing the spine. Norton realized this when Pickering did not stand up out of the black, red-streaked water with the retrieved rifle. Pickering once said to Norton, "This is *their* boonies, man, not ours. They can see us in the bush but we can't see them."

Norton watches Redmond cross the parking lot, thinking, I can see him but he can't see me, then forgets both Redmond and Pickering and goes to his apartment where he will kick the flimsy door open, blame it tomorrow on burglars.

A memory works its way up out of the lower swamps of his ravaged brain: *Didn't he crack open the window before he locked himself out?* *Dumb fuck*, he thinks. All he had to do was rip out the screen, slide the window all the way open, and climb back in. He wouldn't even have to report it to management. Who needs a screen in winter, anyway? If Redmond is Dumb, Norton is Dumber. But if he *had* remembered the open window, then he would have had Schopenhauer for the evening, not Svetlana, and he can have Schopenhauer any time he wants. So, there *is* a god, a comic god, he thinks, and his sacred name is Joke's-On-You. Norton laughs at himself, at his blitzed brain, at fate, at anything that resembles a systematic plan, cosmic or otherwise. He thinks of Voltaire—another favorite—who said God is a comedian playing to an audience that is afraid to laugh.

Norton rips the screen out of the frame, Frisbees it into the parking lot below, then slides the window all the way open and climbs into his apartment. It's still hot as a sauna, the heat ducts relentlessly blowing hot wind into the small rooms. He takes a bottle of Negra Modelo out of his fridge and sits down on his sofa with *The World As Will and Idea*. Norton has moments when he thinks he understands it, moments when he knows he does not. Either way, he knows it doesn't matter. Words won't solve it. They never have.

Norton, slick as a seal with sweat, reads until the words stop making sense. He puts the book aside to think about Svetlana. He'd see her again, of course. Maybe they'd bump into each other in the laundry room. Maybe he'd visit her some evening while Redmond shopped for videos. Maybe he'd ask her to sit for a portrait: *The Russian Bare*. But palochky? There would be no palochky tomorrow. The price was a little too high.

HERBIE

ↆ

There is always one moment in childhood
when the door opens and lets the future in.

—Graham Greene,
from *The Power and the Glory*

Why the Tears, Miss Earhart?

Uncle Ferris came down from Seattle to live with us in Oakland while he looked for a job. He'd been working for Boeing but had been fired for reasons he glossed over and glamorized in his favor. He'd caught someone stealing tools, he said, but instead of turning the man in, Uncle Ferris, who was a tool shop foreman, beat him up. This was early in 1945. The big war was almost over.

My mother only half-believed the story—the fighting part. "Even when he was a kid he'd stretch the truth to make himself look good," she said. Then, in a darker tone, she added, "There was a woman involved, you can bet on it, Herbert." She called me Herbert when she wanted me to understand that she was speaking to me as grown-up to grown-up. Otherwise it was Herbie.

I turned eleven that year, the year I learned how babies were conceived, which had been a subject of uninformed argument between me and my friends. But Frankie Sutton's mother was a registered nurse and he had indisputable proof, obtained from his mother's library of medical texts. One text called *The Human Reproductive System* had red, white, and blue maps of the penis, vagina, and surrounding organs. There was a full-page illustration of frantic white pollywogs attacking the planetary ova. Another page showed a properly inserted penis—complete with veins and sperm channels—in the red vagina, also veined and channeled, impressing the viewer with the notion of perfect, predetermined fit.

My stepdad, Dave, acted as though Uncle Ferris was welcome in our house, but he didn't like the idea, even if it was only for a month or two. Ferris could be trouble, according to Dave, and he wanted no part of him. Mom wasn't crazy about Ferris moving in either, but she couldn't turn away her own flesh and blood. Blood is thicker than water, she said. On the other hand, water doesn't clot. That's how she put it. Besides, it was only temporary, and Ferris already had some good leads.

Even though the war was winding down, there was still a manpower shortage. It didn't take much to land a good-paying job. People from all over the country, especially people from the South, had moved into the Oakland Bay area to work in the defense industry. Mom was working in the Kaiser shipyards as a welder and Dave sold ice cream from a Good Humor truck.

Uncle Ferris would go through the newspapers every morning, circling job notices in the want ads with his big green fountain pen. Then he'd take the East Fourteenth Street bus into downtown Oakland and come back in the late afternoon, his tie loose, his suit coat over his shoulder.

"The trouble with him is he expects to be a foreman just because that's what he was in Seattle," Mom said to Dave over dinner one night. "You don't walk into a place asking for the foreman's job." Uncle Ferris was at the table, but Mom spoke about him as if he were in another room.

"I know how to handle men, you see," Uncle Ferris said, holding his fork up and pointing it at Mom. He was not a big man, but he gave the impression of size. He had a large, square head and wide, powerful shoulders. The span and bulk of his shoulders made him look shorter than his five foot eight. He had a wide, generous smile, and his mass of dark wavy hair gave him an aura of wildness. But he had a melancholy streak, too. I'd often find him sitting alone in the living room with a magazine in his lap, staring off into the vast distance through threads of cigarette smoke as if he was watching a dream recede.

"Now that the war is history, for all intents and purposes, what good jobs are left will be grabbed off by the boot-lickers," he said.

"There's always that excuse," Mom said. "Admit you're just lazy. It's always been in you to be lazy."

Uncle Ferris drew himself up, both fists on the table. "I have never been lazy. I am simply indifferent to certain species of labor, as any self-respecting man should be."

"I'm sure something will turn up," Dave said, more hope than certainty in his voice.

"I'm looking for opportunity, Dave, not servitude." He sneered a bit after saying this.

Dave nodded agreeably, even though this remark was an insult directed at him. Dave was not a forceful man, though I could tell he was fuming behind his agreeable face.

We lived in Sobrante Park, a housing tract in south Oakland, not far from San Leandro. The developer who built these "Victory Homes" had used green wood, and the floor under our icebox had warped. We kept a drip pan under the icebox to catch the runoff from the melting block of ice, but it often overflowed, soaking the floorboards. The green oak had separated and twisted so that you could see the dirt crawl-space under the house. We always had trouble opening and closing doors and windows, which changed size according to the weather. When the wind blew, you could feel it in every room except the bathroom. It wasn't much of a house, but it was the first house Mom had ever owned, and she was proud of it, warps and all.

Mom and Dave argued a lot over Ferris. It was March, and he'd been with us for a month. They had only been married a year and I hated to see them fight. Before she married Dave, I'd been living in the Upper Peninsula of Michigan with my grandmother. Fear that I would be exiled back to Michigan made me hide from their fights. I'd go into my room and turn on my radio, a three-tube kit I'd gotten for Christmas. It wasn't much of a radio, but with the proper coils plugged in I could tune into all corners of the world for news of the war.

I had dreams of becoming a radio operator aboard a navy ship. I'd memorized the Morse system and listened to the perfect code the naval stations transmitted to ships around the world twenty-four hours a day. I eventually became competent enough to read messages that were intended for the fleet. The messages were just meaningless groups of numbers and letters, but the fact that I could copy them thrilled me. It was as if I had a real part in the war.

Recurring fantasies put me aboard a destroyer, cutting toward the periscope of a Japanese submarine. Depth charges rolled from the deck as I pounded code into the big brass key in the radio room, describing another sure kill to the radio operators at KTK, the naval radio station in San Francisco. Once we headed for a Japanese-held island on a secret mission after I had received information from a beautiful Eurasian girl who had managed to find a radio to call for help. At one point in my fantasy, I found myself alone with this girl in a cave on the enemy-occupied coral island. Her name was Laura, a name I favored, and we kissed and promised to love each other forever even if Japanese interrogators forced betrayals from us through torture. The red, white, and blue diagrams of the penis and vagina from *The Human Reproductive System* found their way into these daydreams, but in a confused, detached way that had nothing to do with me or Laura. It was as if the organs of reproduction existed apart from this romantic daydream, energizing it from a safe distance. A radio somewhere in the background played the ballad "Laura" over and over as we held hands, waiting for the Japanese soldiers to find us.

Uncle Ferris had been a shipboard radio operator on a Portland-class armored cruiser before the war, and for this reason he became my hero. He had sailed all the oceans of the world in an eight-year period from 1929 to 1937, a period of relative peace. Mom said he'd wanted a career but had been kicked out of the navy with a bad conduct discharge for fighting and insubordination. Uncle Ferris hinted at a darker cause. "They had to get rid of me, you see," he said. "I knew too much, Herbie."

We were in my room when he said this, listening to Radio London. The room was faintly illuminated by the orange glow from the three vacuum tubes of my shortwave receiver. The light made Uncle Ferris's face craggy with shadows. His eyes glinted black and dangerous.

"Remember Amelia Earhart?" he said.

How could anyone forget Amelia Earhart? Next to the Hindenburg disaster, she was the greatest air mystery of all time.

"We found the wreckage of her Lockheed Electra out on an atoll, near Kwajalein Island," he said. "She was alive, Herbie. She was brought aboard our ship. A short time later, we received orders to return to San Diego. One night I saw her on the foredeck, next to the turret that housed the eight-inch guns. We radio ops worked in shifts, you see, and I was having a cigarette on my break and there she was, Amelia Earhart herself, silhouetted against the turret." He leaned close to me. His breath was thick with cigarette smoke and the boiled cabbage and fried Spam we'd had for dinner. "Herbie, I tell you this in strict confidence: Amelia was crying, and her tears were bitter. It broke my heart to hear it. It breaks my heart today, just to remember it."

I tried to picture the scene, Uncle Ferris smoking cigarettes out on the deck of the big cruiser, Amelia Earhart herself next to him, crying bitter tears. In my mind it wasn't Uncle Ferris and Amelia Earhart, it became me and Laura.

"She was coughing badly, Herbie," Uncle Ferris said. "She was in a bad way. She'd been without food and water for days. She should have been down in sick bay but she was a strong-willed, heroic woman, as you know. I approached her and ventured to ask 'Why the tears, Miss Earhart?' She looked at me and saw that I was the sort of man that can be trusted. 'There's going to be a terrible war,' she said. 'They're planning it in Washington and London. It's been agreed that a war would be just the thing to end the economic depression which has destroyed the wealth and spirit of the civilized world. War would launch both England and America into a new era of industrial and territorial expansion.' Herbie, I could not believe my ears, but now here it is—the biggest war in the history of the world, predicted so ably by Miss Earhart, who had played a serious, if unwitting, part in its inception. Her navigator was a government plant—an agent—sent to photograph small South Pacific islands to determine their suitability as landing fields for our medium- and long-range bombers. He confessed everything to her, you see, thinking they would not be rescued. Of course, she had to be kept from public view."

He paused—a pause filled with significance—and lit another cigarette. Radio London was fading in and out. I tuned to another station. The announcer spoke French. I didn't understand a word of it, but the idea of the French language echoing around in my small bedroom gave me a sense of my own worldliness.

I don't think I actually believed Uncle Ferris's story about Amelia Earhart's navigator and the true reason for her flight around the world, but even so it shaped my thinking for years afterward. I came to regard all major world events as manifestations of secret government plots. The newspaper-reading public never had a clue as to what these world events were all about. They accepted the reports at face value. I did not. I understood that devious things had taken place in darkened rooms. Reading between the lines became second nature to me. Headlines such as "Scientists Baffled by Signals from Space" set me to thinking of the unbaffled ones, working in their labs, who had already deciphered the coded signals but were not free to tell the public what they meant because of the shocking nature of the messages.

When Uncle Ferris smiled, a gold incisor gleamed. His blue eyes twinkled with his superior knowledge as if he knew dark secrets, mine included. One of his eyes was bigger than the other. When he talked to you, his left eye became wide and staring while the lid of the right eye drooped. It was an inquisitional stare that gave the impression that he questioned everything you thought you knew.

"You are not going to be a vigorous participant in life, Herbie," he said after regarding me in this way for an unbearably long time. "I don't mean to pass judgment on your future, Herbie, and I admit I could be mistaken. But in my opinion, you are destined to be a passive observer, useful only if you are able to see the things the vigorous participants in life miss."

He drew so deeply on his cigarette the paper crackled. He blew out a cloud of smoke and more smoke curled from his nostrils. Then he added, "Life assigns us roles, you see. The trick, Herbie, is to discover your role early on so that you can be fulfilled in life. Many do not discover their roles until it is too late. These are the ones who at the end of their brief time on earth complain, 'I've missed the point. Jesus, I've missed the point.' I, myself, am both shrewd observer as well as vigorous participant. I knew this from day one. It is a rare combination that should one day carry me to great achievement. I just need to bide my time, you see."

After the war in Europe ended in April, Uncle Ferris stopped looking for work. He spent his days in the house reading magazines and newspapers and smoking cigarettes. I came home from school one day to find him sleeping on the sofa, a live cigarette burning a hole into the cushion. I picked up the cigarette and carried it into the kitchen. I meant to throw it into the trash after having doused it under the tap, but instead I held it in my fingers in the way Uncle Ferris would have held it. I took a drag and choked on the smoke, then took another. I'd had a bad day at school. The cigarette made me feel older, closer to being an adult and free of school.

There were a lot of Portuguese kids in our school. They were the sons and daughters of fisherman who lived in San Leandro, the little town south of Oakland. The Portuguese girls were far more advanced in every way than the Anglo boys. Two of them invited me into the cloak closet at the back of the classroom after the teacher had left the room during morning recess. "We want to show you something really special," one of them said.

The mystery of girls and their really special secrets turned me into an obedient robot. I followed them, my heart pumping. As soon as we were in the cloak closet they grabbed me. They were bigger and stronger than I was and they got me down on the floor. One of them pinned my arms, the other sat on my stomach. I smelled them as they switched positions to take turns pressing their full breasts against my bony chest. The smoky odors of menstrual flow and underarm sweat, mixed with Portuguese spices, stung my eyes.

"Oh, lookie," the one pinning my arms said. "Herbie's crying." I wasn't crying, but I was in distress. I had a hard time holding back.

Not tears but pee. Eventually, as the Portuguese girl bounced, I
spotted my jeans. I had to go through the rest of the day with
two wet spots the size of a half-dollar on the front of my pants.
Frankie Sutton, who knew more about sex than any of us, said
they did this because they liked me. "It's called dry fucking,
Herbie," he explained.

I smoked Uncle Ferris's cigarette down to a stub. I felt dizzy—
not dizzy-sick, but dizzy in a good way. I decided that I would
become a pack-a-day man, just like Uncle Ferris, observing life
through lazy threads of cigarette smoke. I saw myself on the foredeck of a cruiser, smoking cigarettes next to the eight-inch guns,
looking out to sea, an observer, but also an active participant.

One evening after dinner someone pounded on our door. Dave
answered it. A large roaring man pushed Dave out of his way
and came into our house. "Where is the son of a bitch?" he said,
filling the house with his roaring voice. He rolled his shoulders
like a boxer, shifting his weight from foot to foot. The muscles in
his clenched jaw were big as apples. He pulled a woman into the
house after him. She was a thin blond woman who might have
been pretty under different circumstances. She had a black eye
and her face was swollen. She was crying.

We'd all been in a good mood that evening. Uncle Ferris had
decided to move on. He felt there was more opportunity for a man
such as himself in Texas, "where they respect a man who possesses
natural God-given authority." He'd made Pullman reservations
for Dallas. Mom and Dave were relieved. I was relieved, too, since
Mom and Dave had been fighting more and more over Uncle Ferris.
The "blood is thicker than water" approach was wearing thin with
Dave. I was afraid the escalating arguments would split them up
and I'd be sent back to the Upper Peninsula with my grandma.
On the other hand I knew I'd miss Uncle Ferris and his stories,
whether they were true or not. It didn't matter to me that his
story about finding Amelia Earhart didn't mention what became
of her after her rescue, or why there had been no follow-up on the
navigator who doubled as a government agent. Was the navigator

rescued too? If so, where was he, and if not, why not? None of this mattered to me. The story was the thing.

Uncle Ferris and I were still at the dining room table when the man and woman burst into the house. Uncle Ferris calmly crushed his cigarette in an ashtray and went out to the living room to meet the man. I followed him. "I believe I am the individual you are looking for," Uncle Ferris said, calm as stone.

"Say it, Mary," the roaring man said to the sobbing woman. "I want to hear it from your lips."

"I believe your dispute is with me," Uncle Ferris said. "Be a man and leave Mary out of it."

"Hello, Ferris," Mary said. She tried to smile. Her lips were stiff with dried blood and her teeth were pink. She seemed embarrassed by her appearance.

"You shouldn't have hit her," Uncle Ferris said to the man. "It's cowardly in the extreme for a man to hit his wife."

"Say it! God damn your two-timing hide, say it!" the man said to the woman. He yanked her arm for emphasis. Her arm was long and thin and I was afraid it would come loose of its socket if he yanked on it again. She started to fall but the man jerked her back upright. Fresh tears streaked her swollen face and dripped off her chin. Mixed with blood, they were pink as they struck the floor.

"This is him," she whimpered. She looked away from Uncle Ferris, as if ashamed of betraying him. "This is the fella I been seeing."

The man twisted the woman's arm hard before dropping it. She moaned. It was a terrible sound. I imagined it was Laura moaning as the Japanese interrogator pushed bamboo splinters under her fingernails. The big man stepped toward Uncle Ferris taking a pugilist's stance. He was at least six inches taller than Uncle Ferris and was heavy in the chest and belly.

"Why don't you calm down a bit?" Uncle Ferris said.

"You go to hell, you damned home-wrecker!" the man roared.

He took a swing at Uncle Ferris. Uncle Ferris ducked under it and hit the man hard in the stomach. The man barked as the air shot out of his lungs and Uncle Ferris hit the man's stomach again. While the man was bent over gagging and trying to catch his breath, Uncle Ferris went into the kitchen and came back with a cast iron skillet. He brought the skillet hard against the man's head as if he was serving a tennis ball. The man dropped like a stone.

"Oh God," the thin blond woman said. "You killed him!"

"No, it would take more than that to kill a man of his size and thick-headedness," Uncle Ferris said. He lit a cigarette and blew the first puff of smoke toward the ceiling. "I'm sorry it came to this, Mary," he said softly. He put his arm around Mary and kissed her swollen cheek. He took her out to the front porch.

The large man stirred. He got to his feet, fell to one knee, then stood. He had no equilibrium and had to move his feet in quick little steps to keep his reeling weight above them. He seemed to be dancing. "What happened?" he said, touching his head gingerly.

"You fainted," Dave said.

"I must have fainted," the man agreed.

I peeked out the front windows at Uncle Ferris and Mary. I saw him wipe away her tears with his handkerchief. The full moon had risen above the rooftops of Sobrante Park. Its chalky light made Uncle Ferris and Mary seem like stone carvings.

This is how Uncle Ferris and Amelia Earhart must have looked as they stood next to the eight-inch guns of the Portland-class cruiser. I could hear the breathy wail of sea wind behind the confident rumble of his voice. He was telling Amelia that she was safe now, that everything was going to be all right—even though all three of us knew hard times lay ahead.

Svengali

Tank Metkovich, an unemployed electrician, looked like Frankenstein's monster. He was six foot four inches tall and his movements were slow and deliberate. His eyes were hidden in the dark caves under the bony knobs of his forehead, and his voice was deep and slow, each word carefully weighed as if it were an object of value and gravity. Unlike the Frankenstein creature, he had a handsome head of thick chestnut hair, Errol Flynn's hair on Boris Karloff's head, which only made him uglier. I couldn't figure out what my mother saw in him, especially since she was married to Dave Keats, my stepfather.

I confronted her about it. I confronted her about all of them. Tank and my mother were in the kitchen, drinking red wine from water glasses. She was sitting on his knees. She was small-boned and looked like a child listening to stories in her father's lap. Tank bounced her up and down, making her seem even younger.

"Keep your nose out of it, Herbie," she said. "Tank and I are just good friends." She ran her fingers through his heavy brown hair. He stuck his tongue between his teeth and blinked his eyes.

"Your mama's right, Herb," Tank said, patting her thigh. "We're just good pals."

Tank lived in a one-room apartment above a bar called Starkey's Cove on lower Market Street in downtown San Diego. She took me there now and then because she didn't like to travel alone on the downtown bus. I'd wait for her in Starkey's Cove drinking Nehis and playing the jukebox while they did whatever they did up in Tank's apartment. She called it "visiting."

Dave Keats knew about Tank but never said anything. He was a good sport about it. Dave had his own lady friends, women he'd visit on his bread route. He'd been a Good Humor man in Oakland for three years, but now he sold bakery products in the neighborhoods of east, southeast, and south San Diego. Breads and cakes were more profitable products than ice cream bars, especially in winter. I worked with him summers, holidays, and sometimes after school. He paid me in doughnuts, breakfast snails, and cheesecake, depending on what he had most of.

Dave knew all about the people who lived in the neighborhoods along his route. Once, in Kensington, he'd pointed out a little white stucco house. "That's where Marla English lived before she was discovered by Hollywood," he said. He filled a basket with French bread and coffeecake and told me to carry it to the door. "You never know—Marla herself might be home, Ace." He called me Ace when we were in the truck together. I liked being called Ace. In my heroic daydreams I was Ace.

Marla English was the biggest celebrity Hoover High School had produced since Ted Williams starred on the baseball team back in the thirties. I carried the load of bread and cake to her door, scared and eager. I'd seen both of her movies, *The Sea Creature* and *Voodoo Woman*. In *Voodoo Woman* she made grown men with loaded revolvers crawl to her on all fours.

I had instant fantasies about Marla—Marla inviting me inside for refreshments, Marla in a bikini asking me to paint her toenails or Coppertone her shoulders. Marla saying, "You're only four*teen*? I don't be*lieve* you! You look all of *eight*een to me! And what excellent musculature! Are you an athlete? A baseball player? You throw high hard ones and sinkers? I bet you're no slouch in the batter's box, either! Say, you look thirsty, Ace! Would you like to come in for a glass of red wine?"

I said: "Ted Williams hit .406 in 1941 and still puts the big numbers up." It was a stupid thing to say, but nothing else occurred to me. "Ted flew combat missions for the marines during the war, and again in Korea." Nothing but the life story of Ted Williams came to mind. I couldn't stop myself. What did you say to Marla English, movie star?

My hormones had kicked in the year before. I had discovered

masturbation but my uninformed fourteen-year-old imagination couldn't supply the technical details of a fully realized erotic episode with a real woman, much less with Marla English.

Her alabaster arms reach out to me. I crawl to her on all fours. I get up and take her in my arms. A hundred violins start playing "Dancing in the Dark." Marla's conical Wonder Woman breasts impale me. Our hips touch, we kiss. Then . . .

Marla said, "Well then, Ace, what exactly do you intend to do with me?" Her voice was breathy and intimate but also stern. She wanted clear answers. My tongue thickened in its dry grotto. I was mute—a humpbacked clubfoot groaner with the IQ of a housefly. No longer Ace, I started making self-mocking chimpanzee sounds.

No one answered my persistent knocking. I stood on Marla English's porch, hiding my boner behind the breadbasket. I smoothed down my cowlick. I sniffed my armpits. I went back to the truck.

"No one home," I said to Dave.

This was a time in my life when I studied advertisements in magazines such as *Popular Mechanics* with the hope of finding ways to improve myself, physically and mentally. I was attracted to ads such as

I WAS ASHAMED OF MY FACE! UNTIL VISIDERM HELPED MAKE MY SKIN CLEAR UP IN ONE WEEK! —from a letter by E. S. Jordan, Detroit, Michigan

or

LET'S GO PAL! I'LL MAKE YOU INTO AN "ALL AROUND HE-MAN" IN THREE MONTHS! ENJOY MY PROGRESSIVE POWER STRENGTH SECRETS! —George Jowett, "Champion of Champions," "World's Strongest Arms," "World Wrestling and Weight Lifting Champ"

The one I responded to was in the classifieds. A small-print ad for magic tricks.

> Learn magic now! Learn ventriloquism! Learn Hypnotism! And, as a free bonus, Mind reading! Send one dollar to Philo Quackenbus, Big Flats, New York.

I mailed my dollar to Philo Quackenbus, and two weeks later my magic lesson—a stapled-together mimeographed pamphlet—arrived.

The easiest magic trick was mind-reading. The trick needed an accomplice, and I got my best friend, George Haberman, to help me set it up. It involved a deck of cards and a little mumbo jumbo to fool the rubes.

"George here can read your mind," I said to my mother and Tank Metkovich. They were drinking wine again at the kitchen table. Dave was down in San Ysidro, selling bread to Mexicans.

"Go play outside," Mom said.

"Nobody can read *my* mind," Tank said. "My mind is a locked box." He grinned and patted Mom's thigh. I could read his mind without the help of any magic trick. His mind sat naked in his grin, in his black winks, in the way he rolled his shoulders, in the weight he gave to his words. His teeth glistened pink with wine. He was drunk. Mom was sitting on his lap, also grinning pink. He bounced her up and down on his knees. She got giddy. They were a pair of open books.

"Oh yes he can," I said. "George can read anyone's mind."

"Take Georgie to the basement and show him your shortwave radio," Mom said.

My shortwave radio hadn't been working for a year. I wasn't interested in shortwave anymore.

"Okay, okay," Tank said. "Go ahead, Georgie, read my mind."

I went to my room and brought back the card deck. I put it on the table in front of Tank. "Shuffle the cards while George goes into the living room," I said.

Tank took the deck out of its cardboard case and shuffled. He was a fancy shuffler. He made the cards hum. He spread them face-down on the table in a straight row then lifted the end card and the cards rose up and fell into each other like dominoes, this time face up. He went back and forth like this a few times, then picked them up and shuffled again. The cards fluttered in his long fingers like trapped moths.

"Now pick a card, any card," I said, not so sure of myself after Tank's display of expert shuffling.

He picked the ten of spades.

"Okay," I said. "Put it back in the deck and shuffle again and then put the deck into its case so it can't be tampered with. Then we all have to concentrate on sending a mental message to George. Clear everything out of your mind except the ten of spades and the Hindu word, Om."

The "Om" was just part of a planned distraction. I picked up the boxed deck and dropped it on the floor with seeming randomness.

"Okay, George," I yelled. "You can come back now."

George came back in, looking like he was in a trance.

He held his arms out in front of him and walked stiff as a rusted robot. He picked up the deck, pulled the cards out of the case, then spread them on the kitchen table until he found ten of spades.

"Presto mondo finito!" I said.

"He heard us," Tank said. "He was listening."

We did the trick again, this time not mentioning the card aloud. It worked again, just as Learn Magic Now said it would.

"Georgie was spying on us," Tank said.

This time we sent George out of the house, across the street. Tank kept an eye on him through the kitchen window as he shuffled and selected a card. I dropped the deck on the floor. Tank put a paper grocery bag over my head when George came back, just in case I was using some kind of signaling system. Tank refused to intone the Hindu syllable this time. But George once again baffled him by choosing the correct card.

Tank got mad. He looked like he wanted to break something in his hands. He didn't like being fooled by a couple of kids. He grabbed both of us by the front of our shirts and lifted us off the floor so that only our toes touched. "I ought to crack your skulls together," he said. His voice rumbled from his muscled throat. He was serious. His eyes were black with murder. I looked at Mom. The expression on my face said: *See what kind of moron he is?* but she was dull with wine.

The trick, according to the Learn Magic Now pamphlet, needed a staircase with at least thirteen steps—one step for each of the thirteen cards in a suit. How you set the boxed deck down was how the "mind reader" knew what suit to pick. Flap end of the case to the right for hearts, to the left for spades, forward for clubs, backward for diamonds. So if the deck was on the eighth step, flap to the left, the "mind reader" knew the mystery card was the eight of spades. We didn't have a staircase so I used the square tiles of the kitchen floor, counting thirteen tiles from the refrigerator to the stove. Tank, who was no Einstein, missed the gimmick. He wanted to cave our heads in. He wanted to spill our brains on the floor. Mom's last boyfriend was worse, though. He was handsome in an oily way, and even though he stole money and some heirloom jewelry from her, she cried for a month after he found another woman to leech from. At least Tank paid his own way.

The part about hypnotism began with a lesson in self-hypnosis.

> Tired of being afraid of your own shadow? You can root out needless fear by convincing yourself that such fears have no basis in reality!

The only thing that really terrified me was giving book reports. Standing up in front of my freshman English class at Grossmont Union High School to discuss *Silas Marner* or *A Tale of Two Cities* made me turn red and stutter. My mind would go blank. My desperate bowels would make colossal liquid sounds. The other kids would giggle. A girl I liked but who had no idea I liked her rolled her eyes every time I stood up to give a book report. Her eyes said, "Do we *have* to put up with this?"

I stared at a candle flame and told myself, "My fear has no basis in reality, my fear has no basis in reality."

> Become the flame! Let the flame enter your being. Repeat "My fear has no basis in reality" until you no longer hear the words. The words must become a drone in the backdrop of your mind. Your mind is now blank and receptive. The words will become not just words but chain mail in your soul.

I wanted to believe it. I burned six candles down to puddles. The next time I gave a book report I didn't stutter. I felt my face get red, but my bowels didn't betray me. Even so, the girl who didn't know I liked her rolled her eyes. I hated giving the report, but the teacher said I did very well. "A big improvement, Herbert. Don't you think so, class?" The class chirped with false approval.

I practiced self-hypnosis whenever I could, candle or no candle. When I worked on the bread truck with Dave, I'd stare at the trembling speedometer needle and pretend it was a flickering candle.

"My fear has no basis in reality," I said.

Dave said, "Come again, Ace?"

I hadn't realized I'd spoken aloud. "Nothing," I said.

"You said something about fearing reality. Are you afraid of being in this part of town?"

We were in Logan Heights, the black section of town. "No," I said.

"You just stay in the truck. You'll be all right. There's nothing to be afraid of. I won't make you carry the basket."

"It's okay, Dave," I said. "I'm not afraid." I got out of the truck with him.

"You never know what to expect among the Negroes," he said. His quick eyes checked out the neighborhood. "You know what they call us? Ofay. We're the ofay, Herbie. That's pig Latin for foe."

Logan Heights was a poor section of town. The street we were on was unpaved and the houses were ramshackle, but other than that it seemed normal. Women were talking on front porches, kids were playing in the street, a few men stood in their yards, watering their lawns or smoking cigarettes. Dave opened the back doors of the truck and slid out trays of snails, dinner rolls, pies, cheesecakes, and bread.

A narrow black woman in a flower-printed dress and black tennis shoes came up to the truck. She stepped close to Dave, her arms folded against her thin chest. She was pretty, in a hungry sort of way. She didn't say anything while Dave filled a bag with bakery goods. He seemed to know what she wanted. He handed her the bag. She didn't give him any money.

"What about my cigarettes?" she said.

Dave rummaged around in the back of the truck and came up with two cartons of Pall Malls. The woman looked at him.

"Two cartons won't last me," she said. "I told you last time, I need four. You wanting me to cut down, Keats? You looking out for my health?"

"I was a little short," Dave said. He looked sheepish. "I'll make it up, Leonora."

"How come you brought the boy?" the woman said, nodding at me.

"He can wait in the truck," Dave said.

To me, Dave said, "Stay in the truck, Ace. Take a glazed dough-nut if you want, we've got too many. I'll be a few minutes."

Leonora and Dave went into a small, paintless house. When they went in, three small kids came flying out. I waited in the truck, eating glazed doughnuts and practicing self-hypnosis. Dave came out after a half-hour or so.

"Leonora smokes four or five packs a day, if you can believe it," Dave said. "I ever catch you smoking, Ace, I'll make you eat the cigarette backwards." He started the truck and we drove out of Logan Heights.

My mother's friend, Liz Corso, lived down the street from us. Liz Corso was a gambler. Sometimes, when Liz wanted to gamble

in Tijuana, Mom would make me babysit Liz's twin boys, Lance
and Sperry, a pair of five-year-olds. Liz liked to call them the
Katzenjammer Kids, after the kids in the Sunday comic section.
But the Katzenjammer Kids were no match for the Corso twins.
The pranks of the Katzenjammer Kids were angelic next to the
trouble Lance and Sperry routinely caused.

The Corso twins were demons. They were on their way to
becoming felons. You could see this early dedication to crime
in their constantly plotting eyes. It was a safe bet that they'd be
in prison before they reached twenty. Probably for murder. This
future history was all there, in their eyes, in their faces, in the
way they behaved toward people, animals, and things.

I hated to babysit them. Once they poured lighter fluid on their
cat and tried to light it. I stopped them. But they were relentless.
When they tried to fill balloons with gas from the kitchen stove so
that they could make fire bombs, I tied them up with clothesline
rope until Liz got home. "We were playing Cowboys and Indians,"
I explained. The bawling twins told another story, but Liz was in
no mood to deal with the whining snots.

I said, "Lance and Sperry are just tuckered out. They were the
James brothers, see, and I was Wyatt Earp. They'd robbed the
Wells Fargo stage, and I had to get them to Tombstone, I had the
extradition papers, then Doc Holiday came along and . . ."

"Jesus Christ," Liz said. "I don't want to hear any tales of the
Old West." She'd lost heavily that night at the Tijuana dice tables
and was in no mood for nonsense. She was a big woman, over six
feet tall and wide as a door, and she lived on her dead husband's
pension. She fished a dollar out of her purse and gave it to me. *Gee
whiz, a whole dollar for six hours with twin turds from hell*, I wanted
to say but held my tongue.

The next time I had to watch them, I brought "Learn Magic
Now" with me. The twins were crashing through the house looking for things to destroy. I ignored them, but when they started
throwing carving knives at the wall, I decided to use them as a
test audience for some tricks I'd been working on.

A glass of water disappears under a handkerchief!
A doily floats in mid-air, defying Isaac Newton!

I'd only worked these tricks a few times and hadn't ironed out
the flaws, but Lance and Sperry were stupid enough to fall for
them. They asked me to repeat the tricks again and again. They
were dumbstruck each time, unable to spot the gimmicks—the
fake water, the stickum on the glass that held it to the tray
when I whipped the handkerchief clear and held the tray so
that only the bottom showed, or the fine thread sewn into the
"floating" doily that was spooled to a spring-loaded reel hidden
in my pocket. It was a good idea to work in front of a stupid
audience, since the practice gave me the confidence I'd need
when I tried it in front of Mom and Tank, or any other adults
for that matter.

When the twins finally got bored with these repeated
tricks, I said, "And now I am going to show you the mystery of
hypnotism."

It was almost too easy. I tied some string to a tea ball and
swung the tea ball back and forth in front of their eyes. "Follow
the tea-ball," I said. "Keep your eyes on the tea-ball." I told them
they were getting sleepy, very sleepy. Their eyelids drooped in
less than a minute. And then they were asleep, sitting up in their
chairs.

I gave them instructions. "When I count to ten, you will go
into the kitchen and do the dishes. You will use soap. You will get
them very clean. You will be very careful not to break any." Liz
always left the sink full of dirty dishes, expecting me to wash
them. She felt the dollar she gave me justified this. In spite of
my warnings to the twins to be careful, I was surprised at how
gently they dealt with the dishes, considering what evil little
swine they were.

When they finished, I said, "Okay. Now go drown yourselves
in the bathtub."

They marched like little soldiers to the bathroom and filled
the tub.

I panicked. I saw that my power was very great. All at once I was afraid of myself and of the mystic powers I harbored. I yelled, "Whoa! Wake up you stupid shits!"

But they didn't wake up. They took off their clothes and got into the tub.

Then I remembered. I'd told them they couldn't wake up until I said the magic words, "Dario Lodigianni." Dario Lodigianni had been a utility infielder for the Oakland Oaks when we lived up north. He'd since moved up to the majors. His name had always fascinated me. It wasn't just an ordinary name; it was an incantation. A few years earlier, in Oakland, my friends and I would skip along the sidewalks chanting, "Dario Lodigianni, Dario Lodigianni," as if the syllables had the power to effect wonderful changes in our lives.

"Dario Lodigianni!" I yelled, and the twins, who were about to do the world a favor by drowning themselves, snapped awake.

"Hey!" Sperry yelled, surprised to find himself in the bathtub. "*You* don't give us our bath! Our *mom* does that!"

I counted backwards from ten and said, "You are sleepy, you are very sleepy!" and they went slack in the water. I drained the tub and left them sleeping there, then read magazines in the living room until Liz got home.

She'd won big at her dice table. She gave me two dollars. When she saw how nicely the dishes had been washed and stacked, she gave me another fifty cents.

"You're a good kid," she said. She gave me a hug, smothering me in the soft ottomans of her breasts.

She went into the kitchen and poured herself a glass of beer. "You want some beer, Herbie?" she said. "You're big enough now for a glass of beer now and then, right?"

She filled a glass halfway with Lucky Lager and handed it to me. She opened her purse and spread her money on the table, a mass of crumpled tens and twenties. "I made it all on pass-line bets," she said, "after I sevened on two straight come-out rolls. Life is funny that way."

I sipped my beer, acting as if I understood.

"It's all blind luck, kiddo," she said. "Fair has nothing to do with it. Once you get that through your head, you'll be all right. You want fair, play baseball."

She saw my confusion. "I'm talking about life, Herbie. Save yourself some disappointment. Don't expect it to be fair and square. What you want is luck."

I finished my beer then told her I had to use the bathroom. In the bathroom I hissed, "Dario Lodigianni!" and turned the water back on. "Your Mom's back," I said. She'll come give you your baths in a minute."

The twins were bewildered for a second or two, then looked around for something to wreck.

When I got "The Disappearing Glass" down pat I tried it on Mom and Tank. I brought in the tray with the glass of water on it. Half the water was real, half-fake. I drank the real water. When I put the glass back on the tray—in the center where the stickum was—it looked as if it was still half full. Then I covered the glass with a napkin, said the magic words, "Presto mondo finito!," and simultaneously whipped the napkin away and dropped the tray so that they saw only the bottom of it. No glass or spilled water in sight.

I couldn't help grinning when Tank's jaw dropped. Mom clapped her hands. Tank recovered quickly and sneered. "Another cheap trick," he said. "You'd better straighten the boy out," he said to Mom, "otherwise you're going to have a carny clip-artist on your hands before long, useless as nipples on a boar."

"Oh, he's just having some fun, Tank," Mom said.

"Tank's mad because he can't figure it out," I said to her. It was a chancy thing to say, in view of Tank's temper.

Tank stood up. He stood in front of the kitchen window and the kitchen darkened. He came at me. I stepped back. He grabbed the tray out of my hand and turned it over. He ripped the glass, half-full with the fake water, off the stickum that held it to the tray. He tossed the glass to Mom.

"See? Cheap tricks," he said. "You let the boy keep this up, he's going to turn out rotten. He's going to think he can get what he wants by pulling tricks."

To me, he said, "Let me tell you something, Herbie. It doesn't work that way. The trickster winds up tricking only himself."

"Ah so," I said, sagely.

He raised his hand as if to slap me. I ducked. But he didn't follow through. I looked at Mom, but she had brought her cup of wine to her lips, her mind already elsewhere.

Mom and I took the bus downtown. She was going to visit Tank. I'd been working on a complicated mind-reading trick. It was a great trick, and I'd wanted to try it on George Haberman that morning but Mom had other plans.

We got off at Horton Plaza then walked over to Market Street. She was dressed up—white blouse, pleated blue skirt, white open-toed sandals, toenails painted fire engine red. She was thirty-six years old but she looked barely thirty. Men whistled at her. A group of idlers on lower Market street howled like starved dogs. One of them yelled, "Ditch the punk, hot-lips, I'll make you happy!" She clutched my arm and smirked at them.

"Bums," she said. "Useless no-goods."

It was still morning and Starkey's Cove was almost empty. She gave me a handful of nickels and dimes and went upstairs to Tank's apartment.

I ordered a strawberry Nehi and put a nickel in the jukebox. Hoagy Carmichael came on, singing "Stardust."

Out of the corner of my eye I saw a man at the end of the bar staring at me. He picked up his drink and moved to the stool next to mine.

"That's my next-to-favorite song," he said. "You want to know my favorite?"

I didn't say anything.

"'Cry,'" he said. "Johnny Ray singing 'Cry' rips me up every time."

I didn't like Johnny Ray. He overdid it. He wore hearing aids that you could see, which didn't strike me as being very cool. I saw him once on TV. He tore off his shirt and fell to his knees as he sang his big hit, "Cry." Teenaged girls in the audience screamed and fainted.

"They call me Sailor," the man said. "What do they call you, kid?"

"Herb," I said.

"I spent twenty-five years in the Merchant Marines," he said. "Torpedoed twice off the Solomons. What're you drinking, Herb?"

"Soda," I said.

"You want a whiskey sour? I'm drinking whiskey sours. I'll buy you one."

He ordered a whiskey sour and the bartender made one and brought it over to me. Maybe the bartender thought I was twenty-one. Maybe he didn't care. I was tall for my age, at five foot eight. In the dark bar I might have been twenty-one.

"You're part Chickasaw, am I right?" Sailor said.

I shook my head.

"You look like a Chickasaw girlfriend of mine, Dilly McGovern. You're not a McGovern from Tulsa, by any chance? You got that same black hair, the short forehead. You got the big Chickasaw nose. I can tell that Chickasaw nose anywhere."

"I'm half Italian," I said. "And half Finn."

"That's too bad," he said. "Dilly McGovern. She was hot, if you get what I mean." He opened his mouth and fluttered his tongue at me. "Drink up, Herb."

I sipped the whiskey sour. It tasted like sweet puke.

He slid his stool closer to mine and put his hand on my knee. He was a short, solid, muscular man. He was wearing a flowered Hawaiian shirt with the sleeves rolled up to the shoulders. His thick arms were blue with tattoos. He made the biceps twitch.

"I'm here with my Mom," I said.

He looked around the bar. "Nobody here, Herb, but you, me, and Gordon Pastelli, the barkeep."

"She'll be back in a minute," I said.

"You're no mama's boy," he said. "I can see that. You're all man, Herb." His hand moved up my thigh. "You got a man-size thing here for old Sailor, don't you Herb?" He fluttered his tongue again and squeezed my thigh.

I looked at Gordon Pastelli, the barkeep. He was busy reading his newspaper.

"You feel like doing old Sailor a small favor, Herb?" He squeezed my thigh harder. I felt his warm breath on my neck.

"I don't think so," I said.

"Don't be stingy with it, Herb."

I scooped up my dimes and nickels and broke away from his grip.

"I'll wait right here for you, honey," Sailor said.

I went up the staircase at the back of the bar. The stairs ended at a short hallway lit by a single globe that gave off about as much light as a candle. There were three doors along the hallway. I tried all of them. They were all locked. I knocked hard on the three doors until I heard Tank say, "Get the hell away from that door."

"Mom, it's me," I said. "I'm going home."

I heard movement. Bedsprings groaned, bare feet scraped the floor. The door opened a crack. Mom was in her underwear. "What's wrong?" she said.

I didn't want to tell her what was wrong. A lot was wrong. "I'm going home," I said. "You can ride the bus by yourself. Or you can have him go with you."

"Tank can't go with me. He has a job interview in a couple of hours. What's wrong with you, Herbie?"

"I'll see you at home," I said.

"You wait for your mother downstairs, goddamnit," Tank said.

"Go to hell, Tank," I said. He came to the door wrapped in a sheet, his face twisted with anger. "The villagers are coming with torches," I said.

He thought about that for a few seconds. Then came at me.

I ran down the stairs three at a time and shot out into the sunlit street. Tank didn't follow me. Neither did Sailor.

I walked to Horton Plaza and waited for the El Cajon Boulevard bus. It was a beautiful day, the air so clear all the downtown buildings stood out in sharp focus against the cloudless sky.

A bus pulled up. It was the Mission Beach bus. I needed to go east not west, but I got on it anyway. It was almost empty. It was early May, too early in the year for beachgoers.

I took a seat across from a man who looked pathetic enough to have been my mother's next boyfriend. He was balding but probably only about thirty-five. He wore a tan suit a size too big for him. His wingtip shoes were badly scuffed. He was reading the want ads in the *San Diego Union Tribune*.

I had the trick I was going to try on George Haberman with me. "Think of a card," I said to him.

He looked up from his newspaper. "Say what?"

"Think of a card, any card. Go ahead."

"I'm not gambling with you," he said.

"Not for money. For fun. Go ahead, name any card."

"Five of hearts," he said, then went back to the want ads.

I pulled a sealed envelope out of my pocket and tapped it against his newspaper. I waved it in front of his eyes, hypnotically. "Take it," I said.

He lowered the paper. He snatched the envelope out of my hand.

"Aren't you going to open it?" I said.

"Maybe I will, Svengali, but not now."

I got off the bus at Mission Boulevard and Pacific Beach Drive, then walked to the amusement park on the pier. The salt breeze coming off the ocean was sharp with a clean, nostril-pinching smell.

I walked to the end of the pier. Deep swells from some far away storm broke tremendously into the pilings. I raised my arms to the wind and felt the wind lift me. I closed my eyes, imagined transforming myself into a gull, and for a moment I *was* a gull.

I thought of the guy on the bus, how he would open the sealed envelope and find his card—*the five of hearts!*—and be dumbstruck. He'd regret he didn't open it when I could have explained the trick to him.

I wouldn't have explained it, of course. I'd let it gnaw at him. I'd let him stay in the dark forever. He was the kind of man who would always be in the dark forever.

"Go to hell," I said to him.

"Presto mondo finito," I said to the wind.

Backsliders

Herbie's stepfather, Dave Keats, had a
B A from Colgate and an M A from Columbia and enough natural
charm and personal magnetism to have been the public relations
director for the pro-Nazi German-American Bund when the war
against Germany was raging, but all he wanted to do was peddle
bakery goods from a panel truck.

During his senior year in high school, Herbie worked evenings
and weekends at a carwash. Dave Keats was disappointed. He
thought Herbie was capable of better things, just as Herbie believed
Dave was capable of better things. They were not close and tended
to regard each other with quiet dismay.

What's wrong with the boy? Dave's expression seemed to say.

What's wrong with Dave? Herbie's expression seemed to reply.

Herbie's mother had run off with Baldemar Salcedo Duarte, a
colonel in the Mexican army, and Herbie and Dave were living
like bachelors in their small east San Diego house.

Dave was depressed, but not so deeply that he could not seek
out the comfort of women. Dave was good-looking in a wounded,
soulful way. Certain women found this quality attractive.

Dave's women would come and go. Some would stay overnight,
some would stay for three or four days. Some melancholy types
found a kindred spirit in Dave; others acted like battlefield nurses,
taking over the cooking, cleaning, and grocery shopping with
unflagging cheerfulness.

One of the women, one whom Herbie liked more than he should
have, didn't fit either pattern. Her name was Kelli Opalka. She
was dark and petite and liked to stay up late and argue politics.
Kelli called herself a "free thinker" and took a radical stance on

nearly everything. She once quoted the ancient Greek philosopher Democritus: "Nothing exists except atoms and empty space, everything else is opinion."

"I said to heck with the church when I was fourteen," she'd told Herbie one morning. Kelli had made omelets stuffed with avocados, cheese, and onions, and they were enjoying their second cup of coffee. It was a fine Sunday morning in April and Herbie was getting ready to go to work at the Aztec Carwash, which opened at noon that day out of respect for its clientele, who went to morning church services.

"I told my mom I couldn't swallow that baloney about transubstantiation," Kelli said.

Herbie looked blank. He'd fallen in love with Kelli, who was only seven years older than he was. He didn't like to see Dave and Kelli hold hands or kiss, and the thought of them sleeping in the same bed gave him indigestion. On the bright side, Kelli didn't seem all that taken with Dave. Her freethinking ways ruled out bourgeois romantic attachments. "Romantic love is just a convenient delusion to domesticate women," she'd said. "It's delusional for men, too. Once they saddle themselves with family, they have to hold some dull job for the rest of their lives to support it. The capitalists need drones, so figure it out, Herbie. Romantic love is a deliberate product of capitalism. The thrill evaporates soon as babies and budgets come into the picture."

"Transubstantiation," Herbie said, managing to keep the syllables from separating into five or six distinct sound groups.

"You know," Kelli said. "Where the wine the priest drinks becomes Christ's blood and the communion wafer becomes his flesh. I told my mom that Eucharist stuff was creepy and no one with half a brain could believe it. She crossed herself so many times she got tennis elbow."

Herbie agreed that the idea was somewhat creepy. He wondered how anyone could believe such implausible stuff. Maybe there was more to it than that. People weren't completely stupid. There had to be good reasons why they believed, century after century, in the impossible.

"But it wasn't just that," Kelli said. "I could probably buy into that pagan voodoo cannibal stuff on some kind of symbolic, emotional level. You know, you eat the god to become more like the god. But I junked all of it—the idea of sin, grace, redemption, and resurrection. Especially resurrection. When I'm dead, Herbie, I expect to stay dead."

Dave lowered the newspaper which had been screening him from the conversation. "Kelli's been to college," he explained. "She's a communist."

Kelli's ideas interested Herbie. He'd never thought much about such things, and nothing like them ever came up in his civics or social studies classes at Grossmont Union High School. His teachers shied away from controversial subjects. College professors were having to sign loyalty oaths to keep their jobs, and it was only a matter of time before they'd require high school teachers to do the same. Herbie's teachers were comfortable only with the airbrushed versions of Life in America as illustrated in textbooks.

Herbie once asked a teacher about the Chicago race riots of 1919, something he'd heard about from Dave, who had taken his master's degree in history. The teacher flew into a skittish rage. "Commie propaganda!" he said. "The commies want us to think it meant something terrible about our beloved country. It didn't mean anything. It was just hooligans, white and colored, letting off steam. Nothing more. But to the commies, everything bad that happens in the USA is evidence of how decadent we are."

Herbie knew that their neighbor, Amedeo Garibaldi, was a communist. The church, with the approval of Mussolini's fascists, had confiscated Amedeo's land in Abruzzi, in southern Italy, and Amedeo immediately embraced social revolution. He was imprisoned for a while in Italy. When he was released he emigrated to the United States, where his politics were also suspect and becoming punishable.

Now and then black Fords with whip antennas attached to their rear bumpers would park in front of the Garibaldi house. Men in gray suits and hats sat in the cars, speaking softly into hand-held microphones. "FBI agents," Dave called them. "Looking for saboteurs." Amedeo Garibaldi was an unlikely saboteur. He was a stone mason, as were most of his communist friends.

"Communists are required to be atheists," Dave said to Herbie. "Someone hears you accidentally murmur a prayer, you lose your party card."

"Go ahead, make fun of me," Kelli said. "But religion's the yoke that keeps the drones pulling together in a straight line. It's the tool of the capitalists. You see a capitalist in church, you know the son of a bitch is snickering behind his sleeve at all the mumbling morons."

Herbie's mother had said much the same thing. She wasn't a communist, but she didn't think much of religion or of capitalists. Her father had been killed in a mine accident in Northern Michigan and the British-owned company gave Herbie's grandmother fifty-six dollars a month in compensation for six years and nothing more after that. Herbie's Finnish grandmother, Elma Luoma—called "Aiti" by her kids and grandkids—had to take in washing to get by. Her kids, those who were old enough, dropped out of school to take whatever odd jobs they could find. Herbie's mother was the oldest of Grandma Aiti's six children. She became a housekeeper at sixteen, a job she ran away from after the man of the house, a pious Lutheran doctor with five kids, put his hand up her dress.

She ran all the way to New York, where she fell in love with and married an Italian gangster. The gangster, Niccolo Fontana, was Herbie's father. Herbie's mother left Niccolo a month after Herbie was born. She'd tried to get Niccolo to go back to Michigan with her. She wanted him to take an honest job in the British-owned iron ore mines of Negaunee. But Niccolo's lifestyle was not suited to manual labor. He slept until noon every day; had a manicure once a week; and dressed in elegant, tailor-made suits, silk ties, and expensive Italian shoes. His Lower East Side childhood had been populated by his personal heroes—Lucky Luciano, Albert Anastasia, Frank Costello, Meyer Lansky, and Benny Siegel. Niccolo thought Manhattan was the hub of the universe. He told

Herbie's mother that she was crazy to think he'd leave New York for a crummy job in the Michigan wilderness. Herbie's other grandmother, Luisa Fontana, had a fit. "My Nicky no work in no *inglese* mine!" she'd said, crossing herself to ward off such a grim eventuality.

"Only suckers break their backs for a living," Niccolo told Herbie's mother. The world was full of suckers, but Niccolo Fontana was not one of them and never would be. He showed her his hands. "You will never see a callus on these hands," he'd said proudly. Soft hands with trimmed and buffed nails were signs of nobility and the intelligent management of one's life.

And that was the end of the impossible marriage. After Niccolo, Herbie's mother went with a series of men—a Jewish mobster, an Idaho gold prospector, a semipro football player, an out-of-work actor, a Greek maitre d', a married podiatrist—winding up at the close of World War II with the overeducated but ambitionless Dave Keats.

She stayed faithful to Dave for a few years, then took up her roving ways again, this time with Colonel Baldemar Salcedo Duarte, commander of a reserve artillery brigade of the Mexican army, and who, at the age of fourteen, fought with Pancho Villa in the Revolution of 1910.

They'd been on an outing in Baja and had stopped for drinks at an Ensenada cantina. Herbie's mother and Dave had a spat and she walked over to Baldemar Salcedo Duarte's table with the sexual confidence and directness of a vamp.

The colonel was dining alone and had been casting cautious glances at her. Herbie's mother was in her late thirties and movie-star beautiful. Like many Scandinavian women, she wouldn't show her age until she was in her sixties. At thirty-eight she could pass for twenty-five. The colonel was smitten. They left the cantina together and disappeared into the Baja California night leaving Dave alone at the bar sipping margaritas.

"You keep talking like that, Kelli," Dave said, "and Senator McCarthy is going to call you before Congress to answer some hard questions."

"I wish the son of bitch would!" Kelli said. "I'd tell *him* a thing or two!"

"And get yourself charged with sedition under the Smith Act. You'll spend a few years in jail making license plates for the proletariat."

Herbie excused himself and put on his work clothes. He had ten minutes to get down to the Aztec Carwash, which was only five blocks away. Herbie liked working at the carwash. It was easy work and he liked his pit-partner, Otis Cooper.

Otis was there when Herbie arrived. "You cuttin it close, young-blood," he said.

"The boss isn't here yet," Herbie said.

"That's why he the boss," Otis said.

Only a few cars came in that morning. The boss, Wendell Pritchett, had called to say he wouldn't come in until closing time, when he'd take the day's receipts home with him.

Herbie and Otis cleaned wheels and hubcaps and whatever dirt they could blast out from under the fenders while two other guys soaped the car. They worked from a pit alongside the cars just before the cars were pulled through the automatic high-pressure spray area by a bumper hook. In the pit, they looked amputated at the hips—legless men, three feet tall. They did seven cars right away, then business died down. Otis and Herbie climbed out of the pit and sat in a spot in the carwash parking lot that was shaded by half a dozen scrawny eucalyptus trees. Otis pulled a slim bottle from his pocket. He offered it to Herbie.

Herbie didn't like muscatel, or any wine for that matter, and started to refuse, but he didn't want to give offense and so accepted the bottle. It was a fortified muscatel and burned going down. He gave the bottle back to Otis, careful not to make a face. Otis took a long, steady drink, his lean throat working. They passed the bottle back and forth.

"Be on you, next time," Otis said.

Otis was a tall, skinny man who, as far as Herbie knew, never ate anything. He didn't bring food to the carwash with him, even

on busy Saturdays when they worked a full eight hours. But he
always had a flask-shaped bottle of muscatel in his pocket.

It didn't take much for Herbie to get drunk. When the next car
turned into the Aztec Carwash, Otis had to pull him upright. "Get
on it, youngblood. We got to make that Buick look like it belong
in the showroom."

After the Buick, business slowed once more to a standstill.
Herbie and Otis sat in the eucalyptus shade again. The two oth-
ers working that day were a pair of football players from Herbert
Hoover High School. They didn't associate with Herbie and Otis.
They sat by themselves admiring their biceps.

Otis was a veteran of the Korean War. He'd been at the Inchon
landing, General MacArthur's brilliant gambit that turned the
tide against the North Koreans until the Chinese army crossed
the Yalu River. Otis once showed Herbie his bayonet wound, a
raised lightning-bolt scar on his abdomen. He showed Herbie his
medals, a handful of them, which he kept in his pants pocket. One
was a Purple Heart. Herbie couldn't imagine taking a bayonet in
the stomach and held Otis in awe. He felt privileged that Otis
would share his war experience.

But Otis puzzled Herbie. Herbie wanted to ask: Otis, you're
a war hero. How come you're working in this crummy carwash?
How come you stay half-drunk most of the time? But he knew
it wasn't his place to ask such questions. Half-drunk himself, he
allowed one flippant remark to escape his lips: "My stepfather,
Dave? He doesn't have a lick of ambition either."

Otis looked at Herbie. His eyes were wretched. The whites
looked like red bleeding meat, the dark centers lightless. "*Either*,
huh?" he said, then chuckled. "You thinkin you a world-beater?
You a fly cat goin to own the bank? Listen up chump—they take
your little white balls before *that* happen. They make you kiss
they pink ofay ass an make you believe you kissin Rita Hayworth.
When you figure out it *aint* Rita Hayworth, it be too late."

Herbie thought about that. Was that why Dave was content
driving a bread truck? Because he'd figured out the game was
fixed and decided not to play? But Dave had all the advantages

of a good education, intelligence, and good looks. He could at least have been a high school teacher or a department manager at Macy's.

"I don't get it," Herbie said, half to himself.

Otis had lost interest in the conversation. He yawned, took a sip of his muscatel. He was only in his mid-twenties but he looked like he was dying of old age.

"What's it all about, Otis?" Herbie asked in earnest. This earnestness about the larger questions was a tendency he'd never outgrow.

Herbie didn't expect an answer, but Otis looked at him for a long moment and said, "Aint *about* nothin."

"What's that supposed to mean?"

"What it say. You lookin at it straight on but you don't see shit." Otis chuckled something up from his lungs and spit it out.

"Things are supposed to make sense," Herbie said.

"Say *who*? They don't have to make a lick a sense. You lookin for what *aint*, youngblood."

Herbie took his time walking home that evening. The moon was up, a chalky disk in the deepening blue. He heard music that seemed to be coming from the moon, a manic tune that made his feet move faster. He felt an urge to skip along to the hard rhythms. He realized, then, that the music was coming from somewhere on his street. As he approached his house, the music took a shape he recognized.

The source of the music was the Garibaldi back yard. Amedeo was having a party for some of his communist friends, all Italians. An FBI car was parked in front of the Garibaldi house.

Amedeo's friends were all good musicians. There were guitars, mandolins, an accordion, and a clarinet. They were playing songs from southern Italy—tarantellas, love ballads, plaintive laments—songs that might have been a thousand years old.

Herbie stood in the alley between his house and the Garibaldi house, concealed by a hedge. He listened to the music, which went from mournful to wildly happy to sentimental. When they finished a piece, the men would talk loudly in Italian, and they would laugh and drink Amedeo's homemade red wine, then strike up another tune.

The darkening air was rich with night-blooming jasmine, the aromas of food coming from Mrs. Garibaldi's kitchen, and the uproar of Amedeo's friends laughing and shouting and retuning their instruments. The FBI agents rolled down the windows of the their black Fords to let the happy noise in, as if they longed to relax their isolated vigil and take part in the festivities.

Herbie sat down on the low stone wall Amedeo had built on the property line. The stones still held the day's warmth. Herbie ran his moonlit hands over the moonlit stones as if the stones were alive and sensitive to his touch. The sensation spread to the fragrant night air, to the small houses of his neighborhood, to the moon itself—all of it was alive and connected and Herbie felt cemented, like a stone, to the center of it. And it came to him that everything was stuck in a permanent mortar. Nothing in it needed to be changed, nothing in it needed to be resurrected. It was an unexpected thought, too fragile and intoxicating to examine closely. It infected him with a wildness that wanted an outlet.

The music started up again, a tarantella that shook the air with its wild rhythm. Herbie stood up and watched his feet kicking pebbles around as they tried to match the speed and joy of the crazed dance. He wanted to sing but the notes were flying past him too fast to be caught.

Someone standing next to him said, "What's your role in this, son?"

A thickset man in a double-breasted suit stepped into the moonlight from the shadows where he had been standing.

"Role?" Herbie said.

The G-man nodded toward the Garibaldi house. His wide face held a narrow smile. He put his hand on Herbie's shoulder and squeezed it in a familiar way. "You see anything we should know about, you give us a call, okay?" He handed Herbie a business card, then gave Herbie's shoulder a hearty jostle.

Herbie studied the card.

"You *do* understand what I'm saying, son?" the G-man said.

"I think so, sir," Herbie said.

The man jostled his shoulder again and went back to his black Ford. Herbie went into the house. Dave and Kelli were watching TV in the living room. Before joining them, Herbie tore the G-man's card in half and dropped it into the kitchen garbage.

A Hot Day in January

Herbie Fontana tried college but it didn't take. He couldn't concentrate; he couldn't apply himself. High school required attendance, not conscious effort. College demanded both, and Herbie couldn't make the adjustment.

His life had no direction. The courses he enrolled in stimulated his interest when he read their descriptions in the college catalogue, but after he'd sat through a few uninspired lectures his interest flagged. He flunked everything he signed up for. Which meant he'd lose his 2-S deferment. He'd be reclassified 1-A, and then the army would draft him. College was a safe haven from the draft whether your life had direction or not—provided you passed your courses.

Even though there was no danger in being a soldier—the Korean War was at a standstill—Herbie didn't like the idea of slogging through infantry training. And so he joined the Air Force, a branch of the service that had some glamour. He liked the blue uniforms, the upside-down stripes enlisted men wore, like the British army, and he liked the idea of being a crewmember of a strategic bomber. Maybe he'd find direction in life by being a gunnery sergeant on a B-36, or—if he could qualify for officer candidate school—navigator, bombardier, even *pilot*.

The recruiting sergeant said all these things were definitely possible, even likely. "Intelligent young men with some college training such as yourself," he said, "are in high demand. There's a crying need for pilots and navigators and you look like sure-fire officer material." He said all this with a straight face and Herbie signed the enlistment papers eagerly and with high hopes.

But he failed to qualify for flight training or officer candidate school. He was nearsighted; had poor coordination, average reflexes, and sub-par math skills; and his leadership potential was next to nonexistent. He was trained instead as a radar operator—a "scope dope"—and sent to a remote early warning squadron in the unglamorous high plains of Northern Montana, six miles from the Canadian border and forty miles north of Havre, the nearest American town.

Life at the radar station was dull. Out of desperation, Herbie enrolled in a United States Armed Forces Institute correspondence course called Intermediate Writing. Herbie thought this might give him the direction in life he was looking for. Maybe he could be a professional writer after he got out of the Air Force. Professional writers made a lot of money and were their own bosses. You didn't have to have perfect coordination, eagle-eye vision, math skills, or leadership potential to be a professional writer. All you had to do was write . . . *professionally.*

Writing professionally seemed like the best possible way to live your life. He didn't have any idea what he'd write about but believed that he'd find his subject matter later. *They laughed at me until I scored the winning touchdown* was Herbie's notion of the type of story he'd like to become famous for—unlikely heroes who save the day at the eleventh hour.

The USAFI materials arrived a few weeks after he sent for them. There was a textbook and a lesson plan. The first assignment was simple enough:

> Describe, in one hundred words or less, your immediate surroundings. Hint: do not use abstract nouns. Limit your use of adjectives and adjectival phrases. Do not opinionate. In short, be direct and be concrete. Make your subject *visible* to the hypothetical reader.

"I can do that standing on my head," Herbie told himself, even though he wasn't sure what an abstract noun was.

Herbie was in the barracks, lying on his bunk, pencil and notebook in hand. He put his USAFI textbook aside and studied Sidney

Osmand, who was lying in the bunk opposite his. Sidney was reading *Nugget*, the men's magazine, and manipulating his genitals through the fabric of his cotton fatigues. He made wincing moans as he studied the full-page color photos of nude women.

Sidney Osmand was the most shameless person Herbie had ever met. He'd seen him walking naked from the showers sporting an erection. He seemed completely indifferent to the social pressures that made normal people self-conscious. Herbie thought: *But I can't get a hundred words out of Osmand playing with himself in front of everybody while looking at pictures of naked girls.*

Herbie put his notebook and pencil away. He got into his parka and walked through the squadron area toward the mess hall. It was a bleak Sunday in January. The wind in this flatland was constant and strong. It was so cold it burned as it struck his skin. It hummed in the overhead power lines. Some power lines were shorter or had more slack than others, and as the wind passed over them the different pitches they produced harmonized in a nonstop mournful wail.

Herbie passed by the flagpole in front of the squadron administration building. In the icy gale, the frozen ropes that raised and lowered the flag snapped against the tall steel pole. The hollow pings they made were the only sounds other than the grieving moans of the power lines. Together, these were the loneliest sounds Herbie had ever heard. They were the sound track for a movie called *The Exile of Herbie Fontana*. It filled him with self-pity. It made him resentful, even fearful. He tried to mute the sounds by tightening the strings of his parka hood, but to no avail.

Herbie in exile had frequent attacks of depression. He had one now. *Why me?* he asked. *Why this?* Why hadn't he been stationed with a strategic bomb group in England or West Germany or Turkey? What had he done to deserve this fate? How could he describe anything in this godforsaken place where there was nothing at all to describe except the empty desolate landscape of boredom?

He looked up into the hard blue sky. Ice crystals gleamed like suspended diamonds. The winter sun was low and weak, a gray button in the fabric of this northern sky. Back home in California the sun would be higher and you could feel its heat through your tee shirt. On a good day you could go to the beach and get a sunburn even though it was winter.

Herbie felt he'd put himself in the hands of sinister forces and that he'd been unjustly banished from the real world. He was afraid this might turn out to be the trend of things to come. It was forty below zero and his nostril hairs stiffened into hundreds of tiny icicles with each breath he took. His eyes burned and the tears the wind drew from them froze on his cheeks.

He went into the warm mess hall. There were still some omelets left over from breakfast. Food was a consolation. He'd gained ten pounds the few months he'd been at the radar station. He asked the cook for a cheese and mushroom omelet. The cook gave him two. "Eat up, Fontana," the cook said. "Otherwise I'm tossing this shit out." He shoveled two omelets on Herbie's plate along with half a dozen hard strips of dry bacon and a stack of cold toast. The cook, a gray-haired corporal, was dirty as a motor pool mechanic. His hands were stained and his fingernails were black. His shirt was crusty with dried sauces and soups and bits of solid food. He'd been reprimanded a number of times by the first sergeant. For a few days after each reprimand the old corporal kept himself clean, but then he gradually reverted to his slovenly ways. He was lazy and stupid and had a mean streak. In civilian life he'd be unemployable.

The mess hall was empty except for a couple of bitter old lifers, Sergeants Doberman and Moomaw. Doberman was in charge of the motor pool and Moomaw was the supply sergeant. Both men were working off their hangovers. Sergeant Doberman looked at Herbie, a sneer of utter disgust on his prematurely aged face. Doberman had enlisted in the army before World War II and drove a supply truck in Europe after the D-Day invasion. He was now finishing his military career at this radar station in the middle of nowhere. He was a small, dried-up man with a keen eye for faults in younger men of lesser rank. He looked like a wizened alcoholic elf playing soldier with no future beyond his next drink.

The hat Sergeant Doberman wore added to this effect. It was a nonregulation hat, a replica of a "trooper" hat worn by the men of George Armstrong Custer's doomed 7th cavalry. Custer's last stand was only eighty years in the past and Sergeant Doberman sometimes seemed to Herbie like a ghost from the Little Big Horn battlefield, which was only a few hours' drive away.

The hat Doberman wore was black with a wide stiff brim. It had a tall, meticulously dented crown. The gold acorn band around the base of the crown identified the wearer as an officer. Doberman wasn't an officer and had never been a member of any Cavalry regiment but the CO allowed him to wear the nonreg hat for no reason Herbie could fathom. Under the tall trooper hat Doberman seemed even smaller than he was, yet he strutted about the squadron area glowering like a veteran Indian fighter—a pint-size John Wayne, defender of Fort Apache.

Herbie sat at a table on the opposite side of the mess hall from the two old sergeants. They were sour men with a lot of free time on their hands. They shot ugly glances at Herbie every now and then, probably complaining about the quality of recruit the Air Force was attracting these days. Once, after a night of drinking in the NCO club, Doberman threatened Herbie. "I'm going to give you a good ass-kicking some day, Fontana," Doberman had said. He was wearing his trooper hat tipped low on his forehead and cocked to one side.

Herbie wasn't afraid of Doberman himself—the old rummy couldn't have punched his way through a sheet of wet Kleenex— but backing Doberman's threat were a pair of no-neck thugs, Orville Stonecipher and Raymond Klecko, diesel mechanics who worked for him in the motor pool. Stonecipher and Klecko were known to have carried out Doberman's vendettas in the past. "Why me?" Herbie had asked, and Sergeant Doberman punched a finger into Herbie's chest and said, "Because you're a candy-ass, Fontana, who's too fucking dumb to know you never ask 'Why me?'"

"Sergeant Doberman is a prick," Herbie wrote. "He's mean as an old dog that's been kicked every day of its life. Not a Doberman pinscher, though he acts like he has to live up to his attack-dog name, but more like a Pekinese or Chihuahua, or maybe a toy bull. He's a peanut-brain moron, a midget goon, a . . ."

Herbie crossed all that out, thinking it was more opinion than description. It was sort of direct, but it was more of cartoon than a realistic portrayal. Herbie visualized a nasty little dog wearing a trooper hat cocked at a rakish angle. But that sort of description didn't have *style*. It didn't create an useful image of Sergeant Doberman in the eyes of the hypothetical reader. "One must always keep the hypothetical reader in mind," his USAFI textbook insisted.

He tried again: "Sgt. D's arms are thin as twigs. When he lifts his cup he sloshes coffee over the rim because his hands shake all the time due to the ever-present hangover. If you find yourself in range of Sgt. D's breath you will be exposed to the dire smell of death at which point you will abruptly turn away from him."

Herbie looked at what he'd written. He didn't like it very much, except for part of the last sentence. "The dire smell of death" had something. It had the feel of professionalism. It had *style*. Ernest Hemingway could have written it.

Herbie was not on duty, but he walked to the operations blockhouse anyway. All six scopes were manned by airmen, some of whom he'd trained with at Keesler Air Force Base in Biloxi, Mississippi. Herbie stood behind Airman Clay Ledoux in the gloom of the blockhouse. Ledoux, a tall lanky boy from Baton Rouge, was half asleep, hypnotized by the relentless sweep of the radar scope's trace that lit up targets as far away as 250 miles. But there were no targets, just the endless turning of the bar of yellow-green light that was putting Airman Ledoux to sleep. The Russians weren't coming. Not today, anyway.

Ledoux stood up. He grabbed Herbie around the neck and threw him down to the floor. "I caint stop myself from fallin to sleep, Fontana," he said. "Wrassle me so's I can wake up some."

Herbie didn't want to wrestle Ledoux but there was no choice. Ledoux was farmboy-strong and Herbie couldn't free himself of his headlock. He punched Ledoux in the ribs. Ledoux didn't let go. He put a counter headlock on Ledoux. Locked together they rolled on the floor.

The shift boss, Lieutenant Padilla, said, "Knock it off, you idiots."

"I'm awake now, Lieutenant," Ledoux said, grinning.

"Really?" Lieutenant Padilla said. "How do you know the difference?" Lieutenant Padilla who was from El Paso, Texas, and had played middle linebacker for New Mexico State University, went back to reading the *Great Falls Tribune* by the dim alligator light at his console.

The blockhouse was dark as a closet, the only illumination coming from the radarscopes and a few dim lights scattered here and there. There was a penny-a-point pinochle game going on the Movements and Identification table on the back dais of the blockhouse. The M & I table was an illuminated map half as big as a pool table. All the airlanes that commercial flights were required to use were represented on this map. Anything flying outside an airlane was automatically considered suspicious. If it was also flying south out of Canada and had no flight plan, F-89 interceptor aircraft were scrambled from the airbase in Great Falls, a hundred miles south.

There were no aircraft in or out of the airlanes. It was another boring Sunday, one of almost two hundred Herbie would have to endure at this remote outpost. Herbie pulled a chair up to the M & I table and sat down. He took his notebook out. He opened it to a blank page. He stared at it for a full minute.

The airmen behind the vertical Plexiglas plotting board at the back of the blockhouse were entertaining themselves by lighting their farts with their Zippos. Blue flames torched out from their skinny butts.

Herbie finally wrote something: "Reason number one for war: Boredom. War is a terrible thing, but boredom might be worse. The one thing war is not is boring." But this was opinion, not description. He tore the page out of the notebook and threw it away.

↓

Herbie went back to his barracks. Sidney Osmand was still lying on his bunk reading *Nugget*. "Listen up, you goldbricks," he said. "You'll give up your dreams of becoming fairies when you hear this: 'Elizabeth's perfumed pubic region was silky against Vernon's dry, trembling lips. He tasted Chanel No. 5 on his tongue and thought it odd that it was terribly bitter and yet, at the same time, so sweetly odiferous—the world was so strangely polarized! Elizabeth, her hands clenched in Vernon's dark curly hair, moaned with wildly soaring pleasure as she pulled him excitedly against the silky weave of her sex.'"

Those few words gave Herbie an instant erection. He imagined that everyone within range of Sidney's voice got an erection. The power of professional writing! The power of words! And not just words, *concrete* words! *Direct* words! Lots of adjectives, though. And opinion. He wondered what the USAFI instructor would make of all those adjectives and the notion that the world was strangely polarized. He'd probably deduct points even though he also had a raging boner.

A few other off-duty airmen had pulled chairs up to a bunk and were playing nickel-limit poker. They slumped over their cards half-asleep. Herbie sat on the edge of his bunk and took out his notebook. "The four players held their cards close to their chests," he wrote. "Some of them were wearing fatigues and others were in their underwear and a few were in civvies, getting ready to go into town on the shuttle. All of them were wearing poker faces."

This was direct and somewhat concrete but, like everything else he tried to describe, boring. Did descriptions of boredom always have to be boring? He crossed out what he'd written, then wrote:

> All the players had boners because Sidney Osmand read
> a hot passage from Nugget about this woman Elizabeth
> pulling this guy Vernon face-first into the silky weave
> of her sex.

Herbie considered these words, then rewrote the first sentence: "All the players had boners that bucked against their shorts like untamed horses . . ." Was that going overboard? Did that create a picture in the mind of the hypothetical reader? He continued: "Lucky for us a surprise inspection was not in the works since the first sergeant, Master Sergeant Basilio Napoli, had gone to Mass in Havre, and Major Dorsey Wilts, the CO, was in Great Falls on business. That's what he said, anyway. It was more like monkey business, ask anyone. Everyone knows Major Wilts is messing with a woman in Great Falls even though he has a wife and three kids in Havre and is highly thought of by Havre businessmen and church leaders. Hard to picture old silver-haired Major Wilts pressing his dry trembling lips to the silky weave of some Great Falls woman's sex, tongue springing into action, his boner bucking against his dress gabardines like a wild horse. Kind of unbelievable, if you ask me. But then, the world is so strangely polarized."

Under these words Herbie wrote "DELETE!!!" He crossed out the offending sentences.

Herbie was somewhat ashamed of himself. He respected and admired Major Wilts, who had been a Mustang pilot in Europe during the war and a Saber Jet pilot in Korea. The major was an ace with four Focke Wulfes, five Messerschmitts, and three Russian Mig-15s to his credit. Major Wilts was a genuine hero, and you didn't make genuine heroes look sleazy. It just wasn't right. It was demoralizing. It was unpatriotic.

Herbie picked up his USAFI text and thumbed it open to chapter 2:

> Here is an example of descriptive writing at its finest: "He was massive but mild . . . large and loose and ruddy and curly, with deep tones, deep eyes, deep pockets, to say nothing of long pipes, soft hats and brownish grayish weather-faded clothes . . ."
> —from the "The Tree of Knowledge" by Henry James

Herbie read the passage twice. He was puzzled by the USAFI textbook's claim that this was descriptive writing at its best. It was practically nothing *but* adjectives! Didn't the textbook writer see that? He put himself in the position of the hypothetical reader. He saw nothing but a list of general qualities, none of which had life enough in it to remake itself into a concrete image in the mind of the hypothetical reader.

Herbie was annoyed. "What the *hell*!" he said. The poker players glanced at him with dull flickers of interest then went back to their cards.

Herbie vowed to find a book in the Havre public library by this James guy to see if he wrote descriptions like this in all his stories. Herbie was reading a detective novel called *The Big Kill* by Mickey Spillane. *The Big Kill* had much juicier descriptions. He thumbed it open to a page he'd dog-eared:

> Her legs brushing the sheer nylon of the housecoat made it crackle and cling to her body until every curve was outlined in white with pink undertones . . .

and,

> Her breasts were precious things that accentuated the width of her shoulders and the smooth contours of her stomach, rising jauntily against the nylon as though they were looking for a way out.

The electrified nylon housecoat electrified Herbie. The precious breasts rising jauntily against the nylon started a tingle in his crotch. He liked this description, it made the girl visible, it stimulated his bodily functions. The palms of his hands were damp. His brain felt on fire. What *more* could you ask of a few words? Why was the James description "writing at its best" when the Spillane description was so much better? Hadn't the writers of the USAFI textbook read Mickey Spillane? He hoped his correspondence teacher would clear such things up.

Herbie was thinking about the electrified housecoat and its pink undertones when someone punched his shoulder. "Let's go to town, Fontana." It was Troy Lowry, a fellow off-duty radar operator. "*The Strategic Air Command* is playing at the Orpheum. Jimmy Stewart's in it. It's the closest we'll ever get to flying in a big old atomic bomber. I called Emma and Anna Opengaard. They want to go with us—kind of a double date. You're still hot for Anna, right? You flog your mule every night thinking about Anna, right Fontana? Or maybe you don't. Maybe you think of her as someone who shits tapioca and pees lemonade, a nice clean churchy girl you'd like to go to Bible study with."

Herbie and Troy had met Emma and Anna—twin sisters—a month ago at the Super Ice Cream Parlor in downtown Havre during a blizzard. A group of girls came in. Herbie and Troy sat in a booth and listened to the shivering girls talk about high school intrigues. During a lull in the girls' conversation, Herbie and Troy introduced themselves to the twins.

Havre High School had one of the greatest names for its athletic teams Herbie had ever heard: *The Blue Ponies*. Back home, the schools all had run of the mill copycat names, like *The Pirates*, *The Spartans*. *The Lions*. Northern Montana College, the local two-year school, also had a great name for its teams: *The Northern Lights*. Both Emma and Anna had broken up with *Blue Pony* football players and were now seeing *Northern Lights* basketball players, but they'd also been checking out the flyboys from the radar station, an exotic population of young men from all corners of the nation. The flyboys were hated by the local boys, who saw them as rivals with an unfair advantage. The local girls saw them as possible tickets out of Havre.

↯

Herbie and Troy caught a ride into town with Sergeant Deloche, who was in charge of the mess hall. Sergeant Deloche had a new Buick Roadmaster and he drove the gravel highway, Wild Horse Trail, to town almost every day even though he lived in the N C O barracks. Sergeant Deloche was a huge man, tall and wide with a prominent belly. He wore a diamond ring on his pinky finger and his thick red hair was oiled with Brilliantine. He looked more like a Las Vegas impresario than a mess hall sergeant.

"You boys headed for one of the locally famous twat shops?" he asked.

"No way, sarge," Troy said. "I don't need to pay for it. There's plenty available for the price of a movie and a cheeseburger deluxe."

Herbie knew this was bullshit, but he admired Troy's quick thinking and easy lies. Troy never seemed to be at a loss for words. Troy was a virgin, as was Herbie. But this humiliating condition could only be admitted by not admitting it. There was a tacit agreement between them not to quiz each other aggressively on the subject of sexual experience.

"Well, stay away from the Silver Dollar," Sergeant Deloche said. "They've got the prettiest girls, but they're Indians and their customers are white businessmen who pay premium prices for a taste of wild meat. Flyboys are not admitted. You mess around there you're likely to get scalped by the pimp, or worse." Sergeant Deloche grabbed his crotch and made a crude uprooting motion. The Buick swerved slightly on the gravel road. "The pimp sees you messing with his Indian girls, he'll likely hack off your little white stones and feed them to you for lunch."

More bullshit, Herbie thought. He'd never heard so much bullshit since joining the air force. What was it with these guys that they had to bullshit you until you were wading in it?

"Big half-breed buck in a pinstripe suit wearing steel-toed shoes and hair halfway down his back," Sergeant Deloche said. "Known to friends and enemy alike as Marvin Head. Carries brass knucks, a lead-filled sap, and a skinning knife honed like a straight razor. You see Marvin Head, you turn and move away fast. They say he kicked a couple of fellas to death years back up in Medicine Hat and scalped another with that skinning knife. No, the twat shop for airmen is behind the VitaRich dairy. A pair of five-dollar girls work it. They're on the Kansas City syndicate's northwest circuit. They don't use a pimp since they're protected by local cops, also on the syndicate's payroll. Syndicate man comes by once a month to collect dues and pay off the fuzz. The girls are a little long in the tooth and saggy of tit but certified clean, and they welcome military men. You might have heard that such women use Polygrip for lubrication, but pay no mind. In any case, like the great French poet said, Pussy is pussy is pussy. Am I right or am I right?"

"I guess so," Herbie said.

Sergeant Deloche looked at Herbie and burst out laughing. Three of his front teeth were edged with gold. He had the most evil smile Herbie had ever seen. Yet the big mess hall sergeant seemed genuinely friendly, even helpful.

"He *guesses* so!" Sergeant Deloche said. "Listen up, airman, when it comes to snatch there is no guesswork involved. It is what it is, upper class to gutter class, twists or no twists."

Sergeant Deloche let them off in downtown Havre. "What a load of B S," Herbie said as the Buick eased away from the curb, the sound of Sergeant Deloche's booming laughter not contained by the big sedan.

Troy didn't say anything. Herbie knew he was thinking about the VitaRich whores because Herbie was thinking about them too. Herbie was also thinking about the pretty Indian girls at the Silver Dollar and wondering if Marvin Head, the pimp who might kick him to death or even scalp him, was real.

Herbie said, "What did Deloche mean by twists or no twists?"

Troy Lowry didn't like to admit ignorance. "It's the way you do it," he said, lighting a cigarette. "Regulation or nonregulation. By the book or wild cards rule."

It was Herbie's turn to hide his ignorance. "Oh," he said. "Sure. I knew that," but he believed Troy was talking in a code he himself had not deciphered.

↓

Emma and Anna Opengaard were waiting for them at the Super. The twin girls were seated in a booth, wearing hooded parkas. The hoods of the parkas still covered their heads. Herbie didn't know which was which. The girls' small identical faces were cowled with imitation fur. They wore ski pants, mukluks, and mittens. This was the only way Herbie had ever seen them. He didn't know if they were skinny or fat, or if they had large breasts or no breasts, round hips or no hips, their feet big or small, narrow or wide, or if their legs were tapered nicely or not tapered and stumpy. The identical white disks of their faces seemed pretty enough, but they were heavily made up and so he wasn't really sure.

Troy, who was from Los Angeles, always acted cool around the Havre girls. He lit a cigarette and blew a cloud of smoke toward the ceiling. "There's a one o'clock matinee," he said. "Or we could fool around until the three o'clock. What do you girls do here in Nowheresville?"

"Let's go to our house first," Anna, or possibly Emma, said. "Mom and Dad drove down to Great Falls to do some shopping. They won't be home until late tonight. We can fool around there for a while, then go to the movie later . . . if you still want to."

Herbie felt a surging pressure in his chest. He glanced at Troy. Troy looked liked he was trying to avoid swallowing his tongue.

"Cool," Troy said, his voice pitched an octave higher than normal. "That's cool."

Emma and Anna lived a few blocks from the Super. Herbie and Troy were wearing their class A blues. They wanted to look sharp for the twins. Herbie wore his red, white, and blue Good Conduct ribbon on the blouse of his uniform. Troy had two ribbons, the Good Conduct, and, since he'd spent a few months in Korea on temporary duty, the blue and white Korean Service ribbon. He also wore his nonregulation Sharpshooter medal, won in basic training. They kept their parkas open so their colorful chest decorations would show. The class A uniform was wool but not meant for subzero conditions. By the time they got to the Opengaard house, Herbie and Troy had closed their parkas against the wind.

The split-level ranch-style was twice as big as Herbie's house back home. One wall was all bookcase. It held hundreds of hard-cover volumes arranged in alphabetical order by the authors' names. Herbie scanned the spines quickly and saw a dozen books by Henry James, none by Mickey Spillane.

The living room had a huge stone fireplace, with a firewood box built into it. The box was full of split cedar and kindling. The wall-to-wall carpeting was thick and white as new snow. The chairs and sofas were overstuffed and expensive looking. It occurred to Herbie that he was in the home of rich people. Rich and educated.

The twins took off their outer layer of clothing. Herbie saw that they were as pretty and as nicely built as he'd hoped. They had shiny black hair cut Cleopatra style. They wore identical blue sweaters, identical gray skirts. Under the mukluks and wool socks, their identical feet were small and narrow, the toenails painted the identical shade of stoplight red.

"Build a fire, Herbie," one of the girls—possibly Anna—said. "I'll go make us some cocoa."

"You got any booze?" Troy said.

The twins looked at each other. "What do you think, Anna? Should we?"

"Daddy has that bottle of Canadian Club, Em," Anna said. "He won't miss a teensy bit of it."

Now that the girls had identified themselves, Herbie kept his eye on Anna.

They sat on the overstuffed sofa in front of a roaring fire, drinking Canadian Club and Bubble-Up highballs. The whiskey calmed Herbie's nerves. He put his arm around Anna and she leaned into him, her head on his shoulder. Emma put a Julie London record on a huge hi-fi console. "Cry Me a River" was the first song. It made Herbie feel romantically maudlin. An image of himself standing on a dock engulfed by fog occurred to him. A ship was pulling away from the dock. The fog turned it into a ghost ship. Julie London's voice filtered by fog was like a whisper from the deck of dim ship. Herbie felt an attack of self-pity coming on.

"Let's dance," Emma said.

Anna and Emma got up and danced with each other, leaving Herbie and Troy on the couch. The same girl in two bodies, mirror images moving the same way, their humming voices the same. It dazzled Herbie. He lost track of which was which. Then Troy got up and cut in. Herbie circled his arm around the waist of the other twin. She pressed herself against him.

"You're Anna, right?" he said.

"Sure," she said. "I'm Anna. Why? Does it make a difference to you?"

"No," Herbie said. "Yes," he amended. "I mean . . ."

She laughed and put her finger against his lips, sealing them. They danced in their socks for a while, changing partners with every song. Then they all collapsed on the long sofa.

Anna (he'd kept track) turned her face toward Herbie. The kiss was almost accidental, an awkward collision of lips, but then the tips of their tongues touched. By the time the second Julie London album dropped from the spindle onto the turntable, Troy and Emma had gone into another room. Herbie bent into Anna, kissing her hard, not sure how far he could go with his hands. Anna helped him. She took his hand and put it on her breast. Herbie's hand jumped, as if it had touched high voltage. "You're *shy*," Anna said, full of teasing wonderment.

"Who? *Me*? Not me," Herbie said, his face red. He put his hand back on her breast. It was a substantial breast. He squeezed it. He felt the nipple rise and stiffen through the fabric.

Anna took him by the wrist. "Not so hard," she said. "You'll make bruises. How will I explain bruises?"

"I'm sorry," Herbie said. Then he wondered who would she have to explain the bruises to. The Blue Ponies? The Northern Lights? He put the demoralizing thought out of his mind.

They necked for several minutes, trading hickeys. It became repetitive and tiring. Herbie's tongue ached. He backed away from her and sipped the dregs of his highball. "How come all the books?" he said, gesturing toward the bookcases.

"Daddy's a professor at Northern," she said. "He teaches English."

"I'll be darned," Herbie said. "Do you know if he teaches books by Henry James?"

"Is that what you want to do?" Anna said. "You want to talk about what Daddy teaches?" She sank lower in the sofa and looked at him with dewy half-closed eyes. She looked totally receptive in a way Herbie had never seen a girl look. He took this to be a signal for him to take further liberties. He kissed her again. Her mouth yawned open.

Herbie put his hand on her inner thigh. Her skin was warm and smooth and slightly moist. Her thighs yielded to his touch. She made a soft sound in her throat when his fingers reached the elastic band of her panties. "Oh no—please don't—not there," she said, her gasps submissive, her thighs yielding more ground. He slipped his fingers under the elastic where they encountered the silky weave of pubic hair and the damp cleft it hid. Anna moaned as if in pain. This startled Herbie. He paused. He said, "Are you okay?" and when she didn't answer he continued his cautious explorations.

It was too much. He couldn't hold back.

He got up and ran to the bathroom, but not in time. Herbie had heard of premature ejaculation but this was ridiculous. His shorts were sticky and his pants were stained. Luckily his pants were dark and the stain didn't show up very well. He mopped up with wads of toilet paper then washed himself at the sink. He waited for the remaining stickiness in his shorts and pants to harden.

Troy thumped the bathroom door. "Let's go lover boy," he said. "We've still got time to make the second show."

After the movie the girls went into the restroom while Herbie and Troy waited in the lobby. Then they walked to the Super. Herbie put his arm around Anna possessively. "I had a great time, Anna," he said.

"Not with me," she said. "I'm Emma."

"Damn. I'm sorry."

"Don't worry. It happens a lot." Emma grinned. It was a sly, playful grin.

↙

Herbie and Troy took the shuttle bus back to the radar station. Troy said, "Did you score, hot rocks?"

Herbie thought about it. "In a way," he said. "What about you?"

"You better believe it, airman."

Since Troy didn't press Herbie to explain what he meant by "In a way," Herbie figured Troy was telling something less than the whole truth himself.

"I think I'm going to marry that girl," Troy said.

"Emma?" Herbie said.

"No, *Anna*."

"You mean Emma. *I* was with Anna."

"That's what she told you? Jesus, they like to mess with a guy. They like to play switcheroo. You were with Emma. I had Anna. I think I like her better."

Herbie was confused. Was he in love with Emma or Anna? "Maybe they played switcheroo on *you*," he said. "Maybe you had Emma and *I* had Anna."

"What's the difference? They're identical."

"They just look alike. They don't have the same *thoughts*. They're not the same person, for Pete's sake."

"I'm going to their house for dinner next Saturday," Troy said. "You're sort of invited."

"*Sort* of?"

"Yeah. Anna said bring the other guy if you want. She calls you the 'other guy.'"

"Did Anna—I mean Emma—say anything? About me, I mean?"

"Not much. Something about you being a real nice guy. Very polite, very well behaved. Nice aftershave, well-groomed. I think you bored the living shit out of her."

↓

Nikita Khrushchev toured Canada. The North American Air Defense Command went on Yellow Alert. Two F-89 Scorpions flew Combat Air Patrol orbits along the Canadian border, ready for Communist tricks. Khrushchev's Tupolev 114, an eight-engine turboprop, was watched closely by half a dozen radar stations. The Russians also used the TU-114 as an intercontinental strategic bomber.

"There he is," Herbie said into his microphone. "Señor Khrushchev himself."

The Tupolev was a bright green glob a hundred miles northeast of the radar station. The Scorpions had their IFF transponders squawking Mode II. Two bars of green light identified each interceptor on the radar screen. Lieutenant Padilla was nervous. He was talking to the pilots.

"Pipestone Red One," he said. "Turn left fifteen clicks, you're riding the border."

"Ah roger, Jesse control," said the pilot.

After a minute, Herbie said, "He didn't turn, lieutenant."

"Fucking hotshot," Lieutenant Padilla said. He keyed his mike. "Pipestone Red One, this is Jesse Control. Vector to two-three-zero, *now*."

"Ah roger, Jesse," said the pilot.

"What this asshole wants," said Lieutenant Padilla, "is to get a quick look at Khrushchev's plane so he can tell his girlfriend he had the chubby little Russkie in his gun sights."

"He turned off his transponder, lieutenant," Herbie said.

"I'll write the fucker up," the lieutenant said. "I'll vector his ass into the Great Falls stockade."

Herbie leaned close to his radar screen. "I think that's him," he said. "We're painting something, right where his transponder quit squawking. He crossed the border into Canadian airspace. He's vectoring north toward Moose Jaw. Maybe he's flipped out and wants to shoot Khrushchev down. Maybe he thinks the Russian premier himself is leading an attack on the U.S."

"In that case you'd better buy a lead jockstrap," Lieutenant Padilla said. He took off his headset. "I'm going to the latrine. You watch those assholes for a while. If the other guy turns off his transponder and heads for Moose Jaw, call Division. Tell them they've got two tourists flying their expensive airplanes. That'll bunch up their shorts."

The Yellow Alert lasted a week. No one was allowed off base while it was on. Airmen with rifles stood guard around the huge radar domes. Some patrolled the perimeter, outside the chain-link fence. Troy called the Opengaard twins and explained the situation. The girls said they could postpone the dinner indefinitely.

"In the meantime, you'll just have to friction-fuck Rosy Palm, your old steady," Troy told Herbie.

The Special Services library had an old anthology of American literature. Herbie found two stories by Henry James. He tried to read them but got lost almost instantly. It was depressing. If this was one of the world's best professional writers, how could he ever hope to be even one of the least? His chances looked slim. He went back to Mickey Spillane and immediately felt better.

Nikita Khrushchev went back to Russia and the Yellow Alert was called off. Things went back to normal. Sergeant Doberman, who had more or less ignored Herbie during the alert, now started harassing him again. He saw Herbie reading the Special Services literature anthology in the mess hall one day and snatched it out of his hand. He thumbed through the book. "You think you're hot shit reading these fairy stories?" he said. "This makes you better than me? Is that your idea, Fontana? You making yourself out to be better than me?"

Herbie ignored the old sergeant. Doberman, for all his talk, had never put his hands on Herbie. Herbie almost wished he would. But then there were Klecko and Stonecipher to consider.

↓

"What plans do you boys have for the future?" Professor Opengaard said.

"The air force is a good career," Troy said.

"I'm going to be a professional writer," Herbie said.

"Really," Professor Opengaard said, offering Herbie a humoring smile. "What sort of professional writer?"

"Stories, I guess."

"A fiction writer, you mean."

They were seated at the Opengaard dinner table. Professor Opengaard seemed amused by the idea of Herbie becoming a fiction writer. He was a large, rumpled man with heavy red cheeks and a yellowing mustache. His nose was crosshatched with broken capillaries. Though he had the girth of a wrestler, he picked at his food, eating very little. He'd had three highballs before dinner and had finished most of a bottle of Rhine wine at the table. Mrs. Opengaard, a thin nervous woman, had served pickled whitefish, scalloped potatoes, pickled beets, and creamed spinach.

"You'll have to be very good if you expect to make a living at the writing game," the professor said.

"I'm taking a correspondence course in it now," Herbie said.

Professor Opengaard chuckled. "Oi vey," he said, winking gravely at his wife. "Another autochthonic genius."

Emma and Anna were sitting across the table from Herbie and Troy. Herbie looked from one girl to the other, wondering which one was Anna and which one was Emma and what *autochthonic* meant. Mr. and Mrs. Opengaard sat at the ends.

"Don't ever marry an aspiring writer," the professor warned the twins. He tapped the air instructively with his fork. "They abandon you for their foolish dreams, or if their dreams are not appreciated by the world at large, they turn like rabid dogs on the ones they love." The professor's pale eyes grew misty, as if he knew these things from his own experience. His wife sighed and stroked the professor's hand. "Most of them turn out to be rotters. Be warned, my dears," he said.

"Daddy!" Anna or Emma said. "That's so unfair! Herbie can be whatever he wants to be. He'll be a very good writer, I just know it."

"Good, bad, deep, shallow, it doesn't matter. Sometimes it's better to be shallow and bad. I'm speaking of the struggle, the bedevilment one receives at the hands of fools. And then there

are the countless brutal rejections. A shallow writer, by appealing to the tastes of the vast unwashed, has a better chance of
making a success."

"Craig wrote a novel, you see," Mrs. Opengaard said. "What is
it called, dear? 'The something or other of a Far Island'?"

"'Ironic Laughter from a Distant River,'" the professor said.
"Never published, alas. I thought it every bit as good as *Tender Is
the Night*. A slight miscalculation."

Herbie was impressed. Here was a real writer. A professional.
Or nearly so. A man who had written an entire novel! The wine
he'd had with his dinner gave him courage. "This Henry James
guy, professor?" he said. "How come he's supposed to be such
an ace at describing things? I think Mickey Spillane is better at
describing things."

"The voice of innocence," Professor Opengaard sighed. "You have,
at this stage of your life, an uninformed mind, Herbie. This 'guy'
Henry James, as you put it, is the master, nonpareil, of nuance and
counterpoint. He orchestrates a fine syntactical reticulum that
catches every scintilla of import in relational strategies. His work
has concentrated depth. One looks into it and sees bedrock. If you
intend to write seriously, you'd better look for models superior
to your Mr. Spillane."

Herbie didn't know what *nonpareil*, *nuance*, *counterpoint*, *reticulum*, or *scintilla* meant. He committed these words to memory so
that he could look them up later.

"Mickey Spillane makes the subject visible in the mind of the
hypothetical reader," he said.

"A trivial accomplishment, Herbie," the professor said. "James
makes this hypothetical reader of yours understand what lies
behind the mere physicality of the visible subject. And he does not,
incidentally, resolve conflicted mendacities with the easy deus ex
machina of indiscriminate gunplay—as in Hemingway's cheaply
resolved Macomber story. Hemingway is another shallow one,
unjustly worshipped by the literary establishment even though
they, of all people, should see that the man is possessed of a
posturing superficiality with a neurotic penchant for violence."

Herbie wondered if Professor Opengaard wrote the way he spoke. He hadn't finished the Mickey Spillane novel he was reading, and so he didn't know how Spillane resolved conflicted mendacities—whatever they were—but he intended, now, to find out.

"Henry James uses a whole lot of adjectives," Herbie said, digging in his heels. "And his sentences? They're like an eighty-car train wreck."

Professor Opengaard sighed. His face sagged with fatigue and boredom, and perhaps anger. "You are ignorant beyond ignorance, Herbie," he said. "Henry James writes with an elegance beyond your powers of apprehension. You can't hope to write until you've read the great works of literature with intelligent respect and with the intention of expanding your understanding. Otherwise originality will always elude you and hack work, at best, will be your lot. I'm afraid you have a very long way to go, young man. And, if I might suggest, *too* long a way. I advise you take up something more suited to your aptitudes and capacities—mechanical work, such as automobile or appliance repair. Perhaps you should make a career of the army."

"I'm in the air force," Herbie said, but the professor was done with him and did not hear Herbie's correction.

Later, lying before the muttering red coals of the fireplace— Professor and Mrs. Opengaard long since retired to their bedroom— Herbie whispered into Anna's or Emma's ear, "I think I know what lies behind the mere physicality of the visible subject."

"Shut *up*," she said.

"Nothing lies behind it."

Herbie was a little drunk from the whiskey they'd sneaked out of the professor's liquor cabinet. "No kidding," he said. "I'm being serious." He swept his hand across her naked body as if she were a white field of superficial mysteries. The phrase "superficial mysteries" came to him unbidden. It seemed very profound, very professional. It gave him a sense of himself that he very much liked. He said it aloud as if the syllables had magical powers. "Superficial mysteries . . . right here, right before our eyes."

"Jesus, stop *talk*ing," she said. "Just put it in."

He did. It was over in less than a minute.

"You get too worked up, Herbie," Anna or Emma said crossly. "You've got to learn to turn your dumb brain off."

"Like the Blue Ponies?" Herbie said.

"Okay, if you must know—*yes*, like the Blue Ponies."

↡

Herbie couldn't sleep. He got up and went into the latrine carrying his notebook and pencil. He'd read Henry James until three in the morning and was beginning to get a feel for James's complicated sentences. Maybe they weren't so bad after all. Maybe the problem was his, not James's. Herbie was impatient by nature and wanted immediate gratification, but to read James you had to be receptive to the way a superior mind worked. You couldn't just pick up a story by Henry James and expect it to read like the Sunday funnies. Herbie was willing to meet the great writer halfway.

He opened his notebook and wrote: "Anna, or perhaps Emma, it was impossible to tell which, but then what did it matter unless he wanted both, a pretty cool idea but not one he could get away with, (he imagined being sandwiched between them in bed!) especially since Troy, his best friend and partner in crime, had a claim on Anna or possibly Emma, looked across the table at him and smiled."

Herbie liked this sentence very much. He was proud of it. It could have been written by Henry James himself. He felt he understood something: A James sentence coiled around its subject until it trapped it like a trout in a net, a "syntactical reticulum," just like Professor Opengaard said. Herbie tried another one:

> Anna—or was it Emma?—he remarked to himself, was all a man could wish for, though he could imagine other situations in which what he might wish for could differ

from what he would have wished for if he had only wished
instead of imagining he wished . . .

He crossed this out. He felt strings of words tangling in his
brain. It gave him a headache. He wondered if Henry James ever
suffered from headaches. He imagined the large brain of Henry
James tied in knots of language and eventually exploding like a
bomb made of words, splattering the walls with ink, not blood.
He started another page but was interrupted by sirens.

↘

Without warning, Division had called an alert. Herbie was assigned
guard duty. He stood on the north perimeter of the radar station,
outside the chain-link fence that surrounded it and on the high
ground above the sewage lagoon. It was thirteen below zero
and the lagoon had frozen over, safe now for ice-skating. The
previous winter a radio tech had tried to skate on the lagoon
in twenty-eight-degree weather. The thin ice gave way and he
drowned in black water—the accumulated bodily wastes of two
hundred airmen.

False dawn turned the radar domes a dusty gray against the
darker sky. There was no wind for a change, and Herbie was
grateful for that. He had on his arctic gear: double-knit long
johns, shin-length sheepskin parka, fur-lined gloves, the double-
insulated bunny boots that made his feet look like clown feet.
The snow under them was crusty and hard as pavement. Other
guards, fifty yards on either side of his position, were sitting,
cradling their M-1s. Herbie recognized the one to his left by his
shape: Raymond Klecko. He looked like a bear, its big head sagged
on its chest. Klecko was asleep.

By dawn the cold had penetrated Herbie's parka and the several
layers of his clothes. He jogged in place, slapping his sides and
chest. He was only scheduled for four hours of guard duty, but
time itself seemed gelid and in danger of freezing. The passing
seconds, Herbie thought, became clots of unmoving ice in a frozen

river. The phrase appealed to Herbie. He took out his notebook and pencil and wrote: "Time clots like ice in a frozen river." The sentence had class. It had a definite professional feel to it. He said it aloud, and watched the words become the visible steam of his breath.

Herbie tried to generate some warmth by imagining himself and Anna, or Emma, lying next to the hot coals of the Opengaard fireplace, the glow covering their bodies like a warm red blanket. A growing bar of heat pressed itself along his thigh as he elaborated the details of this scene. Herbie took out his notebook again.

"What the fuck do you think you're doing, Fontana?" Klecko said. Klecko, surprisingly stealthy for a heavy man, had walked over to Herbie's position.

"Just making some notes," Herbie said.

"Notes? What about? *Me?* You think you caught me fucking the dog? You gonna make points off me taking a snooze, you fink?"

Herbie thought about that possibility. "You're not supposed to leave your post," he said.

Klecko grabbed his crotch. "I've got your post, pissant," he said.

Klecko grabbed Herbie by the parka and threw him down. When Herbie got up, Klecko said, "Hit me, Fontana. Take a shot. That's what you want, isn't it?" Klecko stuck his chin out.

"Fuck off," Herbie said.

Klecko put his gloved hand on Herbie's face and squeezed his mouth into a pucker. "You'd rather suck dick, is that it? You want to blow me, Fontana? Isn't that what you California fruits like?"

Herbie put everything he had into the punch. His fist glanced off the wide jut of Klecko's chin. Klecko stepped back, laughing. "Maybe you got some balls after all," he said. He punched Herbie in the stomach. Herbie felt the impact through the layers of arctic gear. It didn't hurt him but it put him on his back, and then he realized he couldn't breathe.

Klecko turned Herbie over and straddled him. "You need to wash up," he said. "Doberman says you come in from town stinking like split-tail. He says you California fruits like to go down on the quim."

Klecko pushed Herbie's face into the hard snow and kept pushing until his face broke the crust. When Herbie was able to sit up his nose was trickling blood which froze on his lips and chin. His breath came back in huge sobs. Klecko, barking with laughter, walked away.

"Fucking moron," Herbie said. If Klecko heard he gave no sign. As Klecko trudged back to his position, Herbie raised his carbine. He chambered a round and aimed at the back of Klecko's head. He put pressure on the trigger. This made his knees weak. He sat down on the hard snow, shaking.

When the sun was a few inches above the horizon, the sky began to fill with vapor trails. "Here they come!" Klecko the merry warrior yelled.

Dozens of bombers, too high to hear, streaked the sky with parallel white contrails from horizon to horizon. They flew south, on their way to turn the cities of America into radioactive ash. Smaller contrails from the Air Defense Command's F-89 Scorpions vectored toward the invading bombers. Herbie could almost hear Lieutenant Padilla, or whoever was on duty, giving frantic headings to the interceptors.

Herbie picked up his carbine. Were the Russians finally coming? Was this the real thing? He couldn't make himself believe it. The bombers were probably B-36s or the newer B-52s, and all this was a practice run to test the air defense system. On the other hand, how could he know for sure? No one had briefed him. He'd just been pulled out of his bunk, handed a carbine, told to put on his arctic gear, and take up a position above the sewage lagoon.

Herbie was still shaking—from the cold and left over adrenaline, but now from anticipation, too. The world could change overnight! Nothing would ever be the same! Would he ever be able to have a life with Anna or Emma? Would he be stuck in this radar base in the middle of nowhere forever, no home to go home to? Home—a glowing crater on the edge of a poisoned sea!

He jotted down that phrase.

Wind, perhaps from a detonated hydrogen bomb, washed over him. It was gale force and warm. He began to sweat. He took off his gloves and parka. The wind blew from the west, from the mountains and maybe beyond, maybe all the way from the coast and its major population centers. Millions could be dead by now, incinerated, with millions more to come. Herbie scanned the sky for the airborne ash of dead Americans.

The hard snow began to soften and shrink. The temperature had gone from thirteen below to forty or fifty above in a matter of minutes. High overhead the contrails of the long-gone bombers—Tupolevs or B-36s or whatever—fattened into bands of red-tinged cirrus. World War Three had traveled south. A pair of Scorpions passed fifty feet over the radar base. Herbie saw the pilots waving. They would go back to Great Falls, and other fighters farther to the south would take up the battle.

"Chinook," Herbie's relief said, an airman who'd been at the radar base for three winters. "The Chinook wind pours down the east slopes of the Rockies and compresses enough to heat up. It happens a few times every winter and melts the whole fucking prairie. It's false spring, but hey, you'll learn to love it."

Herbie walked back to the barracks. The streets of the radar squadron were running with melted snow. The sun was higher now and almost hot. Two airmen in tee shirts were tossing a football back and forth.

Back in his barracks, Herbie took out his notebook. He wrote: "Two airmen tossed a football back and forth in the warm atomic wind. What else was there to do? Boredom was now a permanent part of the landscape and nothing could be done about it. All the interesting places—L.A., San Francisco, Denver, etc.—had been blown to smithereens. All humanity were now trapped in the vast landscape of everlasting boredom where nothing interesting would ever happen."

Herbie thought this might be the beginning of a story. He'd call it "A Hot Day in January." He liked the sound of it. More Mickey Spillane than Henry James, but he'd worry about that later.

ABOUT THE AUTHOR

Rick DeMarinis is the author of eight novels. *The Year of the Zinc Penny* (W. W. Norton & Company, 1989; Seven Stories Press, 2004) was a 1989 New York Times Notable Book. *Borrowed Hearts* (Seven Stories Press, 1999), his definitive short story collection, includes stories from his three previous collections, together with uncollected work predating this volume.